P9-CQN-445

Poison Ivory

**Center Point
Large Print**

**This Large Print Book carries the
Seal of Approval of N.A.V.H.**

Poison Ivory

A DEN OF ANTIQUITY MYSTERY

TAMAR MYERS

CENTER POINT PUBLISHING
THORNDIKE, MAINE

This Center Point Large Print edition
is published in the year 2009 by arrangement with
Avon Books, an imprint of HarperCollins Publishers.

The text of this Large Print edition is unabridged.
In other aspects, this book may vary
from the original edition.
Printed in the United States of America.
Set in 16-point Times New Roman type.

ISBN: 978-1-60285-615-8

Library of Congress Cataloging-in-Publication Data

Myers, Tamar.
  Poison ivory / Tamar Myers.
     p. cm.
  ISBN 978-1-60285-615-8 (library binding : alk. paper)
  1. Timberlake, Abigail (Fictitious character)--Fiction.
   2. Antique dealers--South Carolina--Charleston--Fiction. 3. Smugglers--Fiction.
   4. Large type books. I. Title.

PS3563.Y475P65 2009
813'.54--dc22

2009027897

1

Snow in Charleston lasts less than half as long as a politician's promise. Therefore, if I wanted to walk in it, I knew I had better hurry. I shook my husband for the umpteenth time.

"Greg, darling, wake up."

He groaned. "Maybe later, hon; now I just want to sleep."

I couldn't blame him. It was only two in the morning. I'd woken up to use the bathroom and was suddenly struck by the sound of complete silence that only a wet, heavy snow can deliver in the middle of a night. Not a dog was barking, not a car engine racing, not even a foghorn was sounding on the nearby harbor. The city of Charleston seemed to be holding its breath while this once-in-a-ten-year event unfolded.

Well, if my beloved husband wouldn't join me for an outing in the snow, then maybe my mother would. After all, she is from the Upstate of South Carolina, where the cold stuff, while still unusual, falls at least once almost every winter.

"Mama! Wake up!"

Mozella Wiggins is a petite woman—just five feet tall—who has been stuck in a time warp since the early 1960s. She "retires" to bed in a proper nightgown, and lays a matching robe, neatly folded, across the foot of her bed. At the first sound of her name she sat up and reached for the robe in one smooth gesture.

"What is it, dear? Is it those shadows on the wall again?"

"Mama! I was six years old, and that willow oak branch was growing too close to the house. You said so yourself."

My minimadre shook her head sharply, as if to clear her brain from layers of sand and dust that might have accumulated on it while she slept. Suddenly she was just as alert as a traffic controller fresh back from rehab.

"Listen, Abby!"

"Isn't it wonderful, Mama?"

Her response was to rush to the window and fling open the solid wood plantation shutters. What she saw made her gasp in delight, and she began to jump up and down like an excited schoolgirl.

"Oh, Abby, we've got to get out there as fast as we can. We have to be the first ones to make tracks in the snow. It brings good luck, you know."

"It does? Says who?"

"My mama and her mama before her, that's who."

"Who am I to argue with my foremothers? Do you have any waterproof shoes?" Mama wears only pumps—even to picnics.

"No. I was hoping you had an extra pair of galoshes."

"Well, considering the fact that I've lived down

here on the coast for the last five years, and it's only snowed once, it's somehow slipped my mind to stock up on them. Do you have a pair of old shoes that you absolutely hate?"

"Don't be silly, dear; why would I buy something I hate?"

Sometimes with Mama one needs to tack, just as abruptly as one might with a sailboat. "Ah, but think of this as an opportunity to buy a new pair of shoes; my treat. Yesterday I saw a huge selection of pumps, with stiletto heels, in the window of Bob Ellis."

"You mean you wouldn't send me to Target?"

"There's nothing wrong with Target, Mama—but yes, you may purchase"—one does not *buy*—"a pair of the statement shoes if you like."

"Sold," Mama said happily, and scurried off to her closet, where, without a second's hesitation, she retrieved a pair of pull-on rubber boots in neon yellow.

"Mama, where'd you get those?"

"These are my snow-walking boots from up in Rock Hill. They're from Target, you know. Anyway, I keep them hidden under my laundry bag, because the color doesn't go with this room."

"But you said you didn't have anything!"

"You asked me about shoes, dear; you didn't ask me about boots. Besides, remember all those times I called you up, when you were living in Charlotte,

7

and asked you to come down and walk in the snow with me. If you had, you'd have remembered these."

"Let me get this straight: you wanted me to drive down in the snow from Charlotte to Rock Hill, a distance of thirty miles, just so that I could walk in frozen precipitation with you?"

"You should be flattered, Abby. I could have asked any one of my many friends instead."

It was time for me to shut up and stew quietly. There was simply no way to win an argument with Mama. If buying her a four hundred dollar pair of shoes from Bob Ellis on King Street was what it took to get her to walk with me, so be it. Mama was priceless. Plus, to be brutally honest, she might not live to see another snow as heavy as this one in Charleston.

The natives of Charleston woke up in a panic. Schools were closed, as were bridges, and meetings canceled. Folks descended on the grocery stores like locusts and cleaned the shelves out of bread and milk. But by noon that same day the sun was out and the temperature was in the mid-fifties. By two o'clock it was sixty degrees and there wasn't a trace of snow, not even against the north sides of buildings.

I'd managed to get a little sleep after my joy walk with Mama, and was pumped when I arrived at my shop, the Den of Antiquity. I sell collectibles and antiques, by the way. Although my inventory now tends toward the high end, I still offer a broad enough range to please most of the discerning tourists—and locals—who wander in.

Okay, so that's not quite true at the moment. A faltering economy, a weak dollar, and high gas prices: these are factors that can hit a tourist-oriented town like Charleston particularly hard. A person can't live without food, but a person can sure as shootin' live without a Louis XIV chair with its gilded wood and Genoese velvet. One might say that business has been a mite slow lately—if one were given to understatement. Fortunately, I'd done well in the past, and had a sizable nest egg put aside. Unfortunately, it wasn't going to last forever at the rate at which I'd been spending. I'd found that one gets accustomed to a certain standard of living, and that it is darn hard to cut out luxuries that somewhere along the line became needs.

"Good morning," I said cheerily to my staff as I breezed in through the back entrance. "Are we ready to make this the best day ever?"

"In a pig's eye," Wynnell Crawford said. She's my best buddy who followed me down from Charlotte with her husband Ed when I made the big move. No matter how sunny it is, Wynnell manages to find a couple of clouds in the sky; but the upside is that at least she gets a bit of shade and is less likely to wrinkle.

"Hey Abby," Cheng said. "Why aren't you out dishpanning?"

"I beg your pardon?"

"You know: sledding down hills—except in a dishpan, not a sled. Back in Shelby we used to use washtubs and inner tubes, but you're so small, Abby, you could fit in a dishpan with no trouble."

"Thanks, Cheng—I think. But as you may have noticed, there aren't any hills in the Lowcountry— certainly not in Charleston—except for the banks along highway interchanges."

Instantly, I regretted having said that. Cheng hails from Shelby, North Carolina, which may be neither here nor there, but she has an imagination that makes Paul Bunyan seem like a dullard by comparison. Her large gray eyes grew even larger, and she licked the corners of her mouth.

"You just might have something there, Abby."

"Uh, I don't think so. If the highway patrol didn't stop you first, you'd get hurt on the rocks and broken glass in the gullies. Nope, sledding down highway banks is not a good idea."

"Ooh, Abby, you can be so silly. I'm thinking about buying up a hundred acres in Dorchester County while we can still get it relatively cheap. Then we bring down oodles of clay from the Upstate—since that's all they have, and they hate it up there—and we create a man-made hill. Only we call it a mountain. Did you know that the highest point in Florida is only 345 feet?"

"I did not know that." Cheng, by the way, has an IQ that is off the charts. Unfortunately, so is her sense of reality.

"Mississippi's highest point is only 806 feet, but they call it Woodall *Mountain*. I figure that with the right underpinnings, we could build this baby at least that high. We could name it Mount Cheng, for instance—or, if you insist, Mount Abby. Although personally, the latter sounds a little strange to me."

"Indeed," I said.

"Cheng, you're nuts," Wynnell said kindly.

"You say that now, but just wait. Mount Cheng will pay for itself—ka-cheng—I mean, ka-ching!" The big galoot laughed heartily. "You see, all we need to do is build a road to the top *and* a restaurant. People go crazy for a restaurant with a view, and this will have the best ocean view of any place along the East Coast, from the cliffs of Maine all the way to Key West. Think about it, Abby, the eastern coastal plain is as flat as a pancake, and then suddenly, halfway to Miami, out of nowhere, rises a giant hill with stunning panoramic views. It wouldn't even matter what kind of food you sold; the restaurant would be packed."

"Hmm," I mused. With the right promotion behind this idea, and if we could get the Highway Department to approve a connecting route to I-95, Mount Abby might possibly become the next South of the Border. It might even surpass that, uh, *colorful* collection of shops as a tourist landmark.

11

Wynnell's enormous brows met in an enormous hedge of disapproval. "It'll never fly."

"Why not, dear?"

"Why do you think there aren't any significant landforms between here and New England?"

"Beats me."

"I'm no expert—like Cheng here—but I'll bet some of it has to do with hurricanes. The first Category Five to come through and Mount Cheng will be Molehill Cheng and your cash register will be twenty-five miles out to sea."

"Hmm."

Cheng stomped a foot the size of Delaware. "Abby, does Wynnell always have to be such a downer?"

"Stark raving mad," Wynnell hissed, but in a kindly way, I'm sure.

I clapped my hands. "We have ten minutes until opening. Do we have any business items to review before then?"

"Oh yeah," Cheng said, and scratched her over-sized head to better help her think. "As soon as I let myself in there was a call for you from that guy at customs—you know, Pepe Peeyew. He said your shipment from Hong Kong arrived yesterday and you can come pick it up anytime."

"Fantastic. Anyone want to come with?" Perhaps it was unfair to ask them to accompany me, as they do work on commission, but I hate going to the docks alone.

"Pass," Wynnell said.

"Not today, thanks," Cheng said.

"Are you ladies sure?"

"Shame on you, Abby," Wynnell said. "You don't like being hassled because you're so darn attractive, so you want one of us to ugly it up a bit for you. I haven't figured it out yet, but that's like sexual harassment or something."

"What?"

I pretended to be both shocked and insulted by my friend's allegation.

"Hey," Cheng said, "just what do you mean, Wynnell? I'm *much* younger than Abby, and I'll have you know that there are plenty of men who prefer my type over hers. Abby's way too short to be beautiful—no offense taken of course, Abby."

"Of course. Well, in any case, I think I'll go by myself today. Sometimes it's nice to be alone with my thought."

"Don't you mean *thoughts,* Abby?"

"No, my head's too small to accommodate more than one thought at a time."

"But Abby," Cheng said, "the dock is full of brawny men, some of whom might wish to have their way with you. While I wouldn't add one iota of ugliness to your quota, I could definitely function as a bodyguard. Here, Abby, just feel my bicep."

"Thanks, but no thanks." There was no need; I'd seen Cheng single-handedly tote large dressers like they were blocks of marshmallow. The woman was as strong as an ox, as stubborn as a mule, and as loyal as a team of huskies. She was just who I needed as a companion for my trip to the docks.

"Please, Abby, pretty please. With Granny Ledbetter's homemade, foot-stomped molasses on top?"

"I guess so," I said. "But give the molasses to Wynnell; she's the one with the sweet tooth."

"I'm going to get you for that," Wynnell growled, but my friend was smiling.

The Port of Charleston is the nation's fourth busiest container port. Even with Cheng along to navigate and read the plethora of signs, by the time we parked in an approved spot and found the right gate, I was a four foot nine inch bundle of raw nerves. Cheng, however, was as calm as a goat in a clover field.

"Whatcha here for?" The man's badge read WILSON CURLY, despite the fact there was not a hair on his head.

I showed Mr. Curly my papers. He read them carefully, checked them against a list, and then engaged in a mumbled phone call with his back turned to us. Finally he addressed me again.

"ID, please."

"You mean like my driver's license? Usually I don't show my importer's license until I get to the customs shed."

"Yeah?"

"Yes," I replied.

"If that's true, ma'am, then whoever was on duty wasn't doing his job. Wait right here, please." He strode away, disappearing behind a gray concrete building to our immediate right.

"What a nice fellow," I said.

"You really think so, Abby? If he doesn't ask me out, I might just do the Lazy Mae and ask him out myself. "

It took me a second. "Don't you mean 'Daisy Mae,' as in the dance?"

Cheng giggled. "You're always so silly, Abby—but clever too, the way you're always coming up with new words and phrases. But seriously, the Lazy Mae dances got their start back in Shelby. Mae's full name was Norma Mae Ida Lupine Madrigot Heising—only she couldn't be bothered to use even Norma, much less the other names.

"Anyway, she was really forward for her time, and not at all afraid of asking the boys to dance with her, but she was the laziest girl you ever did see. So her daddy built her a little platform on wheels that she could stand on while the boys pushed her around on the gym floor. Sometimes they pushed too hard and Lazy Mae fell off; that's where the expression 'pushover' comes from."

"How very illuminating," I said.

"Would you like to know how the phrase 'Liar, liar, pants on fire' got started?"

"Some other time, perhaps."

Much to my relief I could see churlish Mr. Curly turn the corner. With him were two security guards. I glanced around to see what interesting spectacle I might be missing.

"Cheng," I said over my shoulder, "do you think those two men over there on top of that blue container look suspicious. The tall one has a hat pulled way down over his eyes."

"Abby, you might—"

"You know what they say: only a fraction of the containers are actually checked. What if they have a nuclear bomb in there?"

"But Abby—"

"You're under arrest little lady."

I would have whirled and faced my accuser, but my hands were jerked behind my back and I felt a set of cold metal cuffs close around my wrists.

2

There are times when life seems to unfold in slow motion. I believe that this is a trick our brains play on us so we have time to think in crisis situations. I remember every second of what transpired next, as if my mind was a film and each frame was duly recorded in celluloid.

Mr. Curly, wielding a badge, began reciting the Miranda clause. Despite the fact that he was speaking, the corners of his mouth were turning up in a smug little smile and his beady eyes shone with pleasure. I thought of interrupting but was too shocked to respond right away, and to be honest, I was quite captivated by the fact that the late winter sunlight backlit a row of hair that marched down the length of his nose. Were those the *only* hairs on his head?

"Did you hear a word I said, Mrs. Washburn?" he asked when he was through.

"I'm sure I did. Although I'm still waiting to hear what I've been arrested for."

"For the illegal importation of contraband goods—as I said a moment ago."

"But you didn't."

"That's right," Cheng said, "you didn't. Abby, what illegal goods did you import?"

"Now who's being silly?" I hissed.

The big gal hung her head.

"Sorry, Cheng." I refocused my energy on Mr. Curly. "You didn't originally state the reason for my arrest, and you darn well know it."

"Are you calling me a liar?"

"Gentlemen," I called over my shoulders to my captors, "did *y'all* hear him?"

The men made no response. I hollered even louder, but they remained as quiet as clams. Now I don't mind stating, for the record, that this sort of rude behavior sets my teeth on edge. A gentleman should always answer when spoken to by a lady—especially if she is his elder. Their failure to answer was extremely unnerving, and on many levels.

Panic set in, and I may have temporarily lost my head. At any rate, the upshot is that I whipped my hands up over my head and whirled around to give those louts a brief lecture on manners. I was able to do to this because I have what I call double-jointed shoulders, and I can rotate my arms 360 degrees with my hands clasped. I have performed this feat many times at parties to amaze and freak out friends and guests. But how was I to know that my diminutive but well-proportioned hands would slip right through those one-size-fits-all cuffs? Bondage has never been my shtick.

Arms the size of pier pilings tried to circled me from behind, but not wanting to be crushed to death, I instinctively ducked.

"She's getting away!" Mr. Curly yelled. "Taser the witch!" Of course, not being a lady, he said it with a B.

"Oh no, you don't!" Cheng bellowed. Without a second's hesitation she threw herself at us, arms and legs outspread. She's five feet ten and weighs at least 180 pounds. In one fell swoop my loyal friend and faithful employee managed to take down all three men—and, unfortunately, yours truly along with them.

It was a brave but futile move. One of the afore-mentioned louts did have a Taser and poor Cheng became its target. I refuse to even let my mind get near a visual memory of the incident, and I'm pretty sure that Cheng, who can be stoic beyond belief, didn't utter a sound. What I do remember is that eventually Mr. Curly ordered whoever was torturing my friend to stop, since she was no longer resisting, and the cuffs went on her instead.

From then on I was too focused on Cheng to pay attention to where we were being taken, or to the length of the trip. Meanwhile Cheng lay face-down in the back of what looked like an army truck. Foam oozed from her mouth. Her eyes were half open.

"She needs to go to a hospital," I said for the millionth time.

"Shut up," Lout Number One said.

"If she dies, I'll testify against you; I'll see that you're convicted of murder."

"If you don't shut up," Lout Number Two said, "I'll use the Taser on you after all."

"My husband's a detective," I snapped. "I have connections." That was only sort of true. Greg used to be a detective, and that was up in Charlotte. Here he was a shrimper over in Mount Pleasant, where he co-owned a boat with his cousin Booger.

"We answer to a higher power," Lout Number One said, and they both laughed uproariously.

"At least let me feel for a pulse."

"You lift your butt one inch off that bench and you're toast."

"He means it," the other one said. "He hates small people."

"Can't you at least tell me what I did?"

"I said 'shut up.'"

I may have complied with my mouth, but my mind kept going a million miles a minutes. With my eyes only partly open, I read the security guards' name tags; I memorized every detail of their hard, unsympathetic faces; and I studied their hands to the point where I could have picked their owners out in a lineup by those alone.

"Whatcha looking at?" Lout Number One growled, when he finally realized what I was doing.

My heart pounded and my throat felt as if it had been sucked of all its moisture.

"I asked you a question, witch."

I tried to swallow. "I—um—I'm trying to decide which one of you is better looking—you or your friend."

"The hell you are."

Lout Number Two leaned closer. "So who is it? Taylor, or me?"

"Definitely you," I whispered.

Lout Number One grabbed the collar of my jacket and lifted me off the bench with one hand. "*What* did you say?"

"I told him that *you're* better looking."

"You got that right." He let me drop and turned his attention to Lout Number Two, whose given name was Hurley. "We gotta get our stories straight, or that witch on the floor could be trouble."

"She's got a name," I yelled. "And you better be taking us to a hospital."

Taylor nudged Cheng with his foot, but Hurley pantomimed kicking her. "She's faking it," he said. "She'll come around just as soon as we get to the station and Big Doris takes over."

I hate to say it, but that was all it took. Sure enough, Cheng sat up and began to groan.

"Where am I? What happened?"

"Didn't I tell you?" Hurley said to me, and gave her a real kick—albeit a fairly light one.

My buddy snarled like a wounded tiger.

"Cheng!" I cried. "It's only going to make matters worse if you don't cooperate with these thugs. They've got the power—for now."

"Sure talks big for such a little thing," Taylor said. "I like that in a woman; it kind of turns me on."

"Oh yeah?" Hurley said. "If she was my wife I'd—"

"Put a lid on it right now," I snapped, "that's what you'd do, because I already have way more than enough to get you both fired. Now it's just a matter of how long do *y'all* want to stay in prison?"

"Maybe she ain't kidding," Taylor said.

"Your grammar is atrocious," Cheng said. "I'm astounded that either of you got hired in the first place."

I cringed. "Cheng!"

"Well, it is. Cousin Johnny Cash back in Shelby

talked just like that, but when he took a DNA test it showed that there was more goat in his goatee than he let on—if you get my drift."

I couldn't help but roll my eyes. "I'm sorry, Cheng, but this time you've drifted right into the ocean; this is one Shelby tale I'm not buying. You may have goat blood coursing through your veins, but Johnny Cash was *not* your cousin!"

Cheng bleated in agreement. "Don't be silly, Abby, of course I'm not related to *the* Johnny Cash, of country/western fame. My cousin's family name was Cashmere when they immigrated to the United States from New Zealand. They dropped the 'mere' because they thought just plain 'Cash' sounded more American.

"That was back in the early 1900s. Later on, when cashmere wool became so popular, you can bet that we were glad that Great-granddaddy Uriah Cash had had the foresight to change his name. As it was, the women on that side of my family had to shave their mustaches before going into town, or risk having them pulled off by greedy fortune-hunters. Auntie Mirabelle even had her sideburns attacked with a straight razor while shopping for fabric at Murphy's Five and Ten."

"This woman is nuts," Hurley said, and both men sat on the other side of the van, facing us.

"Thanks, Cheng," I said under my breath. "That was just over the top enough to put the scare of God in them."

"But Abby, I meant every word."

"You big lug," I said affectionately as I scooted over a few inches.

It seemed to me that we drove at least as far as Columbia, the state capital, which is an hour and a half away, so that when we finally stopped at the City of Charleston Police Headquarters on Lockwood Boulevard, I was plum amazed. When the van doors were opened, at first I couldn't believe my eyes. But sure enough, there, across the street, was the Joe Riley Baseball Stadium and Brittlebank Park, and beyond them, glinting through the trees, the broad expanse of the Ashley River.

For some incomprehensible reason, most first-time visitors to Charleston are surprised to learn that the Atlantic Ocean begins at the confluence of the mighty Ashley and Cooper Rivers (just off Charleston's famed Battery). Just why it is that geographers have failed to address this important fact in our schools' textbooks is beyond me. Unlike some of my co-Southerners, I don't subscribe to the "Yankee plot" theory, but I must say, it is mighty suspicious when the facts stare you right in the face on a daily basis.

Now where was I?

Oh yes, I would have dropped my hank of alfalfa if I'd been Cheng's relatives. Not only were we in front of the police headquarters, but my husband, Greg, was standing there, dressed to the nines in his Sunday suit. He stepped forward.

"Mrs. Washburn is my client," he said, clenching my arm.

"Greg!"

"Are you an attorney?" Mr. Curly seemed to have popped out of nowhere.

"Her attorney is on her way. I'm acting *in parentis horriblis*."

"You better be on the up and up is all I can say."

"To the top," Greg said.

Mr. Curly grabbed my right arm and began pulling me to the main entrance. It felt like his fingers were going to separate the flesh of my triceps from the bone, and I cried out in pain. One cannot, therefore, blame my dear husband for objecting.

"Get your filthy hands off her, you dirt bag, or I'll take you for every penny you have. And when I'm done bleeding you dry, and the papers have had their fill of police brutality, then I'll come after you for incontrovertible conflagration. You won't be seeing sunshine this bright until you're so old they have to wheel you outside with a flannel blanket in your lap."

Stunned, Mr. Curly fell back. Greg didn't hesitate a second. With the confidence of a former law enforcement officer, he marched me into the police headquarters, all the while whispering into my ear.

"Booger's brother-in-law, Slate, works at the docks. You remember Slate, don't you? Drinks too much, bad teeth, but is twice as nice as a church

24

bus full of nuns. Anyway, he recognized you and called Booger. Lucky for you, we'd decided to take the day off and go clamming up the Wando. We were just minutes away. Don't look around, but Booger is sitting over there in the parking lot, keeping tabs on us, just in case our little ruse went sour. Meanwhile I have a call in to the very best attorney in all of the Southeast, and that includes the border states and D.C. Again you lucked out, because he just happened to be vacationing down at Kiawah Island Resorts, and is on his way as I speak. He should be here any minute."

"Greg, I wasn't even trying to get the cuffs off. You know how my shoulders rotate, and how small my hands are."

"Didn't I suggest that you join the circus?"

I struggled to keep a straight face. I felt safe now that I was with my cunning, and apparently well-connected, husband. At the same time, however, it felt like the eye of a hurricane. So far, I'd only seen the weak side of the storm; the worst was yet to come.

3

Perhaps it was thanks to Greg, but Cheng and I were processed quickly, and then thrown into a cell packed with prostitutes. Although there seemed to be a million of them, there were at least so many that there wasn't enough room for them to all sit on the four bunks, so they leaned against the walls and sink, and one very large one sat on the toilet (I never did learn if the seat was up or down). It seemed like they were all waiting for their lawyers as well, and some were being disturbingly vocal. When they saw us, they pounced like the wild dogs I'd seen on the Discovery Channel, their teeth bared, saliva dripping in anticipation of fresh meat.

"Well, well, what have we here?"

We said nothing. We made no eye contact.

A woman with particularly large feet planted herself right in front of me. "Does yo mama know yo're a streetwalker, li'l girl?"

It seemed like everyone—except for Cheng—roared with laughter. Of course I was infuriated, but I realized the futility of trying to win every battle that came my way. So what if they mocked me? I would save my energy for bigger things.

"She's not a little girl," another woman said. "She's a doll. That's why she don't answer."

"I don't care what she is," Miss Big Feet said, "but if she don' want her ass whupped, she best be answering me."

"Abby," Cheng whispered frantically, "please cooperate."

"You hear that little girl? Doll? Whatever you is? You listen to yo friend, girl, unless you want me to rearrange yo face foh you. We don' like no Barbie dolls in here."

When I *was* a little girl, Mama said I was stubborn. When I got to be a teenager I graduated to willful, tinged by mild rebellion (I wasn't always where I said I'd be, and I did try smoking cigarettes—briefly). As an adult I've eased into being comfortably contrary when I feel that I'm being pushed around. But other than that, I've always been the epitome of the Southern lady: gracious and calm. If I identify with any character in *Gone With the Wind*, it would have to be Melanie.

Miss Big Feet extended an index finger as fat as a Cuban cigar and mashed it into my forehead so hard I nearly lost my balance. "Answer me, girl!"

That's when Mama's karate lessons came in handy. Not that I'd taken them along with her, mind you, but she'd made me sit through enough of them to learn how to throw a stomach punch. My fists might be tiny, and my arms short, but I caught my tormentor totally unawares.

Miss Big Feet emitted a very satisfying gasp, swayed like a radio tower in a Category Five storm, and fell over backward. Her enormous stilettos, when suspended in the air, appeared totally surreal. She might just as well have been waving a pair of high-heeled canoes around. The other prostitutes convulsed with laughter.

"Ladies!" The single word was bellowed like a command, and it was followed by the clanging of a nightstick across the bars of our cell.

Cheng and I froze in position, like in the childhood game of Statues, but most, if not all, of the other women hooted and jeered at the prison guard. Even Miss Big Feet—once she was helped upright—got into the action.

The guard's face turned the color of pomegranate pulp. "You," she screamed, pointing at me, "you come with me!"

The women—and I refuse to call them "ladies"—convulsed with laughter. They slapped their thighs, stomped their feet, and whooped with delight. When one of them leaned against a wall to catch her breath and then slipped to the floor, they screamed their approval. At least as entertainment, I was a resounding success.

Another guard appeared to assist with my removal, although my actual removal was non-eventful—well, except for the rude catcalls that followed me down the hall.

"Hope to see you soon, little girl, but not on my street!"

"Hey you! That's right, you! You like yo sugar brown, or white?"

"Don't pay no attention to her. I'm gonna take you home so my daughter can play with you, on account of I can't afford no Barbie dolls."

But it was the last thing I heard before we turned the corner that really got to me.

"Abby, please don't abandon me!"

I was ushered brusquely into a windowless room and told to wait. The center of the room was occupied by a long, institutional-style table, around which six functional chairs had been placed. I chose a chair facing the door, and frankly, at that moment, I was glad just to be sitting. How quickly one's priorities can change, I thought.

After exactly twenty-two minutes (by my watch) the door opened, and a split second later so did my mouth. I stared, but for who knows how long. I was utterly shocked by who I saw standing there.

"You know, Abby," he said, "I always thought you were ravishingly beautiful, but to be brutally honest, you would be a mite more attractive if you closed your gaping maw."

I brought my petite lips together for a second. "My mouth's too small to be a maw—but never mind that. What are you doing here?"

"Abby, is that any way to greet your ex?"

"But Greg said he was getting me an attorney!"

"And so he did; you're looking at him."

"I'm looking at a man in a two thousand dollar suit, who practices law up in Charlotte. I repeat my question, Buford: what are you doing here?"

"Abby, Abby, Abby, I see you haven't changed one iota. You're still the little spitfire I married . . . what was it? Twenty years ago?"

"Twenty-six. Our daughter, Susan, is twenty-five. You do remember her, don't you?"

"Vaguely. Don't we have a son as well?"

I tried mightily not to smile. As husbands go, Buford might have been the slime on the ooze on the muck at the bottom of the pond, but at least he'd always been a decent father—given the circumstances.

"Seriously, Buford, are you licensed to practice law in South Carolina?"

Buford pulled out a chair and eased his ever growing bulk onto it. He'd been buff when we met at the water park, back in the days when we were both college students. Since then success had gone to his head, and biscuits and chicken fried steak had gone to his stomach, and one had to squint to get a glimpse of the same Buford Timberlake I'd said "I do" to at the Episcopal Church of Our Savior up in Rock Hill just over a quarter of a century ago.

"Abby, I'm sorry to be the bearer of such bad news, but you've been charged with a federal crime, not a state crime. And yes, I am qualified to represent you in front of a federal judge."

"*What* federal crime? I don't even know the charges."

"What do you mean you don't know the charges? Weren't they read to you?"

" 'Contraband goods.' That's all I've been told. For all I know, I'm being accused of importing lipsticks made in Shanghai that are fifty percent lead—which I'm not!"

A smile pushed Buford's jowls apart in an agreeable fashion. "Hell's bells," he said, "I think we just caught ourselves our first break. This arrest is not going to stick."

I felt woozy with relief. "It's not?"

"Nope. Now we just have to worry about the second set of charges. They're *not* federal, by the way."

"Since I'm having trouble following any of this, please explain."

"It concerns your behavior in the holding tank."

"Buford, I am *not* a prostitute. Not that I'm judging those women, mind you, but my business is still very successful, and I'm still happily married, and as monogamous as a goose."

"I can't say I'm happy for that last bit of news, but I'm not surprised either. Anyway, you're not accused of being a prostitute—you're being charged with inciting a riot."

I couldn't believe my ears. The day was going from awful to extremely horrible. Was there an even worse category waiting for me around the next bend?

"That's patently false," I protested. "A riot? The women were just laughing. How does that constitute a riot?"

"According to the guard, they were out of control because you had physically assaulted one of the other detainees."

"Is that what I am? A 'detainee'?"

"Well, you haven't been arraigned yet. But you will be—on your new charges—in about an hour." Buford's jowls jiggled again. "You can be grateful that I'm well-connected, Abby. Congressmen, senators, heck, even the President is a golfing buddy these days. You know what they say, don't you? A little charm goes a long way."

So does a little fertilizer. In my opinion Buford had always been *too* well-connected. In college he had channels through which to *obtain* papers, rather than have to write them. Even when he was in law school (which I helped put him through, by the way), we socialized with judges, small business owners, and even the ministers of some of the area's larger churches. Sometimes I rode with Buford to a bar at the edge of town, where he met men who wore sunglasses at night and dressed in dark suits. On those occasions I nursed watered-down glasses of rum and Coke and danced by myself.

When Buford passed the bar he quickly became a force to be reckoned with. In no time at all he made partner in a criminal law firm and his circle of contacts began to extend nationally. Having been raised in a small town, I'd grown up with the concept of the good old boy network, so I wasn't taken by surprise. But as much fun as it might sound to meet congressmen and -women, senators, and even the occasional governor, hosting them is a lot of work, even if you hire a caterer.

Why, there was that one time he brought home a drunken Texas oilman who had aspirations to be President . . .

"Abby, have you been listening to a word I've said?"

"Uh—mostly. Be honest, Buford: you do have a tendency to pontificate."

Buford frowned and his eyes disappeared behind newly acquired folds of fat. "Call your mama, Abby, and have her bring some clean clothes. Tell her to make it a dress—a suit, if you have one. Heels, but not too high, and hose are a must. Got that?"

I saluted. "Yes, sir!"

"I'm doing this for our children, Abby. So be a smartass, I don't care; but our children don't deserve to have a convict for a mother."

"I'm sorry, Buford. This is all so surreal—us *here,* in a jail."

A fleshy hand reached across for one of mine. My instinct was to jerk it away. Not only was Buford supposedly happily married, but he'd traded me in when I turned forty to a woman who was twenty years old and at least twenty percent silicone. But I decided to give him the benefit of the doubt; perhaps he really was just being kind.

After a very awkward minute or two I pulled gently out of his grasp. "Buford, I ordered a rosewood commode for Mama's birthday. Since when has rosewood become contraband?"

"That's just it, Abby. The crate that you came to pick up *didn't* contain rosewood—in any form—it was ivory."

"Ivory? But I didn't buy any ivory. It's illegal to import ivory, unless it's more than a hundred years old, or the tusks in question are one's hunting trophy."

"Exactly. But *someone* in Charleston has been on the receiving end of a great deal of illegal ivory. That's why the Feds may have come down a little hard on you."

"A *little* hard on me? Buford, your children's mother was practically beaten into the pavement—"

"They beat you?"

"No. But they tried to handcuff me. They also swore at me. And they were anything but gentle with Cheng—formerly known to you as C.J."

He nodded; I'm not sure he was still listening. "Now here, take my phone and call your mama. And while we're waiting for her to show up, I'll have the matron take you someplace for a shower. You certainly can't appear in front of a judge smelling like that."

I did the pit sniff test and nearly passed out. "I'll tell Mama to bring some deodorant," I said. I swallowed a huge lump of pride. "Buford, thanks. Really. This is awfully nice of you. Just so you know, I insist on paying you your regular going rate; no special breaks for me just because I'm an ex-family member."

His jowls quivered, his double chin trembled, and he licked his lips with a tongue as pale and unappetizing as boiled cow's liver. "There's no need to think about payment just yet, Abby. I'm sure we'll come to an understanding once this little unpleasantness is behind you."

I reeled, just as surely as if I'd been slapped.

"Buford, are you suggesting that payment be—uh, of a personal nature?"

"And why not?" Buford said. "After all, we are both over twenty-one, aren't we?"

"And *married!* Have you lost your marbles, or did the sun on Kiawah Island bake your brain?"

"I see that you're as feisty as ever; don't think that I've forgotten how it used to be for a minute. We were like ferrets in bed: always nipping at each other—"

"Stop! I'm getting sick to my stomach."

"Good times, Abby. As far as I'm concerned, we can share plenty more."

"What about your wife?"

"She left me."

"Buford, you didn't!"

Although he did have the decency to blush, the color was fleeting. "I only cheated once; besides marriage to Catherine was a mistake, Abby, you shouldn't have encouraged it."

"*Encouraged* it? You came to me for moral support, and that's what I gave you."

"Just the same, you know what kind of cad I am. You should have put one of your tiny feet down."

"If my tiny foot was wearing a more pointed shoe, Buford, you would be begging me to put it anywhere but your backside."

"Golly, how I miss you, Abby."

"I'm calling Mama, Buford. And I'm telling her to bring my Jimmy Choos."

4

The good news was that Buford is one of the best lawyers in the entire Southeast. The really good news was that he is extremely well-connected, and that the judge before whom I was to appear was the brother of Buford's college roommate. Don't ask me how the system works, but the key element in my retelling of that morning's events is that I didn't even have to make a courtroom appearance—although I did have to shower under the supervision of the matron, and dress in the clothes that Mama brought (they weren't what I'd requested).

The bad news is that Buford immediately began pressing me for a date—even though Greg was right there—and the really bad news was that Mama did nothing to keep the two men apart. In fact, she seemed rather stimulated by the idea of two men simultaneously pursuing her daughter.

"Abby," she said, right in front of them on the courthouse steps, "did you know that there are actually cultures where the women have more than one husband? They're called Pollyanna, I think."

"Mozella," Greg said softly, "I believe the word is polyandrous."

"Well, I was close," Mama said. She reached up with a gloved hand and felt the hat she was wearing. Satisfied that it was in place, she plumped the starched crinolines that kept her full-circle skirt inflated. "I heard about this custom from a missionary woman who spoke at our church. The poly-uh-whatever wife gets to do the choosing. Personally, I think that the prospect of being rejected would be just awful. I mean, not everyone is as lucky as you."

"Mama! What is that supposed to mean?"

"You know perfectly well, dear. Here you are—little, itty-bitty you—and here is big, handsome, strong Greg, and here we also have the very wealthy, powerful, and dare we say, well-connected Buford Timberlake, and both of these gentlemen would gladly throw their cloaks over a puddle to keep your slippers from getting wet. You must admit—not every woman has this choice."

"But I don't have a choice! I'm happily married, Mama. And shame on you for even suggesting that I might be willing to entertain cheating on my husband. And even if I did—which I'm *not*—it wouldn't be with the man who cheated on me."

"There, you see, Buford," Mama said, "my daughter has publicly rejected you yet again. At this point any decent man should feel humiliated. Do you feel humiliated, Buford?"

Jowls jiggled as Buford attempted to grin. "Not at all."

"Snakes don't feel humiliated either," Mama said. "That's why we call you Timber Snake."

The forced grin froze and Buford stared at Mama

with his beady little eyes until she waved a glove in front of his face. Then he took forever to clear his throat.

"I wasn't aware of that nickname," he said at last. "Nevertheless, I choose to take it as a compliment."

"It isn't meant as one," Mama said. "Come on, Abby—Greg—let's go."

"Why Mozella," the snake in question said, "you've got even more spitfire than your daughter. How could I have been overlooking something this good all of these years? How old are you? Fifty? Fifty-five?"

"I'm forty-eight," I shouted loud enough for all of Charleston County to hear.

Mama patted her ubiquitous pearls. "But dear, I got married very young."

"But not when you were two! Or even seven years old."

"Well, you don't look a day over fifty-five," Buford said, "and I ought to know. Between this wife and the one before, I spent enough time in the waiting rooms of plastic surgeons to write a book on the aging process and what one can possibly hope to achieve by surgery. I'm telling you, Mozella, my hat is off to whomever did your face. That guy, or gal, is a genius."

Mama twittered shamelessly. "You silly thing, Buford, now just hush. You know when I was born; you did my will."

"I can't remember dates, Mozella. Boy Scout's honor."

"Well, in that case I guess I should be kind and put you out of your misery. Next Tuesday is my birthday, and I will be turning sixty-four."

I started to correct her, then decided to just let it go.

"In that case, happy birthday!" Buford exclaimed.

"Come to think of it, your children will be calling to wish me the same, so why don't you stop by and—"

The right combination of brow lifts and eye rolls from me, and my sweet, strong husband got the message without me uttering a sound. He slipped behind Mama and picked her up by the elbows. Then walking bowlegged—so as to avoid her kicks—he carried her the rest of the way down the courthouse steps and halfway back to the car.

Thanks to the strangely detached world we live in these days, folks hardly noticed. A family of round tourists from one of the square states clapped, a couple of people driving by honked, and some old dude in a tie-dye T-shirt and a gray pony-tail said "Right on, dude" before mumbling something about the end of the world, but to my knowledge no one called the police to report a kid-napping, and certainly no one confronted us directly.

As for the Timber Snake, although he slithered away quietly, I knew him well enough to predict that he would strike again.

Cheng had not been charged with inciting a riot, so she was released before I was. Still, she'd been through a grueling day—and on my account, no less. Therefore I was quite happy to give her the week off that she requested to visit her family up in Shelby, North Carolina, and I insisted that it be with pay. And since I am not the best person at taking care of myself, my darling husband insisted that I also take a week off—which I did. We flew down to Vieques, Puerto Rico, where we did some fabulous snorkeling, lay about in the sun, and engaged in some horizontally challenged marital bonding.

As a result I returned to the Den of Antiquity glowing with sun-damaged skin cells and eager to get back to work. Wynnell Crawford, my dearest friend, not to mention my trusted employee, grabbed me the second I planted a size four boot over the threshold of the shop's rear door.

"Abby, that man from the news was just here looking for you."

"Matt Lauer?"

"You know Matt Lauer?" Wynnell's voice had risen to a frightening pitch.

"No; it was wishful thinking. I did meet our local weatherman once—we were both judging sandcastles for Piccolo—but I can tell by the look on your face that that is not who you mean."

"You're right about that, Abby. This is the guy who arrested you and hauled you off to jail. Mr. Curly, he said his name was. Who is he, Abby, one of the Three Stooges?" Ever supportive, my buddy draped her arm around my shoulder and squeezed me tightly. "I told him you were taking a cruise around the world and called me last night as you were sailing away from the Palagados Islands."

"Hmm. Are those anywhere near the Galapagos Islands?"

"Well he seemed to get the drift. You don't see him here now, do you?"

"I haven't been inside the shop yet, Wynnell. Apart from Mr. Curly, how is everything? How are you? How is Cheng?"

"Cheng called to say that she won't be in until tomorrow—if that's all right."

"I wonder why she didn't call me."

"Because you might have said no."

"Good point. How have sales been?"

"Sales are always down in February, Abby, you know that. But I took advantage of some of the quiet times to work on our displays. Cheng simply doesn't have the knack for it—I mean, either you have the gift for it, or you don't—and you've never claimed to have an eye for staging."

"Staging?"

"You know, like they do in model homes, when

41

they set up tableaux. Come on, I'll show you."

My knees felt weak, but meanwhile my heart raced. Wynnell is a good person, and a loyal friend, but she was born without taste—bless her heart. Every time she's taken it upon herself to set up a display, I've felt compelled to quietly dismantle it. It's either that or run the risk that she'll hear the rude comments of some tourist and have her heart broken.

"Don't worry, Abby," she said. "You're going to like what I've done. And anyway, we better get out there on the floor, because the register is untended."

The U word was motivation enough, and I trotted along behind her, willing myself to be calm. Whatever she'd done, I could gradually undo—I hoped.

Wynnell had indeed taken advantage of the February lull. Her husband, Ed, is an avid fisherman, but not a professional like Greg. He usually fishes with bait and tackle off the pier on Folly Beach. Occasionally he goes trout fishing in the mountains of North Carolina, and on even rarer occasions he forks out enough money to indulge in deep-sea fishing off our own coast.

Judging by Wynnell's displays, either Ed had given up his hobby or purchased a great deal of new equipment. Hip boots, rods and reels, tackle boxes, lures of every description, these were spread across every flat surface or stuck into any cranny that would hold them—whatever best applied to them. Frankly, it looked more like I was running a disorganized garage sale than a high-end antiques store.

"What do you think, Abby?"

I bit my lip, trying to buy some time. "It's uh—very—uh—"

"Mrs. Washburn."

The male voice coming from my right was familiar, but I couldn't place it before I made the mistake of turning to see who it belonged to. I recognized the man instantly, and my hackles were hiked so high I nearly achieved liftoff. Only once before—the second time I discovered Tweetie's lipstick on Buford's collar—did I ever get so angry so quickly.

"S-you!" I sputtered.

"Take it easy, Mrs. Washburn, I'm not here to arrest you."

"Then get out of my shop!"

"Yes, ma'am, but I need to talk to you."

"Go!" I pointed to the door.

"Ma'am, I'm sorry for how it went down earlier; you see—"

"You heard my friend," Wynnell said. "You go, or I'm calling the police."

"Wynnell," I whispered, "I think he is the police. Or the FBI. Something like that."

"Well, I'm calling someone," Wynnell said.

"You mess with my friend, Abby, and you mess with me. I wasn't such a picky eater when I was little, so as you can see, I've grown a bit since I was six."

"Wynnell," I protested, "I'm not a picky eater anymore, and it has nothing to do with being short."

"Oh yes, it does. You missed out on all those vitamins and minerals—and calcium. You need calcium to make bones, Abby, and you never drink milk."

"That's not true. I had milk with my raisin bran this morning—okay, so it was yesterday morning. And I love ice cream, and all sorts of cheeses."

"Mrs. Washburn," the horrible Mr. Curly interjected, "what I have to say to you is extremely important."

"Then why don't you take out an ad in the *Post and Courier*. Maybe a full page ad. That should do for an apology. Don't you think so, Wynnell?"

"Yes, ma'am," Mr. Curly said, "if that's what you really want. But this is about something far more important than that. Might I talk to you alone?"

"Ha! I don't think so. The next thing I know your goons will jump out of nowhere and I'll be hauled off in a paddy wagon again. This time I'll probably have fishing wire wrapped around my extremities."

"Very well, Mrs. Washburn; if that's what you

like. But what I am about to tell you is classified information. That means that your friend here, Mrs. Crawford, can't go blabbing it around to her friends."

"Mrs. *Crawford?*" Wynnell and I chorused.

"How did you know my name?" Wynnell demanded.

"Because you, ma'am, have also been one of the subjects of our investigation."

5

I called Greg and told him about my unwanted visitor, and then I locked the door, so as not to involve anyone else in the drama that had once been my life. In the meantime Wynnell poured cups of her infamous coffee. With her as my witness, I ushered the hateful man back to the break room, which is barely more than a cubbyhole furnished with a Craftsman table and four matching chairs. On one of the three principal walls there is a poster of *The Scream*, which, at the moment, seemed to be fitting.

Motioning for Mr. Curly to take a seat, I plunged right in. "As you know, sir, the case has been dropped."

"And therefore no double identify," Wynnell said sternly, as she plunked a mug of coffee so close to him that droplets splashed on his sleeve.

"Ma'am?" he said.

"She means double indemnity."

Wynnell sniffed. "That's what I said."

"Yes, ma'am." He turned to me. "Mrs. Washburn, again I apologize for my behavior on the dock. There was no excuse for it."

"There certainly wasn't."

"I was completely out of line."

"Just be glad she's not suing you for false arrest," Wynnell said. "Uh, you aren't—are you, Abby?"

"The jury's still out on that." I laughed feebly. "Get it?"

"Very funny, Mrs.Washburn."

"I don't get it, Abby. Then again, I'm not a suck-up like he is."

"Wynnell, dear," I said, "with a friend like you, who needs more?"

"I don't get that either, Abby."

Mr. Curly took a sip of his coffee. His eyes bulged and his lips puckered. He tried mightily to swallow. After a few seconds he wisely spit the brew back into his cup.

"What's the matter?" Wynnell said. "Don't you like my coffee?"

"Ah—hem, hem." He made several attempts to clear his throat and then whilst swallowing in rapid succession, pounded on his chest with a closed fist. "It has a lot of flavor, ma'am."

"Doesn't it, though?"

I felt the blood rush to my head. Once before Wynnell had taken an extreme dislike to a customer who had treated me rudely and "flavored" the woman's complimentary coffee with a liberal dash of Tabasco sauce. That woman was a doyenne of Charleston society, and ever since that fateful day, my faithful friend has been blacklisted (not that she stood much of a chance before that day).

"Wynnell," I said, "is this your special blend?"

"It is."

"Perhaps you will be so kind then as to remove the cup and bring him some water. Make that a *sealed* bottle of water."

Wynnell's eyebrows have never been plucked or trimmed, and she struggles with hormone issues. As a consequence, when she scowls, a bristling black caterpillar takes shape on her forehead, stretching from temple to temple in an unbroken line.

"If you insist," she said, but she didn't move.

"*Now,* please."

"Oh, all right," she huffed. "But you," she said, pointing a finger practically in Mr. Curly's face, "better not try any funny business with our Abby. There are cameras hidden everywhere, and if you beat up on her, I'm taking video evidence to one of the morning network shows. And maybe Dr. Phil. He'll give you what for. He doesn't cotton to men brutalizing women."

The second she was out of earshot Mr. Curly got down to business. "Since the—uh—incident—on the dock, I've checked around, Mrs. Washburn.

You're thought of highly in this community, but what's more important, you have an impeccable record. So again I apologize." He paused, but not long enough for me to comment. "You see, I've been working on this case for going on almost five years. It seems that large shipments of illegal ivory are coming through the Port of Charleston, but sporadically, and the person—or persons—on the receiving end—are never the same."

"Whoa, run that by me again, please. How can you tell something like that is going on if the recipient keeps changing, etcetera?"

"Mrs. Washburn, the Port of Charleston handles thousands of tons of cargo every day, and it is impossible for the U.S. Customs Office to inspect but a tiny fraction of that cargo. Since 9/11 we concentrate on detecting anything that may be a threat to public safety—"

"Like a nuclear bomb?"

"Yes, that too. And besides issues of public safety, of course we screen for drugs, for they pose a threat to society as well. Looking for contraband imports, such as ivory, is low on the list. However, during these five years we've been lucky on four occasions and happened upon shipments of ivory, all of it originating in Hong Kong. And all of it headed to different addresses here in the Charleston area."

Wynnell slipped back into the room with a bottle of Aquafina and a scowl.

"Anyway," Mr. Curly said, "stated recipients, like you, all checked out to be innocent parties, but unlike you, none of them ever showed up at the dock; they were completely unaware that their names and address had been used. That's what makes your case so different."

"Yes, but like I told you, I showed up to collect a rosewood commode, not contraband ivory."

Mr. Curly chuckled. "You're serious, aren't you?"

"Of course she is!" Wynnell snapped.

"You'll have to forgive her," I said. "One of her grandparents was a Yankee; she just can't help herself."

"Why, I never!" Wynnell said. "Abby, you take that back."

"Well, its true, Wynnell. And there's nothing wrong with that; it's not like it's a disease."

"I don't know," Mr. Curly said before Wynnell could react. "My wife started hanging out with a retiree from up North and was recently diagnosed with acute Connecticutitis. All of a sudden she wants to vacation in New England."

I fought back a smile. "Mr. Curly, I don't think charm is going to work. You were there; you know how you treated me."

"Like garbage," Wynnell said. "And you treated C.J. even worse than that."

Mr. Curly frowned. "Who is C.J.?"

"The woman who was with me: Miss Cheng.

C.J. was what we used to call her. It's a long story."

"Might it be pertinent?"

We shook our heads.

"Perhaps I should be the one to judge. These shipments *are* coming through Hong Kong, and Cheng is a Chinese name. Perhaps Mrs. Cheng has connections through her husband."

"It's *Miss* Cheng," Wynnell hissed, "and she's from Shelby, North Carolina."

"What?" he said. "They don't have criminals in Shelby? Although I must admit, one would never guess that she was Chinese simply by looking at her. I mean, *is* she?"

While I am all for not being ashamed of one's ethnicity, I am still not convinced that in polite society one should not express undo pride in one's origins. For either we are born into a tribe, having had no say in the selection process, or else we selected our own group before birth. In the latter case, whichever group we preselected—white middle class, British royal family, one of Brad and Angelina's children—isn't really special, because we could have *all* been that. In any event, for the most part one's ethnicity is a private matter, but Mr. Curly was going to get the answer Cheng would have most likely given him.

"She's part Chinese, part Russian, and part goat."

"Ha ha. Stonewalling me, eh? Mrs. Washburn, I really am trying to be nice."

"Mr. Curly, what exactly is it that you want from me?"

"Mrs. Washburn, may I speak to you alone?"

"You most certainly may not," Wynnell said.

His reaction was to smile. "I admire loyalty like yours, Mrs. Crawford. Mrs. Washburn is a lucky woman."

"Wynnell," I said, summoning up some sugar, "I have no doubt that I'll be just fine here. But I'd be eternally grateful if you'd straighten up the jewelry case to the left of the register—the one with the amber pieces in it. I had a customer just before closing who couldn't make up her mind, and as a consequence the display is a bit of a mess. It was worth it, though. She ended up buying that Latvian piece with three flies embedded in it."

Wynnell whistled. "Way to go, Abby. I didn't think anybody was stupid enough to pay three thousand dollars for a chunk of sap with insects stuck in it."

"It was top-notch amber dredged up from the Baltic Sea, and two of the flies were mating. How sweet is that?"

"Please," Mr. Curly said, "I have other cases to work on."

Wynnell sighed loudly, but nonetheless complied with our wishes. Still, I wouldn't have been surprised to learn that she'd paused just outside with her ear pressed to the door.

"I'll get right to it," Mr. Curly said. "Are you

familiar with The Singing Panda up the street? Forgive the stupid question, how could you *not* be?"

The Singing Panda! Now there was a store name chosen merely for its ability to tantalize. For one thing, giant pandas don't sing, but *if* they did, they'd most probably sing in Chinese, not Italian. Yet it is Italian opera that one hears playing on the sound system. The merchandise, however, *is* Chinese, and is several steps above your average gift shop. A few pieces are, in fact, of such high quality as to raise eyebrows amongst the other vendors on King Street. Where exactly was this stuff during the Cultural Revolution?

"Yes, I've been in there a few times," I said. "He has some nice things. But frankly I think he would have been better off locating in a more cosmopolitan market. Charleston is still a Southern town. There is only so much Asian influence you can add without destroying the local flavor."

Mr. Curly nodded. "Do you know the owner? Eric Bowfrey?"

"I've seen him a couple of times at business events, and once or twice at a party, but I wouldn't say that I know him."

"Still, do you have any impressions of him that you could share?"

"Nice kid."

"Kid?"

"He can't be more than thirty; that's a kid to me."

"He seem strange?"

"Yeah, but—if you already know about him, why are you asking me?"

"Please. Just answer my question."

"Well, he's extremely quiet. Mostly just keeps his hands in his pockets and smiles. And no matter what the occasion, he wears a forest green sweatshirt with the hood up. Then again, if I had eyes as green as his—Oh, and those dimples. I could eat custard with a spoon out of them."

"Mrs. Washburn, the green-eyed boy with the bottomless dimples came down to the dock yesterday afternoon and signed for a large shipment from Hong Kong. I had a feeling about that lot so I had him open it. It was all run-of-the-mill stuff—some of it not too bad, and all of it on the bill of sale—except for a rosewood commode. When the kid saw it, the first words out of his mouth were, and I quote: 'What the heck? I didn't buy that!' "

"Too bad for the kid," I said, "but I fail to see how this relates to me."

"I doubt if that's so," Mr. Curly said. "On the day when—uh, you unfortunately landed in jail—you said that you were expecting a commode. Instead you got ivory. Perhaps this is *your* commode."

"Mr. Curly," I said politely, "for the sake of argument, let's say that you are correct. Thank you for notifying me, but to be honest, my illegal incarceration has taken the bloom off of that rose. I no longer wish to have anything to do with a Chinese

53

commode. In fact I'm going to stay away from any foreign imports for a while."

"I understand, Mrs. Washburn, but believe me, your experience was atypical. I'm sure that as a successful businesswoman, you know that."

I shrugged. "Am I to believe that you took time from your busy schedule terrorizing minuscule middle-aged women just to inform me that someone else got a set of dresser drawers that were intended for me?"

"And to ask your help in setting up a sting."

"What?"

"It's a kind of trap, Mrs. Washburn. There was even a movie by that name—"

"I know what a sting is! I just can't believe you want me to be part of one."

"Oh." A light seemed to have gone off behind Mr. Curly's eyes. He stood slowly. "In that case, I apologize for your time, as well."

"No, you don't get it! I'd *love* to be a part of a sting! When do we start?"

"We already have," he said with a smile.

6

My hunk of burning love keeps a schedule that is in tune with both the tide and the season. But the one thing I count on is that he is always home when I trudge in at the end of the day. Not only that, but he usually waits with a drink in his hand. Sometimes he even has a drink ready for me.

That day was no different. "Hey, darling," he said, and gave me a passionate kiss on the lips.

Immediately the other male who lives in our house rubbed his hairy body against me, as he vocalized his pleasure. I would have picked up my fifteen pound cat, Dmitri, but this was one of those days Greg had thought to make me a drink.

"It's called a Pom-Pom," he said. "I thought it up myself."

"What's in it?"

"Two parts pomegranate juice and one part pomegranate liqueur, and a twist of lime."

"Where did you find the pomegranate liqueur?"

"I didn't, so I used vodka."

I took a sip. It was tart, but not unbearable. After a few seconds the astringency abated and my mouth felt fine again, so I took another sip.

"Did you and Booger have a good day?" I asked.

"So-so. We're taking some tourists on a pleasure ride tomorrow. They want to see what it's like to be out over the Gulf Stream. You want to come along? We'll be doing an onboard picnic."

"Thanks, but no thanks."

"Oh come on, hon. Ever since I bought into this boat you've been complaining that I don't take you out on it enough. Besides, have you heard the weather report?"

"No."

"Near record warmth."

"That figures. Snows one week, gorgeous weather the next."

"So come, already."

"Sorry, Greg, but I promised—there's just some work I have to do."

"Don't say that I never ask."

"Okay. Where's Mama?"

"Uh—I think your drink needs refreshing, Abby. Here, let me have it."

"It's fine. Just tell me where she is? Is she out seeing friends?"

"Yes—uh, no. I guess I'd have to call him more of an acquaintance."

There are times when I don't catch on right away, but I'm not completely brain dead. "Greg, dear, something smells fishy, and it isn't just you and your work clothes."

"Honey, sit down—please."

My legs wobbled over to the nearest chair—a genuine Louis XIV—and the rest of me obligingly followed.

"Sweetheart," Greg said once I was seated, "your mother has a mind of her own; I'm sure you know that."

I nodded mutely.

"And she can be very contrary."

"Uh-huh."

"I've always said that she reminded me of George W. in crinolines. Of course your mother keeps her body hair to a minimum."

I gave him a weak smile. When he trots that joke out at dinner parties he at least gets polite laughter. Don't get me wrong, Greg loves Mama, but now that she lives with us, he feels entitled to some mild humor at her expense.

"Abby, your mama is out to dinner with Buford." He almost whispered the B word.

I wasn't shocked; thanks to his buildup, I'd almost seen that coming. In fact, my immediate reaction was relief—relief that she hadn't run off and married my ex-husband. That would have been an icky situation, not only for me, but for our children, Susan and Charles.

"Why is she doing this, Greg? Why is Mama dating Buford?"

Greg set our drinks down and knelt beside me. Wrapping me in his arms, he pulled my head to his chest and smothered it with kisses.

"Now honey, let's not get ahead of ourselves. She's not *dating* him; they're just having dinner. And this is the first time—that I know of."

"And the last!"

"But to answer your question, for some reason your mother has a very low boredom threshold. Couple that with a strong need to compete with you and . . . well, I'm surprised this hasn't happened before. Remember that time she ran off to become a nun?"

"They rejected her for wearing curlers under her wimple and for whistling on the stairs."

"She definitely was not an asset to the abbey. I don't think she'll be an asset to Buford either. If he really has his eye on a public office, he can't afford a scandal like dating his ex-mother-in-law. Even though she is very attractive—in her own way."

"*You* think so?"

"Well I should hope so. You favor her, don't you? Yeah, I know you don't dress like you're the Beave's mom, but you share the same features, and the same nice proportions—uh, but of course you look younger and nicer. Don't they always say that you should look at a woman's mother to see how *she'll* look in twenty years?"

I asked for my Pom-Pom back, and then downed the glass in two gulps. "Make me another please."

"Whoa, are you sure?"

"Quite."

It was quarter past eleven, and I was sitting on the front steps (it was so warm that I needed only a light sweater) when I heard a woman's voice approaching from my left. Ours is a very quiet street, and since there are no bed and breakfast establishments anywhere near, a human voice at such a late hour is quite the anomaly. The speaker was either talking to her dog or speaking into her cell phone. In either case, she was not from around here, because behavior such as this was just plain rude, and my neighbors are all very polite people.

"No, I will *not* free them; I don't care what Mr.

Lincoln says!" There was something odd about her accent, something I couldn't put my finger on.

I stood quietly, hoping to spot her.

"In case you have forgotten, sir," she said, her voicing rising, "it was my father's money that bought them. It is his largesse that we depend on even now. And it would be my father's wish—were he here—that I continue to be cared for in the manner in which I have always been accustomed."

Okay, now it made sense; the woman was an actress rehearsing a scene about the emancipation of the slaves. We have several theaters in town, and Hollywood loves to use our colonial and antebellum homes as backdrops for their movies. In fact, great chunks of the film *The Patriot* were set here, just two blocks from my house.

"If that's how you feel, Mr. Broderick, then perhaps you *should* return to Illinois."

There! At last I could see her. She was much taller than I—but who wasn't—and wearing a period costume. Under the streetlights the dress appeared to be a rich blue, perhaps silk, and the skirt ballooned in all directions, no doubt supported by barrel hoops. She wore her dark hair swept up off the nape of her neck, and atop it a blue-feathered hat that matched her dress.

"Sir, do you jest? Benjamin and Alice are *my* children! You are but their stepfather; you cannot take them to Illinois with you."

I stood very still. The woman was now passing

just inches directly in front of me, but she seemed totally unaware of my presence. I could hear the rustle of her dress and smell the combination of old sweat and lavender water.

"No, sir, you cannot make me choose! You cannot!"

It was then that I noticed that the woman in blue was too preoccupied to duck, or sidestep, the overhanging bough of a live oak tree. She walked right into it—and then *through* it. I mean that literally! Leaves, twigs, even wood as thick my wrist, passed right through her head, neck, and chest.

"If I give up my slaves," she cried, "then I shall have to give up this grand house, for we will never be able to afford so many servants—not on your salary, sir!"

I sat back down on the steps. I wasn't afraid, mind you, just somewhat entranced. For some reason Charleston has more than its fair share of Apparition Americans. As one local medium expressed it: unhappy people here don't die; they just become invisible part of the time. Of course not everyone is misfortunate enough to see those who have only partially passed from this life—nonbelievers seldom do—but at the same time, there are those among us who are particularly sensitive to their continued presence. I just happen to be one of them. And although this was by no means my first encounter with an Apparition American since moving to the Lowcountry, it was by far my longest.

"Abby," another voice said, "what's the matter? You look like you've seen a ghost?"

I looked up to find Mama standing so close that I could see my reflection in her black patent leather shoes. "Mama! Where did you come from?"

"From across the street; my date dropped me off."

"Aha, so he *was* your date!"

"He was my dinner date, dear. Although frankly, the exact terminology for my evening's companion is none of your business."

"The heck it isn't. Mama, what did you—"

But Mama had swept past me and was on her way into the house. Extracting any more information from her on the subject was going to be as futile as the press trying to get the truth from the White House. I was going to have to wait until either she tripped herself up or felt the need to gloat.

Tomorrow I would start my unofficial undercover work. It was time for me to go to bed.

7

When The Singing Panda opened its doors, it was an instant success. The name alone elicited a good deal of press, but the higher-end Asian goods seemed to really hit the spot with the nouveau riche who were flocking onto the Lower Peninsula and buying homes south of Broad Street.

S.O.B.'s, we call these folks. South of Broaders. To be honest, I am one of these.

While a pleasing aesthetic can be achieved by mixing quality Asian pieces into a traditional decorating scheme, quite often designers are asked to incorporate mass-market resin pieces that are commonly available at home decorating stores. The truth is that many of these fake antiques are more attractive and durable than the real thing. A hundred years from now these resin beauties will take on a value of their own—perhaps—but they won't be traditional Asian antiques. For the real thing, go to The Singing Panda; there, you'll find treasures that managed to escape the Cultural Revolution.

As I pushed open the door of The Singing Panda, my senses were immediately confronted by two things: loud Italian opera and thick Chinese incense. I glanced around through the haze, and thankfully, rather quickly, spotted the owner down an aisle to my right. He was dusting with a feather duster.

Can you turn down the volume? I mouthed, without uttering a sound. This is a little trick I play on Mama when she starts pretending she can't hear something. The fact is, she could hear a frog fart in Fargo—if she wanted to—pardon my indelicate language. Since Mama's ear pans work extremely well, this sudden "glitch" sends her into a panic.

Apparently Eric Bowfrey was a pro at lip-reading. Mind-reading too. He not only turned off the music, but he made a show of carrying a bowl of lit joss sticks into the back room, and then closing the door on them.

"How may I help you?" he said when he returned. As usual, he was dressed in a lightweight green burnoose, the hood up. His face had all the serenity of a sitting Buddha, yet his vivid green eyes managed to sparkle. As for his dimples, they were every bit as deep as I'd imagined, so I did a little more on-the-spot imagining, and pressed some finely cut Colombian emeralds into them.

"My name is Abilake Timbergail," I said. "I mean, it's Abigail Washburn, but Timber Snake is my business name—please, just call me Abby."

"I'm Eric," he said softly. "I know who you are, Abby. You have that fabulous shop: the Den of Iniquity."

"Uh—it's the Den of Antiquity. Iniquity is my *a*vocation, not my vocation."

His face didn't change. "Are you serious?"

"Are you stoned?"

"I'm at peace with the world, Abby. I speak only the truth. This makes me vulnerable to sarcasm and the butt of jokes, but I have worked hard to be where I am. This is where I wish to stay."

"I'm not trying to dissuade you—Never mind; it's an admirable state of affairs. Eric, can we talk?"

"Aren't we talking now?"

"Yes, but a customer could walk in any minute. I mean, like, can I take you to dinner after work? Can we meet for a drink? That type of thing?"

"Abby, I eat only raw organic produce that was picked at midday when the plant is least likely to be actively growing and thus the least likely to experience pain. Did you know that most plants grow at night?"

"No, I didn't. How fascinating."

"At any rate, everything I eat, I have to grow myself, or else have it especially shipped into Charleston; long story short, I can't eat out. And of course, I don't drink. Yes, I know that red wine is supposed to be beneficial, but in the making of most commercial wine, grapes are tortured."

I thought of Lucy and Ethel stomping on the grapes in an old *I Love Lucy* episode. I could just hear the grapes shrieking in pain as the pair clowned around. What an absolutely insensitive person I was. Could this soft-spoken man be right? And what if it was just a matter of time before scientists proved that it was only a small step from being *infruitane* to being inhumane?

"But," Eric, said, his voice barely above a whisper, "this shop is mine, and I am free to do with it as I please. And what I please is to close now for a few minutes so that we can talk here—if that suits you."

"It suits me to a tea."

The tea wasn't jasmine, but English breakfast, and served in hand-painted porcelain as light as paper and as transparent as Greg's mind the week before Christmas. Pottery might have gotten its start in the Near East, and glorious glazes perfected in China, but it was an Englishman by the name of Josiah Spode II who thought of adding powdered animal bone as fifty percent of his porcelain component. Eric also brought a plate with warm blueberry scones and a glass bowl filled with clotted cream.

"Have you ever had clotted cream?" he asked.

"Never."

"Spread it on your scone like butter. I picked that up at the Mount Nelson Hotel in Capetown. Believe me, it's worth the calories."

"Eric, you shouldn't have."

"It was no trouble. I bake my own scones every morning before I come to work."

"No, I meant you shouldn't have brought out just two. I skipped breakfast and I'm hungry enough to eat both."

He laughed. "There are two more back there; I never know who's going to drop in. So, Abby, what's on your mind?"

"Before I get to that: aren't scones made of wheat, and isn't wheat thrashed?"

"The word is 'threshed,' and this wheat isn't, it's handpicked. Mozart is played while the milling takes place, to ease the pain of the grain being crushed. However, the cows much prefer the Beatles. *Abbey Road* is their favorite album."

His green gaze never wavered, which meant he was telling the truth—at least in my book. What a peaceful face! What was it that drew one in? Was it the perfect skin, or the slight smile that tugged at the corners of his full, bow-shaped lips? Forget about putting emeralds in his dimples. Fill them up with clotted cream and—

"Abby. Are you all right?"

"Never better. Why?"

"You look sick. Perhaps you should stick to the tea. And without milk."

"I'm fine. If you think I'm going to pass up the chance to eat a nontraumatized scone, then you're crazy—uh, nothing personal." I took a deep breath. "But about why I'm here in the first place—you did hear about my arrest, right?"

"No."

"What do you mean by 'no'? Of course you did! It's all anyone in Charleston could talk about for days—correction, it's all they *still* can talk about."

His eyes never flickered. "I don't listen to gossip."

"But surely people say things—"

"I ask them to stop."

"No radio? No TV?"

"I play music, Abby. Only music. I don't have time to listen to the commentary other people want to impose on me."

"You're either too good to be true or too true to be merely good. Would you like to meet my daughter? She's twenty-five, has straight teeth, and good breeding hips."

He grinned wide enough to show me that his own teeth were rather nice. "Thanks, but no. I've taken a vow of celibacy."

"Well, it was worth a try. Anyway, I was arrested because a rosewood commode that I ordered from Hong Kong turned out instead to be a shipment of illegal ivory."

"I may have a partial explanation," he said, his voice as calm and soft as pillow talk. "Please, follow me."

I carefully set down my delicate cup and did as bade.

Eric Bowfrey's storeroom was disgustingly organized and clean. Susan and Eric would not have been compatible.

"Here," he said, stopping at a neat row of small tables and chests. "Is this what the commode was supposed to have looked like?"

"Why yes, that's it!"

"For some reason it was sent to me."

I admired the beautiful chest of drawers; the craftsmanship was superb. "If this isn't what you ordered, then what was?"

"Black lacquer tea tables—three of them. With mother of pearl inlay. One was already spoken for."

"Ouch. Do you suppose that this commode will work as a substitute?"

"I doubt it; this client is very specific. Abby, since the commode *is* what you ordered, why don't you take it off my hands? At cost, of course."

"Well, I—"

"I insist, Abby." He leaned toward me and lightly touched my arms with fingers that were as long and slender as tapers. And even though my arms were covered, his fingertips felt like flames. I jumped. "I'm sorry, Abby, did I startle you?"

"No, no—I mean, yes. I'm just a silly old woman, I guess." The heck I was; I was only forty-eight.

"You're not old at all, Abby. You remind me very much of my mother, and she won't turn sixty until September twenty-first."

I swallowed enough foolish pride to add a dress size; it was a good thing I was wearing slacks with hidden stretch panels that morning. "You seem to be a very knowledgeable *young* man, Eric. What do you know about the ivory trade?"

"I know that the ban has been so effective in some of the countries that have enforced it that elephants have become a problem."

"What do you mean?"

"Have you been to Namibia, Abby?"

"I regret to say that I have not."

"Chobe National, which is right on the Zambezi River, is one prime example. It is chock full of elephants. There simply isn't enough for them to eat, so they strip the bark off the trees and eat that. But trees have to have bark that extends contiguously around them or they die. The place is full of bleached trees—but lots and lots of elephants. For now."

"So what is the solution? To kill some of them?"

"That—or relocation. The problem, for the elephants, is that the human population keeps growing and expanding its range. Finding areas large enough to support breeding populations of elephants is becoming more and more difficult. They're having the same problem in India with tiger preservation."

"So that's the story in the countries that lived up to the ban. What about the countries that didn't participate?"

"You mean like the Congo? And some of the West African countries? Their elephant populations really took a beating. You see, African elephants are different from Asian elephants in that the females have tusks. An entire breeding population can be wiped out just because somebody wants a fancy carving or *real* piano keys."

"What about trophies?"

"Not surprisingly, the ban makes an exception for trophy hunters."

"What do you mean by 'not surprisingly'?"

"Gun lobbyists."

As a daughter of the South, I'd been raised with

the belief that hunting was an inalienable right, because the pursuit of game and the pursuit of happiness were one and the same thing. Since then I'd become intellectually opposed to the unequal match of bullets versus beast. But early cultural conditioning was a powerful force to be reckoned with, and I knew that the best thing for me right then was to change the subject.

"Eric, do you get a lot of your merchandise from Golden Tiger Exports?"

"Come again?"

"The company in Hong Kong; the one that mistakenly sent you the rosewood commode intended for my mama's birthday."

"Oh. To be honest, Abby, I don't do any of the ordering. My aunt handles all of that; this is really her shop. I've got a forty percent interest and I sell and manage the employees—we have two shop assistants, and a pickup and delivery man."

"What days does your aunt come in?"

"She doesn't. She's able to keep track of inventory by computer codes. When something sells, she knows about it immediately."

"Who usually picks up the shipments? And who unpacks them?"

Eric grinned sheepishly, which was the closest yet he'd come to losing his cool. "The delivery man almost always picks them up, and Tina and Marisa unpack them. I'd like to blame it on a bad back, Abby, but I'm a terrible liar; you'd see right through me. The truth is that I'm the laziest man this side of the Mississippi, and possibly the other side as well. If it wasn't for the money my grandfather left me, I'd be living on the street somewhere."

"And not with your aunt?"

"Lady Bowfrey is poison."

"*Lady?* Does she really have a title?"

"Titles aren't recognized in America."

"And since your name is Bowfrey, then you have one too, don't you?"

"It's a silly, antiquated system, based on whose ancestors were historically the most brutal. And the answer is no, I don't have a title."

"Aha, but you still haven't *denied* that she has a title. Come on, Eric, give us the royal scoop."

"Let's just say that if she did have a title, it would most certainly *not* be royal, but minor aristocracy."

"Then give us the aristocratic scoop."

"Abby, it's unhealthy to gossip."

"But it can be so much fun."

"Only in the short run. You still have to answer for it; maybe just not in this incarnation."

Until that morning I hadn't a clue that I could find green eyes so tantalizing. I also hadn't fully appreciated just how irritating a moral extremist could be. Even if I wasn't a happily married woman, and even if I was twenty years younger— I would still enjoy a good steak and some chitchat with my friends.

Eric's homemade scone tasted like I would imagine a lump of Carolina clay might taste. I forced down three bites and covered the remainder with my napkin.

"You don't like it?" he said.

"Tiny person, tiny tummy, but you are some kind of cook!" I said it with enough enthusiasm to make it sound like a compliment. I've had to go this route before when faced with ugly babies, and it has always worked.

"Thanks. I can give you the recipe if you want."

"That would be lovely. Would it be possible to have your aunt's phone number and address as well? I'd like to talk to her about some concerns I have with Golden Tiger Exports."

"No prob," he said. "She travels a lot, but she's home this week. Why don't I give her a call now and introduce you over the phone?"

Why not? Some of my best decisions have been impetuous ones. Then again, so have most of my worst ones.

8

When I returned to my shop I saw immediately that a small, but very vocal, herd of female tourists, dressed in wrinkled shorts and faded T-shirts, had taken over. It is women like these who are the bane of our nonmercantile citizenry. We are a conservative city, and save clothing such as this for gardening, or the beach—certainly not for shopping.

And we do *not* move in herds. Nor do we ever shout to each other, all the while pretending that the shop owner and her assistants are incapable of hearing our critical comments.

There are fine ladies and gentlemen that we welcome as visitors to our beautiful historic city, and then there are the tourists. The latter come in degrees of refinement—or lack thereof. Those toward the bottom of the scale climb our front steps and peer into our windows. They open our gates and wander into our gardens; they even pick our flowers. I suppose those acts might even be forgivable, depending on the age of the transgressor, or some other mitigating factor. However, when they park in spaces that are clearly marked RESERVED, that takes the red velvet cake!

I tried to slip unobserved to the back room, but before I was even halfway there I felt a huge hand clamp down on my shoulder. "I'll be with you in just a minute," I said as I tried to pull away.

"Abby, it's me!"

I pivoted. "Cheng! You're back."

"Only I'm not Cheng anymore; you can call me C.J. again. In fact, that's what I insist you call me—unless I'm drunk; then you can call me a cab."

I grabbed her oversized paw and pulled her into an alcove formed by two armoires and a highboy.

"What are you talking about?"

"When I was home just now—back in Shelby—I learned that the story about my Chinese father was totally false. Ditto the one about my Russian mother. I'm as American as lingonberry pie."

"I don't understand."

"Aunt Nanny got drunk one night on some clover wine and confessed that the story about the touring Chinese students with their Russian interpreter—that was all made up. I was really their baby all along and they just didn't want to admit it because they weren't married."

"So Nanny Ledbetter is your honest-to-goodness mother?" I'd met Nanny, and could attest to the fact that she was the salt of the earth. As for Billy, he'd been pushing up daisies for some time, and was no doubt adding some salt back to the earth.

"Yes, but I'm not speaking to her; she's a liar."

"But she's a very sweet, gentle woman nonetheless."

"Don't nag me, Abby—please."

"And then there's her rather unusual DNA to keep in mind."

C.J. giggled. "Ooh, Abby, you're such a tease. You always make me feel better—no matter what."

"Is that so? Then how about taking a ride with me out to the Old Village of Mount Pleasant."

"Sure thing. When?"

"Now."

"But then who will mind the store?"

"Wynnell—if I ask her right."

"Abby, I hate to have to tell you this, but Wynnell just went home."

"She *what?* Is she ill?"

"She said that she's sick of tourists mocking her accent. One of them called her a 'li'l ol' honey chile,' so then Wynnell called the tourist a Yankee Doodoo Dandy, and then it kind of went downhill from there."

"*Down*hill?"

"Don't worry, Abby, I pulled them apart before any second punches could be thrown, although if you ask me, Miss Yankee Doodoo Dandy had it coming to her. If she follows through with her threat and sues, I'd be happy to testify on Wynnell's part."

I hugged the big lug affectionately. "Thanks, C.J., you're a trooper."

Not too many years ago one had to cross the Cooper River on a bridge constructed out of— what appeared to be, at any rate—giant metal Tinker Toys. Now one can practically sail over on an eight lane highway suspended by cables; in fact, the South Carolina Department of Transportation proudly proclaims that the Arthur Ravenel Bridge is the longest cable-stayed bridge in North America.

When I first visited Mount Pleasant as a little girl, traveling with my family on our way to the beach, it was a sleepy village of fishermen and their families. Our initial glimpse was not of buildings, but of marsh grass waving in the harbor breezes. Now visitors are welcomed by waves of hotels and office buildings, and the "it factor" that brought development is no longer there. The charming village is now bursting at its seams with retirees "from up the road a piece," and the roads are so congested it takes twice as long to get anywhere as it did ten years ago.

The core of Mount Pleasant is known as the Old Village, but unfortunately even some of the old is being replaced by new. The smaller homes on the oak- and palm-shaded streets are being snapped up by the wealthy. The small homes are then razed and replaced by much larger ones. And since these new homes conform to stricter building codes regarding the flood plain, they're built on stilts. Of course not every small homeowner wants to sell. As a result, some of the nouveau riche of Mount Pleasant literally look down on their neighbors.

Lady Bowfrey lived in one of these elevated monstrosities that was sandwiched between two cinderblock homes that seemed barely more than cubicles by comparison. There was an elevator in the middle of the concrete pad, beneath the building, and we were instructed to take it to the third floor. That, we soon learned, was because the front door had never been used, and appeared to be stuck shut due to dried paint.

When the elevator door opened it was immediately clear why Lady Bowfrey never used the stairs. Without a doubt Eric's aunt was the largest woman I had ever laid eyes on. If I had to guess, I would say that she weighed six hundred pounds at the very least. She met us in a motorized wheelchair that was larger than some energy-efficient cars I've seen on the streets lately.

"I can read your mind," she said without a preamble.

"Excuse me?"

"Even though it's fine print, I know exactly what you're thinking. So here are your answers: three hundred and fifty-four, and because I want to clear up any misunderstanding regarding my nephew, I've already taken the liberty of calling Gold Tiger Exports and giving them a piece of my mind—believe me, I chewed them out good. As a result, they will be refunding you the full amount, plus they will plan to ship you another commode, one equal in value to the first. And don't forget that my nephew, young Eric, will be delivering the rosewood one that he signed for, to your shop this afternoon. Do you have any questions?"

C.J. raised her arm and waved her hand like an excited schoolgirl who'd gotten her first right answer at the end of the term. "Me, me, me! I've got a question. Ask me?"

Lady Bowfrey regarded C.J. through hooded eyes. I noticed that the imperious figure was decked out in a black silk kimono, embroidered with red and white cranes, and that she wore a pair of Kelly green chopsticks tucked into a neat bun of auburn hair. Her hair color, by the way, came from a bottle.

"Yes?" Lady Bowfrey asked C.J.

"What is three hundred and fifty-four? At first I thought that might be your weight, but then I thought what a silly goose I was, because Cousin Tatum Ledbetter back in Shelby weighs more than that, and she's *much* smaller than you. So then I thought that if I added the words hundred thousand to it, I would get the amount you paid for this house, but Abby has a friend who lives two blocks over and she paid a million and a half for hers, and it's smaller than this and didn't eat up nearly as much marshland. Which leaves me just one question—well, for now at least—did you yell at Gold Tiger Exports for selling illegal ivory?"

"C.J.!" I was shocked, appalled, and proud—all at the same time.

Lady Bowfrey whipped a chopstick out of her do, and using it like a conductor's baton, jabbed the air with it. Her quick, precise movements punctuated each syllable of her staccato speech.

"We haven't even met, you rude woman. How dare you insult me inside my own home? Please tell me that you are *not* Abigail Timberlake."

C.J. giggled. "Of course I'm not. Our Abby is—"

"Then leave my home at once."

C.J. flashed me a questioning look. "Go," I whispered. "I'll be all right."

"You hurt one hair on her tiny little head," C.J. said to Lady Bowfrey, "and I'll be all over you like red on rice."

"The expression is 'white on rice,'" Lady Bowfrey sneered.

"No ma'am, not back home in Shelby. You see, Granny Ledbetter was slicing some tomatoes one day—"

"Skedaddle," I hissed. *"Please!"*

When she was gone I apologized for my friend's shocking behavior. "She's been going through some big changes lately," I said.

"I think that's called life," Lady Bowfrey said as she stabbed the green lacquered stick back into her bun. From what I could see, she managed to get it precisely back into its original hole on the first try.

"True," I said. "But she's in the middle of divorcing my brother, the priest, then she gets arrested for ivory smuggling, and then just this week she finds out that she isn't Chinese, like she thought she was. That's a lot of stress."

"This woman is your friend?"

I nodded. "One of my very best."

"Have you ever considered the fact that she might be nuts?"

"Without a doubt she is. But then again, who doesn't have a friend or relative who's a bit on the strange side? I dare say that your nephew, Eric, dances to some rather original tunes."

Now that Lady Bowfrey was no longer conducting, her hands were folded across a surprisingly flat chest, and resting atop an enormous stomach. Her eyes narrowed for a second, which I chose to interpret as a smile.

"Eric is a fool. He's the late Lord Bowfrey's youngest brother. My husband died of leukemia last year; now I'm all young Eric has. I suppose I could throw money at him and let him waste his life entirely, doing things like smoking pot—but I refuse. Since he has traveled a bit, and has a broad education, I thought the least he could do is run my shop for me. You see, I love the idea of owning an antiques store, but I have physical limitations."

"I understand."

"You *do?*"

I smiled reassuringly. "Mama has a friend whose knees have given out. One has been replaced, and she's about to have the other done. But she says—and everyone who's had it done backs her up on this—if you're going to have both knees done, have them done at the same time, because its not the surgery that's painful, but the physical therapy that follows."

"Why I never!"

"Then you still have time to get them both done together."

"It's not my knees, you idiot! You just assumed

that because I'm slightly overweight. If you must know—which, of course, you don't—at times I have trouble catching my breath." She proceeded then to pant; I wasn't sure at first if it was a demonstration, or if the symptoms were real. "There," she finally gasped, "you see what you've done?"

"I'm sorry," I mumbled. "Perhaps I shouldn't have come. In any case, I should be going now. Thanks for seeing me, Lady Bowfrey."

"You're leaving?"

"I really need to get back to my shop."

"But you can't go—not just yet. I mean, I don't often get visitors; not ones I like, at any rate, Abby . . . may I call you that?" She didn't wait for an answer. "You have a lot of chutzpah, but you're not Looney Tunes like your friend from Shelby. And I don't mean to sound like a whiner, Abby—I eschew self-pity—but life can get very lonely for us shut-ins. Because of my income level I can't even get Veal on a Wheel to come out and serve my meals. Abby, sometimes I feel like I'm in solitary confinement."

"Veal on a Wheel? I know you're only joking about the name of a fine organization, but please, do not associate it with veal. Do you know what terrible conditions veal calves have to endure just to be on someone's dinner plate? They're taken from their mothers as newborns; they're never allowed to sit or lie down, run or even walk, so that their meat remains tender; and they're fed an iron-poor diet so that they become anemic in order that their meat will be a pleasingly pale color."

"Oh, I know all that. But consider this: those calves would never have even been born in the first place were it not for the purpose of becoming veal on our dinner plates. So which is better for them, not to have lived at all, or to have lived with a few restrictions? And bear in mind that these calves have no expectations."

"I believe the same thing was once said about human beings born into slavery."

"You see, Abby, you are so delightfully gutsy. I think I'll keep you."

"I *beg* your pardon?"

9

As a friend. One can never have too many friends, can they?"

"It sounds like you collect them."

When she laughed, Lady Bowfrey's eyes disappeared altogether, and her jowls shook. With her mouth open that wide, I noticed for the first time that she had the tiniest teeth I'd ever seen on an adult woman. To be brutally honest, they reminded me of the front teeth of a kitten, the ones found between the incisors.

"Abby," she sputtered at last, "but you and I *are* collectors, are we not?"

I felt the need to get out of the house. Without as

much as touching me, Lady Bowfrey was beginning to suffocate me.

"My companion is waiting for me outside," I said.

"*Her?* Late her wait; she was rude to me. Remember?"

"C.J. is rude to everyone, and then you get used to her." I inched back toward the elevator.

"Well, I doubt that I ever could. Besides, don't you want to know what I said to the management of Gold Tiger Exports about them buying and selling banned ivory?"

"Yes, of course." The elevator doors were still open and I stepped gratefully back onto the platform.

"Abby, please don't go!"

"I really have to."

"You'll make me angry if you go."

"Ta ta, cheerio, and all that sort of rot," I said breezily, whilst exercising my false bravado.

But when I finally got back to the safety of my car, my hands were shaking like those of a drunken televangelist come Judgment Day.

"Abby, I have an idea."

C.J. and I were seated on the deck at Coconut Joe's on the Isle of Palms. A sheet of clear plastic protected us from the winter wind, but it wasn't cold enough to warrant the management turning on the outdoor heaters for the noon lunch crowd. I will admit that I'd been staring judgmentally at a smattering of tourists, but understandably so. Tourists cavorting in *swimsuits* on the beach in South Carolina in February? Come on, give me a break. We're not Miami!

"They're going to freeze their nipples off," I said.

"That's nice, Abby. Did you hear what *I* said? I have an idea."

"Unless maybe they're from Canada. Remember when—before gas prices got to be so ridiculous—it seemed like half the tourists used to be Canadian? The other half was from elsewhere in South Carolina, and the third half was from Ohio."

"That's three halves, Abby; there can only be two halves of something."

"I know; it was just a joke."

"Unless you're Cousin Ripley Ledbetter from up in Shelby, North Carolina. He was born with a third butt cheek, only it wasn't on his bottom, but across the top of his skull. When he was growing up the other kids used to call him 'fathead' and 'wiseass.'"

I shook my head. "Sorry, C.J., but this Shelby story makes even less sense than some of your others. I mean, if the fat was on his head, what made it a *butt* cheek?"

"Trust me, Abby, you don't even want to know—although I'll give you a hint: his own mother once called him a potty-mouth."

I groaned. "That would be a very crude reference

for a cozy novel—although perhaps I'm being unduly prudish in my judgment, given the anything goes aspect of family hour television these days."

It was C.J.'s turn to shake her massive head. "I swear, Abby, I love you bunches, but sometimes you make less sense than a congressman preaching ethics."

"*Touché, ma chérie.* So please, just tell me your idea."

"It's very simple, Abby. You just put an ad in the *Post and Courier*, under the antiques and collectibles section, and then sit back and wait to see who takes your bait."

"Uh—that's a brilliant idea, C.J., but just whom am I fishing for, and what the heck am I using as bait?"

C.J. sighed. "Ooh, Abby, I keep forgetting about the difference in our respective IQ points, on account of you're so well-spoken for a person who is merely above average in intelligence. You would be fishing for ivory collectors and, of course, the bait would be ivory."

"Of course." I was a bit miffed at my pal's remarks, and rather than respond immediately, I decided to cool off for a moment by turning my attention back to people-watching. As if on cue, a rather cadaverous, yet extremely flabby, woman appeared on the sand dressed in a thong bikini. Her buttocks—she had only two cheeks—hung down on either side of the thong like the twin jowls of a bloodhound. With every jaunty step she took, they swung to and fro, proclaiming to all who saw her that here walked a self-confident woman of a certain age, one who knew no shame. It was all I could do to keep from running after this clueless soul and offering to buy her a beach cover-up.

"Abby, are you mad at me?"

"Whatever would give you that idea?"

"Because you have that look."

"That 'look'?"

"You know, like you're about to cry."

"No, I'm not mad—not anymore. But I don't sell ivory, C.J.; you know that."

"Yes, but the people reading your ad wouldn't have to know that. You could say that you're expecting a huge shipment, and that early birds could have first choice—something like that."

"So you're purposing a sting."

"Exactly!"

"Have you thought about who is likely to get stung? We're not in a movie, C.J., or some characters in a zany mystery novel. Mr. Curly would be on me faster than chickens on cracked corn."

"Not if you tell him first what you're doing."

"You mean get his permission?"

"Well, you're on the same side, aren't you?"

"Yes, but—okay, C.J., let's suppose—and we're just supposing here, that Mr. Curly agrees to this, and I arrange for a bogus ad. What should I expect to learn from this? Just because someone wants to buy ivory doesn't make them a criminal."

C.J. clapped her hands several times. It was a gesture borne out of frustration, I'm sure, but nonetheless it garnered unwanted attention from the other diners.

"Ooh, Abby, you've got to use your imagination. This won't be an ordinary ad; it will be for a large collection of ivory, and anyone interested will have to initially respond to a P.O. box. That's the kind of thing that will get the attention of someone trading in ivory big-time—not a little old missionary lady who's hoping to sell a single figurine. Then, one by one, you interview the respondents in a neutral location. Of course you'd have somebody with you: somebody big, strong, and worldly, for security reasons."

"Like Greg?"

"Don't be silly, Abby. We can't tell Greg. Face it, we can't even tell Mr. Curly. You know how men are when it comes to rules. I was referring to me, Abby. You and I could pull off this scheme, just as sure as a hog will head for a wallow."

An order of coconut-crusted shrimp arrived, and I munched on those while I cogitated on C.J.'s proposed ruse. It made a surprising amount of sense. And I could just hear Greg telling me what a stupid idea it was, which made it all the more attractive. Don't get me wrong: Greg and I have a very happy marriage. It's just that I don't like being told what to do, even if the orders I've been given are still all in my head. I've known my darling husband long enough to know what he *would* say, and it was those observations that I found myself reacting to.

"Okay," I said. "I'll do it."

"Ooh, Abby, really?"

I smiled. "You, young lady, better learn some kind of martial arts—and fast!"

"Abby, have you forgotten that I know shiitake?"

"Isn't that a mushroom? How do you plan to protect me with a fungus?"

C.J. appeared crestfallen.

"But then again," I said, "what do I know about martial arts? Or mushrooms for that matter? I get the two mixed up all the time."

My buddy perked up. "Then we're on?"

"You bet," I said.

I dropped C.J. back off at the Den of Antiquity after swearing her to secrecy—both about the upcoming "sting" and lunch at Coconut Joe's. If I had to pick one of my two best friends to save from drowning, it would be Wynnell. She is, after all, my *very* best friend, and I've known her longer. Besides, she can't swim. She also has a jealous streak as long as the Indianapolis 500.

Wynnell, like just about every single one of us, can be easily distracted, if the conversation is turned around so it focuses on us. When she asked where we'd eaten lunch, I told her that I'd never seen her hair looking quite so beautiful, and I asked her to write down the names of all the products she used, along with the name, phone number, and address of her hairdresser. While she was busy doing that I slipped out the front door and across the street to The Finer Things.

This antiques store lives up to its name. You won't find 1950s bird cages and velvet Elvis paintings in The Finer Things (or in my shop either, for that matter). To gain entrance to this upscale purveyor of good taste one must be "rung in." And this is a privilege that is not doled to just anyone—although to be sure, race is not a factor.

Once you are in, however, you are treated like royalty. The staff bows and scrapes to you while offering champagne, coffee, canapés, and a host of other treats. In the background the soft, seductive tones of classical jazz weave a trance-like spell that soon becomes a snare. In the end, well-dressed tourists who merely meant to browse find themselves leaving after having spent such outrageous sums as twelve thousand dollars on a worn leather ottoman that never got near a real Ottoman; or thirty-five grand on a crystal chandelier that may—or may not—have graced the dining room of the thirteenth Duke of Ulcer, or Worcestershire sauce, or whatever.

The masters of seduction are the owners, and my dear friends, the Rob-Bobs. Rob Goldburg shares the title of "best friend" along with Wynnell. He is stunningly handsome: in fact, a lot of people think that Pierce Brosnan looks exactly like him. Rob hails from Charlotte, North Carolina, and is the epitome of refinement.

Bob Steuben, on the other hand, has a big heart. The fact that he comes from Toledo, is bald, pigeon-chested, has exceptionally large feet, and wears thick black horn-rimmed glasses, doesn't seem to have put Rob off in the least. The two have been a couple for fifteen years, and are every bit as monogamous as any two Southern Baptist preachers you can randomly find. Did I mention that Rob has a bass voice as deep as the Mariana Trench? Perhaps that is something else Rob loves about his partner.

At any rate, I was lucky that it was Rob himself who rung me in, and not one of the gatekeepers they hire from the drama department of the College of Charleston. I was in no mood to confront an actor playing the part of a snooty doorman, yet feeling far too good to want to send anyone home in tears (I'm ashamed to say that the latter has happened before).

"Hey Abby," Rob said as he bent low to kiss me. "To what do we owe the honor?"

"Hey yourself, good-looking. Can't friends just drop in on each other?"

"It's a lovely idea in theory, but we're both in business, and it's the middle of the day. My maydar says there's a crisis brewing in the Kingdom of Abbydom."

"What, pray tell, is maydar?"

"Mayhem radar. So, am I right?"

Although I was slightly offended, I responded with brave chuckling sounds. "Wrong! I just wanted to check on how things were coming along for Mama's surprise birthday party."

Rob swallowed and tried to clear his throat. When an attempt to whisper proved unsuccessful, he pulled me into his office and closed the door.

"Abby, I tried talking sense into him, but you know how he is."

I felt light-headed and needed a place to sit. I knew from experience that the chair behind Rob's desk was by far the most comfortable, so I slipped into it.

"Are you saying that *Bob* is planning to cook?"

"Abby, darling, the caterer bailed out. It only happened this morning. I tried to call you: I *did* call you, as a matter of fact. Where've you been?"

"Nowhere—the beach—I mean, you didn't call my cell."

"That's because you keep changing it, and I don't have the new number punched in. But not to worry, Abby, I made Bob promise that the menu will be very down-to-earth this time. 'Comfort food,' I said. Things that a native of Rock Hill, like Mozella, is sure to enjoy."

"No eye of newt?"

"Nary a one. For the moment Mr. Gingrich gets to keep all three of his."

"You're bad," I said.

"I try. And another thing: he won't be doing the cooking by himself. He's planning to invite the top chefs of Charleston to come in and make it a joint affair. Abby, this should be *the* social event of the season."

I managed a smile. I was writing a blank check for all the expenses, and while Mama was certainly worth any amount of money, I still wasn't convinced spending that much money on one night of food and drink was the way to go. Yes, it would help the local economy, but given the hunger elsewhere in the world, it felt indecent.

Rob must have noticed me equivocating. "Say Abby, you mind if I ask you a question?"

"Ask anything you want; but I reserve the right not to answer."

"Understood. What were you *really* doing this morning?"

"Probably getting into a whole lot of trouble."

Rob sighed. "Okay, darling, have it your way, but just remember that if you get in over your head, I'm always here to help you dig your way out."

"Thanks, Rob. That means more than I can say."

"And Bob would say the same thing too if he were here right now; but he's helping a customer."

"Thank him too. And remind him that I want comfort food for Mama on the twenty-eighth, not wallaby steaks with lingonberry sauce and fricasseed iguanas."

"Don't worry, we're never serving that menu again; we never could decide if iguanas took a red or a white wine. Talk about a stressful evening!"

Before I could change my mind, which would mean having to look for another caterer, I bade Rob a fond farewell. As soon as I was out on the sidewalk again I called the number for the *Post and Courier*, Charleston's one, and only, daily newspaper. It was time to put C.J.'s diabolical plan into action.

10

I wouldn't characterize myself as the impatient sort, nor am I lazy by any means. It's just that once I have a plan of action in place, I can pretty much rationalize taking shortcuts if they'll get me to the end result quicker. For instance, why rent a P.O. box for the initial contact? Why not just use my cell phone number? After all, a really determined criminal can stick a gun to the head of a post office worker and make him, or her, cough up my address.

As for notifying Mr. Curly of our plan—well, I certainly intended to do that. At *some* point. But isn't there a well-known saying about erring first, and then asking for forgiveness? What if Mr. Curly was against the plan? Then what? It's not like he was getting anywhere, and he'd been working on the case for years.

At any rate, the woman who worked in the advertising department of the paper said she probably couldn't get my ad in until the day after next, but when my cell starting ringing before seven the next morning, I knew exactly what was going on. All I can say is thank God that Greg was already out for the day fishing with his cousin Booger.

"Hello?"

"Are you the ivory lady?"

"In a manner of speaking. I swim, but I don't float."

"What?"

"Nothing; that was just a little soap humor."

"Is this some sort of a scam? You're not one of those Amway dealers, are you?"

It was one thing to offer ivory for sale in print; it was quite another thing to push it over the phone. But in this case the ends justified the means, and believe me, I can't be nearly as mean as my friend Magdalena Yoder up in Pennsylvania, and she's a sweetheart in a curmudgeon's clothing. As long as I didn't lose sight of the fact that I was merely role-playing, I was in no danger of losing my way.

"Sir, I'm offering a collection of choice ivory artifacts to serious collectors. You may, or may not, realize that this puts me in a tenuous position. If at any time I feel that *you* are wasting my time, I will simply hang up on you."

"Ma'am, I assure you that I am a serious collector. Are you selling whole tusks, or carved pieces? African or Asian? Live ivory, or dead?"

Live ivory? What on earth was that? Perhaps it was a trick question.

"To whom am I speaking—if you don't mind my asking?"

"Not at all. My name is Conrad Stallings. And you are?"

"Hortense Hogsworth," I said, without pausing to think. As I have never met a Hortense or a Hogsworth in *this* life, it has occurred to me that perhaps I was saddled with at least one of those names in a *previous* life—bless my heart.

"Are you English?" Conrad Stallings asked.

"No, sir: red-blooded American all the way back to before the Revolution on at least one line."

"But surely Hogsworth is of English derivation. I have a particular fondness for the English, you know. My late wife, Janet, was English: born in Malaysia, schooled in Hong Kong, but still English—funny how that goes. Have you ever been to Southeast Asia, Miss Hogsworth? Or should I call you *Mrs.* Hogsworth?"

"I'm not particular; one's as good as the other. Mr. Stallings, I was wondering if we could meet for lunch. I'm really not very comfortable discussing business over the phone."

"Yes, I suppose that could be managed."

"Speaking of Asia, there's a Chinese restaurant

on King Street called Chopsticks. Do you know it?"

"Do I know it? It serves the only unadulterated Chinese food in Charleston, if you ask me. The others offer either upscale Asian fusion or Chinese barf bag buffet—pardon my graphic description."

"No pardon needed. If I see iceberg lettuce or Jell-O squares in a buffet line, I leave and go somewhere else. In all seriousness, I'd rather eat at Chucky Cheese's with a million screaming kids for company than shovel down a lot of tasteless gunk that's supposed to be Chinese."

"You're a woman after my own heart, Miss Hogsworth. Just tell me when, and I'll be there."

"Noon too soon?"

"That's a lot of O's for one short sentence."

"I beg your pardon?"

"Never mind. That will be fine. Can you bring some samples and a portfolio?"

"Absolutely," I said. Then I panicked.

"Now what do I do, C.J.? He wants to see my wares. Duh! Why didn't we think of that before?"

"Calm down, Abby, we did."

"We *did?*"

"When I was in the Atlanta airport last week I saw a display of contraband ivory. It was very nicely done, so I took a picture. Anyway, last night I photoshopped it, along with some other photos I found on the net, and then I dug up an old album I wasn't using and put you together this." C.J. bolted from the break room and returned a few seconds later with what looked like a professional catalogue of select ivory pieces for sale—including asking prices. The girl was an absolute miracle worker! I made up my mind then and there that at the next presidential election I was going to write C.J.'s name down on my ballot—should there be a spot for it.

"C.J! How can I ever thank you?"

"Change the name of your shop, Abby."

"What?"

"The Den of Antiquity just doesn't work; half the people get it wrong. You should answer your own phone sometime."

"I do, dear." She had a point. Folks did tend to say "iniquity" instead of "antiquity," just because they were more familiar with the former. Although frankly, I didn't really mind, since "iniquity" did have a certain cachet.

"And while I'm on the subject, Abby, you should change *your* name as well."

"What?"

"You can't seem to decide if you're a Washburn or a Timberlake. No wonder Buford still thinks he has a chance. So Abby, I think that maybe you should change your name to Hortense Hogsworth. And you know what? It seems to suit you."

"C.J., look closely at my ears. Do you see smoke coming out of them?"

"Maybe just a little from your left ear."

In order not to laugh, I had to bite my tongue. *Hard*.

"Well, keep watching them, because I'm starting to get mad. By the way, where are the actual ivory samples?"

"Ooh, don't be silly, Abby. You don't want to be caught with something contraband, do you?"

"But C.J., as wonderful as this book is, he's going to want to touch and feel the goods."

"That's where I come in, Abby—I'm your safety net. You see, you're going to be wired. And you're going to tell this guy that you think that maybe you were followed—but just for a little bit. In order to be on the safe side, you left any hard evidence back in your car. Explain that you wanted to check him out first; it's not like you'd show your samples to just any old Tom, Dick, or Bildermouse who answered your ad."

"I think that's Harry, C.J."

"What's hairy?"

"I mean the third name; it's not Bildermouse—or whatever it was you said."

"That's exactly what I said, of course. Everyone knows that. Those are the three most common names for boys in the English language."

"They *are?* I don't mean to be contentious, C.J., but I've never heard the name Bildermouse before."

The big galoot cocked her head. "Hmm. My bad,

Abby; those are the three most common names for boys in *Shelby*."

I knew better than to argue. C.J.'s Shelby stories were like religious beliefs—or presidential facts, for that matter. No amount of "proof" was going to change her mind.

"Okay, C.J., so you're going to be listening in on our conversation?"

"You betcha, Abby. And if he gives you any trouble, I'm going to give him a Dutch burr."

Wisely, I declined to ask what that was.

Not only does Chopsticks serve delicious food, but it's reasonably priced, and the foyer was packed with College of Charleston students picking up their carry-out orders. I managed to slip under, and through, them relatively unscathed—I got whacked once up the side of the head with an order of egg foo yung—to the back room where the tables are located.

When I was much younger a bad case of nerves would cause my digestive tract to rebel. Now anxiety makes me ravenous. That explains why I was midway through a plate of spicy Szechwan beef when Conrad Stallings arrived promptly at one.

There were about a dozen other diners in the room, but he headed straight for me, his hand extended. "Miss Hogsworth?"

I am not a huge fan of pressing body parts just before, or during, meals. Especially during the flu season. Instead of responding in the Western manner, I laid my chopsticks across my plate and folded my hands together. It was a gesture of respect that I'd observed Asians perform many times on television.

Unfortunately, Conrad Stallings did not withdraw his hand. Like a moray eel, it bobbed and darted under my nose as he all but demanded that I shake it like a proper American. And this from a self-confessed Anglophile!

"It's a very nubile hand, Mr. Stallings," I said. "You must be very proud of it. And nicely manicured as well."

"And you are the height of arrogance, Miss Hogsworth."

"I apologize if I have offended you; it's just that I don't shake hands at mealtime. With *anybody*. Direct contact is the number one way colds and flu are spread."

"I'll have you know that I have neither!"

"Perhaps you have no symptoms, but at this very moment you might well be carrying a virus you picked up, and of which you are still unaware."

"Harrumph."

"*Harrumph?* Nobody says that anymore, Mr. Stallings. I happen to find that utterly charming."

He stared at me, which I took as an invitation to stare back. He was, bless his heart, a very unattractive man, with a concave face and a pickle for a nose. His lipless mouth was pulled back in a sneer, and the deep lines across his forehead extended high up his smooth shiny dome. What little hair he had was white and confined to the back of his head, and extended no higher than the tops of his ears.

One cannot blame a man if he was born so ugly that his mama had to borrow a baby to take to church. That is no fault of his own. But surely Conrad Stallings was responsible for his wardrobe choices; he was dressed like an English memsahib from a 1930s movie depicting the declining days of the Raj. Khaki shirt with epaulettes, khaki shorts, knee socks, he was even holding a cork helmet in the hand not proffered.

"Miss Hogsworth," he said at last, "are you mocking me?"

"Indeed, I am not. Please sir, be seated."

He nodded his acceptance, withdrew the bobbing moray eel, and settled into one of Chopsticks' molded plastic chairs. "Any specials today?"

"A broccoli something or other, but I didn't pay attention. Mr. Stallings, would you like to see the catalogue I brought?"

"In due time, Miss Hogsworth. First I'll read this menu, and then I'll get around to reading you."

11

*E*xcuse me?"

"I'd like to read your palm, Miss Hogsworth."

"Why?"

"To see if we're compatible, of course—and, to be perfectly honest, I have to keep my bases covered. My first wife, Amelia, had a very short lifeline. That is something that I learned only in retrospect from her sister. When I think of the grief I might have saved myself—"

"Mr. Stallings," I said, pointing my bosom toward his face, so that C.J. was sure to catch every word, "do you read the palms of everyone you do business with?"

"Huh? What a ridiculous thing to say. Of course not! What would be the point unless I was considering marriage?"

I jumped to my feet. One of the few pluses of being so short is that I didn't have far to go.

"M-Marriage? What on earth gave you that idea?"

"You did, of course."

"How?"

"You practically propositioned me, Miss Hogsworth. Did you not claim to be red-blooded, and then invite me to lunch in the back room of a restaurant?"

"Yes, but—"

"And that business about the hands; your obstinacy is nothing if not provocative."

"Then it's nothing! C.J., are you there?"

"Even now you reference someone I don't know just to make me jealous. Miss Hogsworth, believe me when I say that it works."

I was trembling with rage and frustration, while he seemed to be purring with satisfaction. "C.J.," I practically screamed, "where the heck are you?"

Conrad Stallings's concave mandible appeared to collapse further as he mouthed a mock, *Oh, dear me.*

"What did you just say?" I demanded.

"That's too bad," he said, "about your boyfriend not being reliable. You'll be a lot better off with someone more mature—like me. Say, does the waitress come back here, or does one have to take one's order up front?"

I glanced at the remains of my lunch, and thought about dumping them in his lap. But I am a Southern belle, born and bred. In addition to being raised to have good manners, I was brought up to be practical. Why waste perfectly good food when there was still enough for tomorrow's lunch?

"Some wet birds do fly at night, but they almost never fly backward," I mumbled. I said it so softly, he couldn't possibly have caught more than two words.

"What'd you say?"

I smiled graciously and left. As I passed the open door to the kitchen I ran into Veronica, the only waitress on duty. Veronica was as Chinese as a basketful of hush puppies, and she often had trouble communicating with the Mandarin-speaking cooks.

"Hi. How goes it?" I said to her.

"Not so good. The owner's wife stayed home today; she usually does the translating. This," she nodded at an order on her tray, "was supposed to be moo shu pork, but I don't see any meat. I'll be happy if I get any tips this shift."

I fished in my purse for my wallet and extracted three twenty dollar bills. "Veronica, this is my tip, and a little extra for special services rendered."

She smiled, and her tired eyes danced conspiratorially. "What am I about to do *this* time?"

"You see that bald guy over there dressed in khaki? The one who's got a helmet in front of him on the table?"

"Yeah, what is he? A Nazi?"

"Just an American who wants to be a British colonist married to woman named Hogsworth."

"A real weirdo, huh?"

"Like you wouldn't believe. Anyway, I want you to totally ignore him. If he tries to wave you over, pretend like you don't see him. Can you do that?"

"With pleasure."

"Thanks."

"Good luck, Abby—with whatever you're up to."

• • •

Poogan's Porch, at 72 Queen Street, was built as a spacious home in 1888, surrounded by a lovely garden and enclosed by a wrought-iron fence. In 1976 the owners sold their home and moved away, leaving behind their faithful dog, Poogan. The charming Victorian structure was subsequently turned into a restaurant, but Poogan remained, claiming a perch on the front porch, from which he greeted customers until his death. The heart-breaking story alone makes it worth a visit. Throw in an Apparition American—Poogan's is haunted—and you have the perfect place to lunch. But even if you've already had lunch, it is worth spending one's calorie allotment on the bread pudding with rum sauce.

I'd made arrangements to meet Pagan Willifrocke there at two o'clock. She said she was in advertising and that I would recognize her when I saw her. Now, I hoped that no one I knew would recognize *me*.

There would have been no such risk at Chopsticks, because none of my social set would deign to dine in such a humble, and anonymous, place unless they were having an affair, in which case they wouldn't have dared speak up. Not so, with Poogan's Porch, which was popular both with tourists and locals, and brightly lit to boot.

I elected to arrive a few minutes late, and was vastly relieved to find that Pagan Willifrocke had already been seated and was waiting for me in the back room. Just as I was breathing my sigh of relief, the hostess piped up again to serve me a dollop of karmic justice.

"You know, Miss Hogsworth, I would swear that you were in here just the other day, only you had a different name. Timberlake—no, that's Justin—Tumblelake, that's it! Mrs. Tumblelake, and you had that really handsome husband, and a kind of strange mother—but not too strange—I mean, you oughta see mine. Anyway, I know that Pagan Willifrocke is kinda like a big deal, local celebrity—"

"She is?"

"Oh yeah, she's in all them car ads. You know, where she bends over the red convertible, flicks her tongue around the corners of her mouth like a sexy snake, and says 'yum.' But like I was about to say, I'm like, totally cool, if like, you and Miss Willifrocke are, like, you know, 'cause my cousin Diane back in Terra Haute, she's a lesbian, and she's about the nicest person you could ever know. She wouldn't abuse you, if you were the last person on earth—oh crap, that didn't come out right, did it? Really, I'm sorry, Miss Tumblelake, I shouldn't have said anything. There—There she is, by the table over by the window."

Holy guacamole! It was indeed the blond-haired beauty who salivated all over the latest model vehicles, promising that no other area dealer could go lower than the one she represented. Much to my surprise she was even prettier in person; she had wide full lips, pronounced cheekbones, and eyes as blue as Newman's own.

Some years ago a wise person told me that even celebrities have to put their panties on one leg at a time. Translation: we're all pretty much the same. Bearing in mind that nugget of truth, I stepped forward and introduced myself—as Abigail Timberlake.

"But I was supposed to meet a Miss Hogsworth," the pretty blonde said in an accent that was clearly from north of the Line.

"Oh that was hog*wash,*" I said. "I was trying to be clandestine about this meeting, but since you're here, and using your real name—well, then it seems sort of silly for me not to, doesn't it?"

She tossed her platinum locks as she laughed. "I suppose so. Especially considering the fact that Pagan Willifrocke is my professional name."

"*Excuse* me?"

"Miss Hogwarts, do you really think that a mother somewhere would name her baby daughter Pagan?"

"I know someone who named her dog that," I said stubbornly.

"I'm sure you do. I see that you brought a book of some sort with you. May I take a look?"

"Will you tell me your real name?"

I could see her surreptitiously eye the door. "Are you a cop, Miss Warthog?"

"I most certainly am not!"

"Do you swear?"

"Cross my heart and hope to die, stick a needle in my eye!"

"Then may I see the book, Miss Piggy?"

"Certainly. Hey, the name is Sweathog—I mean Hogsworth—no, Timberlake. Do you see what you've done?"

Pagan Willifrocke flashed me an expensive smile. "I can be naughty at times, even wicked. One thing you should know about me, Miss Timberlake, is that I have expensive tastes. I live on Sullivan's Island, but I'm tired of the so-called 'beach house' look that is *de rigueur* for a house on the coast. Quite frankly, I'm sick of sea-foam green, and I think that pelicans are hideous birds. I don't want any of that crap in my house. My decorator is doing the entire house in a black and white theme.

"The formal living room is going to have black walls, high gloss, with white cotton sofas, and white objets d'art. Do you know what an *objet d'art* is, Miss Timberlake?"

"I am not a rube, Miss Whatever-your-real-name-is."

"I prefer Pagan Willifrocke. If I told you my real name, I'd have to kill you." She then produced the obligatory laugh, but it didn't sound convincing. "Anyway, Maurice—that's my decorator—was going to commission some white fiberglass sculptures, but then I saw your ad for the ivory. I don't normally read that section of the paper, but I needed some for the bottom of Ivory's cage. Ivory's the name of my new cockatoo that I got just for the living room—because he's white, you know. That's almost like a sign, isn't it? Now where was I?"

"Pleasantly lost in space?"

Pagan laughed. "You forgot to say 'bless your heart.'"

"Sorry; please consider it said. Miss Willifrocke, what do you know about ivory? Where it comes from? How it's collected, etcetera."

"You may not be a rube, Miss Timberlake, but I'm not the stereotypical dumb blonde. Were you expecting me to say that it grows on ivory bushes? I know that it comes from elephants. But here's the way that I look at it: any ivory that you have to sell, obviously comes from elephants that are already dead. It's not like I'm putting an order in to a poacher."

"Yes, it is, because once I sell this shipment, then I'll turn to my supplier, and he'll turn to his source, which *is* the poacher."

"Are you saying that you *don't* want to sell to me? This is really weird, Miss Timberlake. I haven't even glanced at your stupid catalogue, and I'm getting this really bad vibe off of you."

"My bad," I said quickly. I didn't much cotton to this expression when I first heard it, but it's grown on me. I certainly like it a lot better than saying, *You're right, it's my fault.*

But it *was* my fault. I'd gone on the defensive and referenced a nonexistent supplier and a source for him. If I ever did resort to a life of crime, got caught, and sang, I might perform an entire opera.

Pagan Willifrocke was about to say something perhaps a tad less than profound—she had an evil glint in her eye—but we were interrupted by Gwen, our waitress. Much to my surprise, Pagan ordered what I did, and nothing more: bread pudding with whipped cream and warm rum sauce. Gwen promised to bring the desserts momentarily and then scurried off.

"Miss Timberlake," Pagan said the second Gwen was out of earshot, "I have a confession to make."

12

There's no need to confess anything, dear; I've already guessed. But I've seen a product advertised on TV that the manufacturer claims can touch up your roots instantly—no muss, no fuss."

"Hissss. I like that! And I thought you Southern women were as soft and sweet as overripe peaches."

"We are. But you have heard of peach schnapps, haven't you?"

"Touché. Anyway, my confession has nothing to do with my hair—which admittedly needs a touch-up, but the fact that I've been dropping by your shop from time to time and spying on you."

"You have—oh, you're just pulling my leg! Miss Willifrocke, I may not be the most observant person in the world, but even I would notice someone like you."

Pagan threw back her head and laughed with apparent delight. "I used a number of disguises: big hats, wigs, scarves, glasses, stage makeup. I must have been in the Den of Antiquity a dozen times."

"Why?"

"Because I was walking up King Street one day and your window displays captivated me. Who does your displays, by the way?"

"Usually I do—although lately my assistant has been taking over."

"And lately the quality has suffered. Anyway, I was so taken with your style that I slipped in to peruse your merchandise, and when I left I said to myself, 'If this woman would decorate my house, instead of the arrogant, dichromatic Maurice, I would be a happy camper'—and I hate the outdoors!

"Look, I know that you're not a decorator, but an antiques dealer, but still, I kept coming back, because I was drawn by your exquisite sense of taste. I just couldn't help myself, and I was learning so much. And then it happened."

As if on cue Gwen plunked down large ramekins

of bread pudding in front of each of us. "Will there be anything else?"

"No," we said in unison.

I glanced fleetingly at my tower of melting whipped cream and breathed in deeply the heady aroma of warm rum sauce. The truth be told, I couldn't resist shoveling a huge bite into my mouth before following through on Pagan's last statement.

"And then *what* happened?" I asked.

"Honestly, Miss Timberlake, your manners are atrocious."

"But this is so good." I smacked my lips. "Go ahead, take a bite."

Pagan Willifrocke took three bites before she could speak again, and even then her mouth wasn't clear of food. "What happened is that I had this brilliant idea for a television series. Of course it would star myself—I am, after all, a well-known TV personality, but you would be my costar."

"Me?" Thank heavens I was between bites.

"Yes, you. Granted, you're uncommonly—uh, petite—but not too unattractive, and like I said, you are a very talented designer. Think what this show would do for your business."

"But I don't even know what this show is about!"

"It would be a show about redecorating Low-country homes, using your shop, and your skills, to bring about the physical transformation, but my on-camera presence, as the narrator, to make the show happen. The series would be called 'Where There's a Willifrocke, There's a Way.' " Her voice had risen an octave and her eyes were shining with excitement. "Oh, Miss Timberlake, can't you just see it?"

"Yes, but—but it sounds like such a lot of work."

"Don't worry about that. There'll be a production crew at your disposal: carpenters, painters, paperhangers, seamstresses, you name it. The truth is that you'll be the real star of the show, but"—she cackled evilly—"I don't care, I want my name in the title and top billing. Let's face it, Miss Timberlake, while it's true that I'm hands down far more attractive than you, I don't have the talent you do. When these fabulous looks of mine start to go, then what will I do? Open an antiques store?" She cackled again.

"What about a career as a motivational speaker? Or perhaps a therapist?"

"Nah, therapists are all a bunch of quirks."

"You mean quacks?"

"I meant what I said. Miss Timberlake, I'm afraid I'm going to have to be pushy on this, but the network is breathing down my neck. They want to get 'Where There's a Willifrocke' on the fall schedule, which means we will have to start shooting immediately." She reached into a large, rather nice, but faux Gucci tote beside her and withdrew several papers. "If you could just put your John Hancock here, it will secure your position on the show until we arrange for you to sign papers formally with our lawyers. And initial it here, please."

"Jeepers creepers, Pagan, this is moving awfully fast. How did you know to bring papers here? You didn't know to expect *me,* did you?"

"Miss Timberlake, I know this is going to sound crazy, but I'm somewhat of a psychic. Now before you get freaked out, I've got to explain what I mean by that: I'm not the woo-woo, here's your fortune, kind of psychic, but I get these really strong feelings, you see. Oh heck, why am I trying so hard to convince you? Why don't I just resort to my backup plan? I know you're tempted to think of them as your competition, but—I don't mean to be cruel here—they're in another class altogether."

"Whom are you referring to? Are you referring to my friends at The Finer Things?"

"The name says it all, doesn't it?"

"Give me those papers!" The Rob-Bobs are my best friends, but they are also my chief competitors, and *they* didn't have a show.

I scribbled where told to, but barely heard another word she said. I might as well have been sitting in Mama's church on a spring day listening to her priest drone on and on about our fallen natures, while outside just plain old nature beckoned me to take a walk along the waterfront.

• • •

It was my cell phone that brought me back to reality. A man's deep voice—a soothing voice, despite a lot of background noise—politely inquiring about the ad in the paper. Yes, I'd said, looking Pagan straight in the eyes, the ivory was still available, and yes, I'd be happy to meet with him. Just tell me when and where.

"You can't do this," Pagan Willifrocke said. She had the temerity to grab my wrist as I stood back from the table.

I snatched the papers with my free hand. "Yes, I can. I didn't even have a chance to read these."

"And you won't!"

The moral to this story, if there is one, is never play keep away with someone whose reach far exceeds yours. Pagan recovered the papers as easily as if she'd taken candy from a newborn baby. Then, upon stuffing them safely back into her faux Gucci tote, she strode angrily from the room, sticking me with the check.

I stared at her retreating bottom: it was disgustingly tight, like a snare drum. "Are you still there?" I said to the caller.

"Yes, ma'am."

"I'm at Poogan's Porch now," I said. "Are you downtown?"

"Yes, ma'am; I have a stall in the City Market."

The City Market is a two-hundred-year-old institution that is a tourist's delight—unless said tourist is claustrophobic, or has a migraine. Then it's like wading in ankle-deep molasses through a maze, while hundreds of very large people pop up right in front of you. At least this is what I hear from my dear sweet husband, Greg. He says he'd rather roll on a bed of hot coals that stretches from Charleston to India than have to look for me in the City Market during the Christmas shopping season.

"How interesting," I said to the soothing voice. "What is it you sell?"

"Velvet paintings."

"Even more interesting. There used to be a woman who sold velvet Elvis paintings, velvet Jesus paintings—"

"I bought her out."

"Wow. So you do the same stuff?"

"A lot of it the same. But this year velvet political paintings are the hot sellers. Velvet Obamas, velvet McCains, of course for a long while there it was velvet Hillaries."

"Cool beans! Are they campy?"

"They're supposed to be. Of course some folks think they're as serious as a three car collision, and that's all right with me too, on account of it's the paintings that pay the bills. Who am I to interpret art—even if I created it? Right?"

"You're darn tooting."

"So, Miss—uh—"

"Nagpa Frockewilli," I said. Perhaps I could think faster on my feet if they weren't a mere size four.

"Now that's a new one for me. What is it, Greek?"

"Israelian."

"You mean Hebrew?"

"Yes, of course. Silly me, I keep forgetting my English translations."

"My name is Phillip Canary," he said. "Like the bird. Hey look, I'll be here until six, so you can just come by anytime you like and we can talk. How does that sound?"

"Super. I'll see you in twenty."

Poogan's Porch is said to be haunted by the spirit of a lonely, frustrated woman. While I am seldom lonely, I do get frustrated from time to time, and it seemed that this particular afternoon the Apparition American resident of Poogan's Porch was doing her best to assist in the process. I'm not sure I can even enumerate all the things that happened to slow my departure—besides my credit card dropping from my fumbling fingers and getting wedged between two boards of the restaurant floor—but it took me much longer than twenty minutes to even leave the place.

Once outside, into fresh, unhaunted air, I strode quickly up Queen Street and turned left on Meeting. Two blocks later I crossed Meeting and went over to where the famed Market Hall stands as a majestic landmark. On the second story of this picturesque building is the Museum of the Confederacy, which is run by the Daughters of the

Confederacy (although I doubt if many of them are really old enough to have been part of it), and behind it stretch the four long sheds of the actual market.

The Charleston City Market is not a flea market, nor is it, as some have suggested, a place to buy upscale gifts at bargain prices. It is, however, the place to buy "something" for that person or persons back home who stayed behind to water the lawn, take in the paper, or scoop the litter box.

If you want to buy an authentic pashmina and spend well over a hundred dollars for it, shop on King Street. Buy an even prettier shawl for a fraction of the price in the City Market. As for the authenticity of either shawl—they both bear very similar, if not identical, labels. Some items are peculiarly Charlestonian, like benne wafers and sweetgrass baskets; some things are generically coastal, like carved pelicans and porpoise sculptures. There are leather wallets, handbags, T-shirts, costume jewelry, and, for at least the last four years, velvet Elvis paintings.

Phillip Canary's stall was exactly where I remembered it. I could see velvet paintings hanging from a clothesline and perched on easels, but I couldn't get anywhere close enough to get his attention because of the crush of people that had gathered to watch him paint. In such a situation, what was a well-bred Southern lady to do? Holler? I think not.

"Achoo!" It was a fake sneeze, but very convincing. I followed it with five more, in quick succession. Although most folks haven't caught on to the role that handshakes play in spreading disease, the sound of a sneeze, especially one that is up close and personal, is enough to make anyone recoil. Every time I sneezed, when someone pulled back in either alarm, or disgust, I slipped right past him. Or her. Before you could say *gesundheit,* I was in the front row.

Phillip Canary had neglected to mention that he was an extraordinarily handsome man. He was built like a quarterback, and his shoulders and pecs strained against a sweatshirt that appeared to be a size too small, although the bright yellow color of the garment was the perfect foil for Phillip's dark brown skin. His tightly curled black hair was cropped short. His skin was clear, his nose broad and symmetrical, and his lips full and well-defined.

He had yet to spot me, so I studied his work. There were indeed a number of velvet Elvis paintings: young Elvises, mature Elvises, fat Elvises, a presumably dead Elvis with wings. There also several velvet Jesus paintings, including a black Jesus, and a black Jesus with Elvis standing together under a rainbow. But it was his political paintings that drew the most comments from the crowd.

"Now looky there, at that painting of President Bush standing in a pit surrounded by all them flames. What in tarnation do you reckon that's s'pose to mean?" The speaker was male, and may well have been from the sticks of South Carolina.

"I think that it means that he's in hell, where he belongs," said a woman, whose rigid control of her diphthongs tipped me off to her status as a tourist from one of the square states.

"Well, he ain't dead, so there."

"Oh my, what do we have here? Nancy Pelosi pole-dancing? Now *that's* disrespectful!"

"Serves you right, missy."

"Hey, watch who you're calling missy, *mis*ter!"

I might have called a time-out on the quarreling, middle-aged children, but Phillip looked up then and we made eye contact. Perhaps he'd seen me leave or enter my shop sometime and I looked familiar. At any rate, he stopped painting, and oblivious to the stares and murmurs of the crowd, he walked over to me.

"It's in the trunk of my car. If you'll keep an eye on my money box, I'll go and get it."

"Get what?"

"Your painting, of course."

"What painting?"

"The nude Hillary. You wanted her on the unicorn, but without Josh Brogan, am I right?"

"Absolutely." I winked. Oh what fun! I'd only met this handsome man, and I'd been recruited to be in on a game of some kind. This was my kind of sleuthing.

Phillip was gone one minute, and upon his return he handed me something wrapped in plain brown paper. Instinctively, I opened it.

"Oh my stars!" I exclaimed. "It *is* Hillary in the nude—and she's riding sidesaddle, no less. You could have at least crossed her arms. When a woman reaches a certain age, those puppies relocate. Really, Mr. Canary, no one looks good with their nipples in their lap."

The crowed roared with laughter.

Emboldened by the thought that I might someday be a stand-up comedienne, I continued. "Who, pray tell, was your model for this depressing take on the female form?"

Phillip frowned. "Why you, of course, Mrs. Dougherty."

13

*W*hat?" I cried in alarm.

That's when Phillip Canary took a really good look at me and his jaw muscles twitched. "Shoot a monkey," he said, "you're not Mrs. Dougherty, are you?"

I shook my head. "Miss Frockewilli."

"Hmm. Is this how you treat everyone?"

"What do you mean?"

"I thought you weren't coming. Twenty minutes—that's what you said an hour ago."

"That is not the case!" I glanced at my watch.

"Oops, sorry! I honestly don't know where the time went."

Our tones must have been somewhat strident, because the crowd just kept getting bigger. Thankfully, that irritated Phillip as much as it did me. He jumped on his stool and clapped his hands.

"People," he boomed. "The show is over. Now move along, please. There are some really fine sweetgrass baskets at entrance to shed three. Don't forget to shop along the way for the most unique gifts you'll find in the Southeast."

Then he hopped down and began turning all his velvet paintings so they faced away from the main flow of traffic. Meanwhile the assembled folk dispersed with a good deal of mumbling and backward glances. As long as at least some of them were jumping to very wrong conclusions, that was fine with me.

"I think some of them suspect something is going on between the two of us," I said.

He turned. "Miss Frockewilli, I don't mean to be cruel, but please don't flatter yourself."

"But I—"

"I'm a healthy young man; I can sense when someone has the hots for me."

"Why you arrogant little twerp. You're not even dry behind the ears. How *dare* you say that?"

"Just so you know, Miss Frockewilli—and I don't think that's your real name—I'm already in a relationship. You might even know her; she was a local celebrity of sorts, before she moved back to Charlotte. Her name is Ramat Sreym."

"The *author?* Ha! Now there's a laugh. That woman couldn't write her way out of a paper bag. Her books are zany—they're like situation comedies. They'll never get her nominated for any kind of award, and everyone knows that awards are what counts. That's where publishers put their money: behind award-winning books—uh, well that's what I've been told."

"Ramat's books are delightful, and so is she. The point is, Miss Frockewilli, that I'm taken."

"Okay, I get your point! And for the record, you're right: I'm *not* really Miss Frockewilli. But listen, if I promise to keep my middle-aged libido in check, can we still discuss the I word?"

"Incorrigible?"

"Very funny. By the way, isn't 'most unique' a bit redundant? Either an item for sale is one of a kind, or it's not."

"Touché." He looked around before motioning me over to a side exit that opened onto Market Street. "Look, if I'd known that you were going to be this much aggravation, I wouldn't have bothered to call."

"Me? Aggravation?"

"We're practically outside, so I know that I'm not hearing an echo."

I took a deep breath, and counted to ten in my head, but it did no good. When I reached ten, I exhaled a good deal of carbon dioxide along with the last of my patience.

"You know, I'm the one who doesn't need this *tsuris*."

"What?"

"It's Yiddish; with a name like Ramat, your girlfriend should know what it means." With that I clutched my indignation tightly around me like a cloak and strode across Market Street.

I knew better than to attempt a conversation, especially with someone whose perception of the world was slightly off kilter, but of course that didn't stop me. The fact that I hadn't been able to reach C.J. since leaving Chopsticks made me want to get in touch with her all the more. It's not that I was worried about the big galoot—she has size going for her, in addition to some awesome brain power—it was purely the fact that she was unobtainable, and I was every bit as stubborn as a Democratic Congress.

But finally, as I passed the candy shop that hands out fresh praline samples—I had two huge chunks—C.J. answered. "International House of Bitter Remorse and Abject Apologies," she said in a remarkably soothing tone. If I hadn't been so angry, and in such a hurry, I would have hung up and redialed, just to hear her say it again.

"C.J.!"

"Abby, I said that I was sorry."

"Where did you go? What happened to you?"

"You'll never believe it, Abby."

"Just try me," I growled.

"Well, you know that a lot of celebrities come to town, right?"

"Yes, C.J. Please get to the point."

"And you know that I have a crush on Rob Lowe, right?"

"No, I didn't know that."

"So anyway, I see this guy walk past the window at Chopsticks who looks just like Rob, so I jettisoned my mission—but only because I thought it was Rob. Abby, I love *Brothers and Sisters*."

"Isn't Rob Lowe a little old for you, C.J.?" Perhaps it was my loyalty to my own jilted brother that made me ask that.

"Don't be so silly, Abby. Rich men marry younger women all the time."

"But Rob Lowe *is* married," I said.

"Praline sample?" A gangly but well-meaning young man lowered a dish in front of my nose again.

"C.J.," I snapped, "we seemed to have gotten off track. Are you all right? And do you still want your job?"

"I'm fine as frog's hair, Abby, and of course I want my job."

"Well, where are you now? In the Rob Lowe look-alike's boudoir?" That was, admittedly, a punch beneath the belt. C.J. is anything but a floozy.

"I'm helping Mr. Hartman load his truck."

"Say what?"

"Mr. Hartman is the man who favors Rob Lowe. You see, I sort of followed him a bit, then he caught on and turned around so we started talking, and when I told him I worked in an antiques store, he wanted to see it. Well, he liked a bunch of the stuff he saw, and he just happened to have his truck, so he bought that English oak bookcase—the one you keep saying we'll never sell—the mahogany sideboard that's signed by William Moore, and that set of six Gothic side chairs. Isn't that a hoot, Abby? All those different periods going into one house?"

"Yes, but think of all that money going into my bank account—ack! You *did* get him to write a check before you started loading, didn't you? Oh C.J., dear, please say that you did."

"Sorry, Abby, no can do."

The pralines passed within two feet and I snatched two in lieu of a stiff drink. "Get one now! Call the cops if you have to."

"Abby, there you go, being silly again. I don't need to get a check from him, because he paid me in cash."

"Huh?"

"And before you have more kittens, Abby—and that really did happen to a woman in Paris in 1926—we went to the bank and he withdrew the money, and I got it directly from the teller, all fifteen thousand dollars of it."

"C.J., I'm so sorry—"

"Oops, gotta go, Abby. Mr. Hartman wants my help in selecting a few smaller accent pieces—you know, like lamps and things."

She hung up.

One of the problems with hailing a cab in Charleston is that it is a walker's paradise. Should a cab eventually come along, the odds of it seeing me are about the same as those of a politician sticking to his, or her, pre-election platform. Thus it was that I was pretty much committed to a long walk back to the Den of Antiquity on King Street, or an even longer walk back to my house.

When a car pulled up alongside me and a young lady rolled down a window and said, "Abby, get in, I'll give you a ride," you can bet that I accepted.

The fact that she looked only vaguely familiar didn't matter—at first. But when I stole a second peek and realized that I didn't know her from the Prime Minister of Canada, I began to panic.

"Uh—you can let me off here."

"Please wait."

"I want out."

"Not yet."

Foolishly, I tried to open the door while the car was moving. Wisely, the car manufacturers had seen to it that I was indeed going to have to wait. I soon learned that even my window wasn't going to budge at my command.

"Who are you?" I demanded.

"My name is Taiga Fünstergarten"—she spelled her name, then added—"with an umlaut."

"Well, Miss Fee-*yoon*-ster-garden—what is it you want? Money? I'll give you my wallet—heck, you can even have my Gucci handbag; just let me out at the light."

"That's not a real Gucci—it's a hideous knock-off. And please, do me a favor, and never try to pronounce my last name again."

"A hideous knockoff? I'll have you know I paid almost fifty dollars for it at A*faux*dables on King Street."

"Like they say, Abby, there's no accounting for your taste."

"*Who* says that? And who the blazes are you?"

"In due time, Abby."

My abductress—for that's how I chose to think of her—was a very plain young woman, with short curly hair that was rodent brown, and pale down-turned lips. She appeared to be devoid of makeup. She was dressed in a gray skirt and a gray blouse, which didn't match, and a pair of sturdy gray shoes that almost matched the blouse. Altogether her ensemble was close enough to being a uniform to make the situation even scarier for me.

"Look, lady—ma'am—whatever, it's not what you think. I'm only trying to help out Mr. Curly."

"Excuse me?"

"You know, help him find the distributor on this end."

"Who's Mr. Curly?"

Poodle poop, I said to myself, and without any alliteration. Maybe this one *was* the distributor. Loose lips sink ships, a wise man once said, but a mouth like Abby Washburn's can get you a life-long invitation to Davy Jones's locker.

"On second thought, Miss Taiga, you'd do well to ignore everything I say. The doctor said I'd have these moments of paranoid delusion if I skipped my medication, but oh no, I wouldn't listen. But I tell you, she is wrong about one thing, I am not violent." I smacked my pitiful excuse for a faux Gucci. "Just because I insist on carrying a loaded weapon with me everywhere I go is no reason to suspect me of violent tendencies."

"You don't fool me, Abby."

"Yes, that one death was ruled an accident, but what about the other four?" I smacked the hapless tote again.

"I used to drive the transfer van for the state psychiatric prison, Abby. Those patients weren't nearly as much fun as you."

"Still, you're not smiling."

"I never smile. Would you, if your name was Taiga Fünstergarten? With an umlaut?"

"Point taken, bless your heart. Will you at least tell me where we are going?"

"No."

"Pretty please? With oodles of sugar on top?"

"You're starting to annoy me, Abby."

"Is that a threat?"

"I don't pack a gun—even a fake one—but I won several wrestling championships in college."

"Men's, or women's?"

"*That* was mean-spirited."

"But can you blame me? I've been kidnapped, made to feel like a fool when you didn't believe my gun shtick, but worst of all, you exposed my Gucci as a fake!"

"I think you might actually be serious."

"You're darn tooting. I've toted this tote with me to countless occasions. For all I know now, I'm the laughingstock of Charleston."

"Calm down, Abby. You need to have perspective. There are a lot worse things in this world than having your friends know that you wear cheap knockoffs—which, I assure you, they do. Think of the hunger, poverty, and acts of personal violence that women all over the world are experiencing this very minute, and here you are stressing over something I said about your bag. Thank heavens I didn't say anything about those silly wannabe Jimmy Choo shoes you have on."

"I beg your pardon!"

"Abby, you sound positively outraged."

"How dare you? How dare you—" I cleared my throat, and in the couple of seconds that this took, I changed my mind. "How did you know the Jimmy Choos weren't the real McCoy?"

"Experience, Abby. I've seen more Jimmy Choos and Guccis and you name the brands—I can spot a designer brand like a forester can spot a maple or an oak."

I turned to better scrutinize the drab woman.

"Abby, I know what you're doing."

"My one butt cheek was going to sleep—that's all!"

"You're thinking, how does such a Plain Jane, one who dresses in Goodwill clothes—that's what these are, Abby—know anything about designer clothes? It's because I see so much of that crowd, that's why. But Abby, I think it's perfectly okay to wear what you do in your circles. I'm sure that no one has noticed. And I'm sorry I went overboard; your tote really isn't *that* hideous, and I take it back about your friends knowing."

I couldn't help snorting. "Do you honestly expect me to believe all that? I mean, even your car looks like it got pulled off the junk heap and then resurrected."

Taiga's down-turned lips actually twitched in what may have been the beginning of a smile. "It is an old car. But it runs well, and it gets me there."

"I know rich people," I said. "You're not one of them."

We'd made several turns by then and were headed up East Bay Street. This made me think our destination might be somewhere across the Cooper

River, so I was totally taken by surprise when she made a right turn onto Calhoun Street, and then a left into the parking garage that serves the South Carolina Aquarium.

"Uh-oh," I said, "you plan to feed me to the fishes."

"I care about animals," she said flatly. If she had a sense of humor, it was as dry as a Carolina summer.

"Abby, we're going on a little walk. I want you to stick with me. Of course you're free to run off, holler, and make a fool of yourself, but you might wish you hadn't."

"Is that another threat?"

My captor did an expert job of parking on the top deck, and then without further ado got out and made her way as close as possible to the side over-looking the adjacent shipyard. I did consider bolting, but it was mid-afternoon and there weren't any other people out on the upper deck, and yes, I confess, I was as curious as a box full of kittens.

"You see that ship down there being loaded?" Taiga asked. She hadn't even turned around to con-firm my presence.

"What about it?"

"Read the name—please."

"S.S. *Taiga*." My heart skipped a beat, but then, thank heavens, common sense took over. "What does that prove? Maybe you work here, you saw the name on the boat, so you tell me that's your name as well, big deal. My name is Statue of Liberty. So what?"

"Abby, sarcasm seldom becomes anyone, and I regret to say that you are not the exception." She opened her own bag, which I *know* came from Target, because I have one just like it at home. "Here, look at my license. As it happens, this was my daddy's first container ship, and I'm getting ready to retire it. I own a fleet of them. Sixteen in all—but they don't all sail into Charleston. Some are Los Angeles–based, while most of them sail between the Continent and New York."

I stared in disbelief. "Why I'll be dippity-doodled," I finally said. "You really are Taiga Fünstergarten—with an umlaut. Or else you've stolen her wallet. Nevertheless, this doesn't prove that this is your boat."

"Ah, my dear Abby," she said. And although she had to be at least a decade younger than me, she sounded like a tired old aunt. "If you represent the best of what this nation has to offer, then we are in worse shape than I thought. Tell me, how many Taiga Fünstergartens are there in the Charleston phone book, listed, or unlisted?"

"Like I said, you could have stolen the ID."

"With a photo of me included."

"That can be doctored."

"I'll grant you that. So come, let's get back in the car and we'll drive around to the dock—although I know that a dock might not be your favorite location right now—and I'll introduce you to the captain. Will that make a believer out of you?"

I know, she could have been bluffing even then, but I pride myself on picking up on the nuances of people's voices, and Taiga sounded resigned, as opposed to anxious. I suddenly realized that she knew that I would eventually believe her; it was just a matter of her taking me through the tedious steps of proving who she was.

"Don't bother yourself, dear; I believe you. But allow me to say, you are the first fabulously rich person I know who dresses like a—uh—"

"Regular person?"

"Yes, but a nonslutty regular woman, and that's how it should be. Nowadays folks go shopping in spandex shorts and halter tops—Never mind that. Why did you kidnap me?"

"Saffron is just down the street. As I'm sure you know, they have fabulous desserts. We can talk over early tea—English style."

Saffron Café and Bakery is one of Charleston's culinary jewels. The menu for the main courses is predominantly Mediterranean, but the desserts seem pretty much American to me—well, except maybe for baklava and the German chocolate cake. Everything, however, is good—no, make that superb. There is no such thing as getting a bad meal at Saffron.

"No thanks," I said. "I just had bread pudding at Poogan's Porch."

"Then have a cup of coffee on me and watch me

eat. It's a better place to set a scene than standing on the roof of a parking garage."

"Say what?"

"You're better off not trying to figure out everything I say; I enjoy trying to be enigmatic."

I shook my head, and then nodded vigorously. "You're definitely an enigma, Taiga Fünstergarten with an omelet. You're—"

"The word is *umlaut,* Abby, not omelet."

"I stand corrected. Anyway, as I was about to say, you're not only enigmatic, you're also a bit ominous. I have the feeling that I really don't have much say in the matter. Do I?"

Taiga smiled broadly.

14

When I observed how moist Taiga's hunk of German chocolate cake was, I decided a thin slice would be the perfect accompaniment for some mid-afternoon perk-me-up coffee. Taiga stuck with her aforementioned tea.

We made small talk until we were both served, and then I got down to business.

"Okay, Taiga, what's this all about? Alfie?"

"Abby, playing the dimwit does not become you; you know his name is Conrad."

"*Excuse* me?"

"My uncle, Conrad Stallings. You just had lunch with him a couple of hours ago."

"Look, I was being droll, not dull—never mind. So he's your uncle, huh? What are you two, some kind of tag team?"

Taiga swallowed and daintily patted the corners of her mouth with her napkin. "My uncle is the only family I have left. I'll be the first to admit that he's eccentric in an upper class sort of way, but he's not crazy, Abby. He's certainly not dangerous. Like many of the old families of Charleston, and throughout the Deep South, he's still living in another era.

"But for Uncle Conrad Stallings—he was my mother's brother—that era happens to be when Britannia still ruled the waves. He married an English tea planter's daughter in Malaya—now Malaysia—after World War Two. It was during the last gasp of the British Empire, but for Uncle Conrad it was like coming home. He's a man born out of his time. Really, Abby, he should have been born two generations earlier.

"At any rate, Uncle Conrad's bride died two years later in childbirth, and then not long after that Malaysia became an independent country. Did my uncle tell you about the house my mother built for him on James Island?"

During her rather long recital I'd been wolfing down my cake. The number of calories I'd managed to consume that day was plum amazing. A highly creative person—like, say, an author—might suggest that I was eating for two, but that would be medically unlikely, given my current stage of life. Whatever the reason, if I continued inhaling carbohydrates as a way to deal with stress, I might soon have to bounce to work, rather than walk.

"No, although your uncle proposed marriage, we neglected discussing where we would live."

Taiga sighed. I'd obviously disappointed her again.

"Abby, no one lives in the house my mother built; it was destroyed by Hurricane Hugo. You should have seen it. My mother had it decorated to look like what an English planter's house might look in the highlands of Malaysia. But what's germane to this conversation is that in the gentleman's sitting room—the den, if you will—she had on display some first rate trophies and a really fine collection of ivory."

I licked my fork for the second time and was considering a quick pass over Taiga's still untouched icing when I realized it was my turn to speak. "Um—let me guess, so the real reason you kidnapped me is so that you could convince me just how badly your *eccentric* uncle needs to buy my ivory collection. Since you're a veritable Miss Money Bags, Miss Fünstergarten, why not just buy him a small African country and let him shoot elephants? That will allow him to feel *veddy* British."

Taiga leaned over the table. At first I thought she might be protecting her cake, but then she started to whisper. "I would have replaced his ivory sooner, but I respected the ban—oh crap, that's not the whole truth. I don't like breaking laws. I might risk millions of dollars in business deals, Abby, but I obey these kinds of laws. Then when I followed my uncle to Chopsticks today and overheard the two of you—well, somehow it didn't seem like such a big deal."

I recoiled in surprise, and my response was anything but a whisper. "You were *spying* on us at Chopsticks."

"I was seated right behind you."

"But I didn't see you."

"Why *would* you notice a frumpy woman in gray clothes?"

"Harrumph," I said. "Tell me, how many times have you heard that word this year?"

"Seven times. I belong to ASS, the Archaic Speech Society. I make a point of using 'harrumph' and other seldom used words at least once a week."

"Back to the subject at hand, dear—"

"Abby, please don't say no, before you've had a chance to drive out and see Uncle Conrad's simulated tea plantation."

"But I—"

"You can bring a friend—like that Amazonian who works for you, or your unibrowed best friend, or your petite mother. Or that cute husband of yours."

"On one condition."

"Name it."

"You buy me a piece of cake to go, for that Amazonian, and another for my shop assistant with the caterpillar eyebrows."

It was a done deal. What's more, when I got home that night I discovered that Taiga Fünstergarten had every dessert in the display case packed up and sent over to my house. My petite mother and cute husband were too busy feeding their faces to be the least bit suspicious.

When Greg and I moved to Charleston five years ago, we asked Mama to move down with us. At the time, she was ensconced in the house that she and Daddy had raised us in, up in Rock Hill. Although Mama had grown up there, and had many friends in the area, the only family she had left was a cousin who raised laboratory rats, and who was, to be brutally honest, a bit squirrelly.

I adore Mama, as does Greg, and she adores us, and for the most part it has been a mutually beneficial arrangement. We provide my mother with companionship and security, and she cooks fabulous dinners and keeps us from ever getting bored. (As my friend Lydia once said, "Your mother is like a short Jim Carrey with breasts.")

Initially I was worried that a senior citizen from a small city like Rock Hill would have a hard time adjusting to the sophisticated likes of one of

America's last bastions of culture. But the fact that Mama is stuck in the year 1959 makes her a perfect fit for Charleston. All she had to do was plug into Grace Episcopal Church, join a book club, and seek out the local chapters of the Daughters of the American Revolution and the Daughters of the Confederacy, and Mama had more connections than a jumbo box of Tinker Toys.

One would have thought that after consuming all those sweets, Mama would have experienced a sugar crash. Instead, she donned a plum-colored satin dress—full circle skirt, of course—with a self-covered belt that cinched a waist that still measured in the twenties. She slipped her tireless feet into plum-colored satin pumps, and since it was still the fifties, and it was winter, she set a plum-colored hat upon her silver head (according to Mama, only harlots and movie stars dye their hair—myself excluded).

"How do I look?" she said.

"Like a million bucks," Greg said, although he was too busy watching *Wipeout* to even glance at her.

"Will your bag be plum as well?" I asked.

"Of course, dear. In my day there was no such thing as overcoordinating. Don't believe those fashionista men on *Oprah*; they have v-jay-jay envy."

"Mama!"

"Oh Abby, you're such a prude."

"And you're such a contradiction; neither June Cleaver nor Margaret Anderson would ever have said that."

"Yes, but both those characters would be dead by now. So tell me, how do I look?"

"Awesome as usual, Mama."

"I do, don't I?" she purred. "It's the prunes, you know. They've been proven to keep wrinkles away."

"Where are you going, Mama? To play bridge?"

"Heavens, no; I gave that up for Lent."

"It's not Lent yet. Is it Blue Stockings then?" That's the name of Mama's erudite book club. She doesn't exactly *read* the books, but she does comment on them.

"On a Saturday night? We may be older, Abby, but we have lives too. Who would want to stay in and discuss some boring book on a Saturday night?"

"Then what *will* you be doing?"

"Give it a rest, hon," Greg said, without tearing his eyes from our fifty-two-inch wall-mounted screen. By the way, when we first bought this monster, it seemed large; now it barely suffices.

That's what tipped me off! I still didn't know if Greg and Mama were in cahoots, but I did know that my dearly beloved tends to take a more enlightened position when it comes to feeding and caring for his mother-in-law. My husband's basic philosophy was that Mama is an adult and can do what she pleases, as long as she is of sound mind and does not unduly hurt herself.

It's the "sound mind" part that we disagreed on most. "Let's not forget, dear," I said, drawing myself up to my full four feet nine inches, "that she is *my* mother."

"Amen, hallelujah, and pass the peas," Mama said, "I hear his car now." She darted into the hall closet like a purple martin, and emerged with a mink stole.

By then my turncoat husband was on his feet, insisting that he help his mother-in-law with the difficult process of laying the stole across her narrow shoulders—a *stole,* for Pete's sake. It's not like it had sleeves.

Fortunately, that meant she was ready when the doorbell rang and I didn't even have to look at the Timber Snake, much less invite him in. Nonetheless, the quiet evening at home together that Greg and I had planned was about to get even quieter than either of us had anticipated.

"Gregory," I said archly, "just so you know, there will be no jumpy-jumpy for you tonight."

"Jumpy-jumpy? What's that?"

"You'll just have to wait to find out."

There was indeed no jumpy-jumpy for Greg, although I was jumpy all night, because Mama didn't return until six in the morning. I slept fitfully, if at all, and would have called the police, except that my ex-detective husband insisted that it would do no good. She was an adult of sound mind, yada yada yada. And when I tried to jump out of bed at six, I found a strong pair of hands restraining me.

"Abby, hon—"

"Don't you 'hon' me. How would you feel if it was *your* mama in my mama's shoes?"

"Shocked and relieved." Greg's mother is—and I will try to put this kindly—a religious fanatic who wears her hair in what he refers to as a "holy-roller bun," and who firmly believes that Satan controls the airwaves. I think Greg would be happy if his mother became Amish, because outwardly she'd have to make precious few changes, but it would undoubtedly make her a kinder, gentler person.

"Greg, I can't take this anymore! The ick factor alone is about to kill me."

Much to the surprise of both of us, I let him put his arms around me. "Abby, we don't know for sure if the ick factor is even warranted. Jumping to conclusions might be the only form of exercise your friend Magdalena Yoder gets, but it can lead to a serious case of egg on the face—and trust me, that's not your best look. Since you seem deter-mined to play the adversarial role, at least allow me to play devil's advocate, and I'll try and get the details. But you have to stay out of it. You hear?"

"I hear."

"You promise?"

"Yeah," I muttered.

I feigned sleep for the next hour, but even Mario Lopez couldn't have kept me in bed when I smelled bacon frying in my kitchen. I hopped out of bed and, without bothering to put on a robe, stormed off to confront my minimadre. Yet when I saw her standing in front of the stove in a pale blue silk dress and a white organza apron, I saw Betty and Bud Anderson's mother, not my own.

"Coffee, dear?" she asked.

"Funny, I couldn't smell that over the bacon."

"It's Virginia ham. Only the best for my daughter."

On her way to get the coffee she peeked into the top oven.

"Mama, what's in there?"

"Why, biscuits of course."

"Mama, what are you doing?"

"What I always do on Sunday morning: I'm cooking breakfast for my loved ones."

"Your loved ones are always asleep at this hour on Sunday morning." I yawned to prove my point.

"Let me stir the grits, dear, and I'll be right with you."

I poured my own coffee and dumped in extra sugar, hoping to get a better jolt. The second I sat down again, a fifteen pound blond male jumped into my lap and started to dance. Well, sort of. Dmitri is always happy to see me awake in the morning, even if he's spent the night in my bed.

And I love him enough to be arrested in at least three states, but it is dang hard to sip one's coffee with a cat's tail whipping across one's face.

While I was setting him on the floor and gently urging him to show his affection elsewhere, Mama resumed her explanation. "If you must know," she said, careful to avoid eye contact, "I'm going to Sunday school this morning."

I sputtered a mouthful of dark, sweet fluid. "Whoa! This I've got to see. I'm coming too."

"I'm going to St. Michael's."

"*Why?* You belong to Grace. If you're going to switch, at least switch to St. Stephen's or St. Mark's." The Episcopal Diocese of South Carolina is, by and large, extremely conservative, and its officials were outraged at the nomination of Gene Robinson, an openly gay bishop. St. Stephen's and St. Mark's have reportedly been much more accepting of gays than most area Episcopal churches.

"The person I'll be attending with does not approve of gays, Abby."

"What do you mean by 'approve of'?"

Mama suddenly found it necessary to stir the grits vigorously.

I jumped up. After all, the ham slices needed turning—or more likely, to be removed from the stove altogether.

"Mama, are we talking about Buford? Because when we were married, he wasn't homophobic."

"Well, he's not dear—not socially. He just feels that in the religious sphere, they should submit to—uh—majority rule."

"Repent and disappear? Mama, the Rob-Bobs are like sons to you. They certainly treat you better than your own son, Toy, whom, by the way, I've always suspected was—uh, never mind."

"Was what, dear? Were you going to say *gay?* Well, I asked him, and he said he wasn't."

"And Toy's never lied?"

"I knew you'd say that, so I asked him again. He said the same thing: no. And even if he was, Abby, you know it wouldn't matter to *me.* You know that I am very tolerant, and I taught you to accept everyone—Why shoot a monkey! My biscuits are burning!"

I waited until she was through fanning a pan of biscuits as black as Buford's heart. "Mama, I believe I'll be going back to bed now."

"But my breakfast!"

"I'm sorry, Mama, but I've lost my appetite."

She sighed. "Maybe it's just as well that the biscuits burned. They turned out extremely heavy for some reason."

"In that case," I said, "take them to Sunday school with you. If you see adulterers, you can throw the biscuits at them."

"I don't think Buford would like that," Mama said, and then despite our mutually hurt feelings, we laughed until we cried.

Greg generally goes to bed with a clear conscience, and invariably wakes up each morning with a mind as empty as a newborn baby's. He tells me that these are good traits, but I'm not so sure about the empty mind. Case in point: the morning Mama burned the biscuits, Greg awoke unable—or perhaps unwilling—to recall that we had quarreled the night before.

"Whatever happened, I'm sure we were equally at fault," he said.

"Grrrr!"

"Oh come on, hon, I'm sure I didn't behave that badly. After all, you didn't have me sleep on the couch."

"We don't own a couch, Greg."

"Well, in the guest room, then. Say, what do you want to do today—besides argue?"

"Frankly—"

"Because I was thinking of going over to Mount Pleasant. Booger and I are finally getting around to putting a head on the boat. It came in Friday, but I didn't get a chance to even open the crate yesterday. Booger will be meeting me at the slip at eleven. You want to come along and watch?"

First of all, it was mighty kind of my husband to invite me to be a part of his day. And while having a head on the *Abby* would make going out on the water a whole lot more fun, staying in dock to watch the men attach a toilet to a redolent shrimp boat was not my idea of a fun way to spend a Sunday morning.

However, some snooping (with my big strong husband safely close by), while not exactly fun, would certainly be entertaining. I took a moment to compose myself. After all, faking nonchalance isn't as easy as one might think.

"Sure, that sounds all right. Hey, why don't I make some sandwiches, and I'll bring a book. Then you guys can work on the boat all you want. I mean, didn't you also want to poop on the deck?"

Greg roared with laughter. "We want to varnish the poop *deck,* darling."

I managed a grin. "Yeah, that was pretty stupid of me. You'd think that I would know better," I said.

"Abby, you're a hoot," Greg said as he reached for me.

"And maybe a fool," I whispered.

15

No project has ever proceeded smoothly from the tools of Gregory Washburn and Booger Smith. First, the hole they cut for the pipes was too small, then too large, then the seal cracked, and on and on the project went—or so I'm told. I don't have firsthand experience because after watching them for only five minutes, I claimed to be bored. Then I casually expressed a desire to stroll over to the Old Village. Greg grunted a response, but since he was a man involved in a repair project, it meant absolutely nothing. Nor did Booger's exceptionally loud belch.

Still, my conscience was as clear as the sky that morning (which was a lot more than Mama could say). Shem Creek was sparkling in the sunlight, the shrimp boats gently bobbing, the sea grass softly sighing, and at least a dozen other clichés were happening all around me, so that by the time I got out of earshot of grunting Greg and belching Booger, I was feeling pretty chipper. When I got to Royal Street, my spirits were positively buoyant.

Of course I was a woman on a mission. The enigmatic Lady Bowfrey was not to be forewarned this time. I'd purposely dressed in winter browns and grays, hoping to blend in with the sidewalks and dormant centipede lawns. Someday I was going to learn to rappel and sharpen my tree-climbing skills, so I could move through the canopy like a life-size, if somewhat deformed, spider monkey. The thing is, no one ever looked up—least of all me. But with the ancient live oaks that still survive in parts of Mount Pleasant, there really is a potential for a highway of sorts in the sky.

"Oops, I'm sorry!" It's that silly kind of thinking that gets me into trouble each time. In this case I'd plowed full force into a woman a good ten years older than Mama, almost knocking her to the ground.

"I'm all right," she gasped. "My dear, you must be one of those writers."

"I beg your pardon?" I put a hand to steady her, but she stepped back to let me know she was fine the way she was.

"Our famous local writers. They wander about our streets with minds off in faraway places. No doubt in their banks accounts, ha ha."

I was too puzzled to respond.

She scanned my face. "Oh dear, you're not one of them, are you?"

"I'm afraid not. Tell me about them."

"Oh, they're a reclusive bunch. Some live here on the mainland, some on the islands. I've run into a few of them in the stores, but I'm too shy to approach them—one in particular; she always seems to be scowling. Although I think I heard she moved to Charlotte—good riddance, I say. But anyway, I've tried to read their books, but I can't get into them. Pat Conroy they're not."

"Well, I'm ashamed to say that the last book I read was *Eat, Pray, Love*. I enjoyed it, by the way. But then again, I'm only an antiques dealer."

"That's where I know you from! The Den of Iniquity, right?"

"Funny that everyone says that. It's actually the Den of Sobriety."

"It is? Then I've been saying it wrong all these years. No wonder all the friends I recommend it to can't seem to find it."

"You're putting me on now, aren't you?"

"Weren't you?"

"I like you, Miss—uh—"

"Dora."

"I'm Abby."

"Are you a newcomer to Mount Pleasant, Abby?"

"No. I don't actually live here; I live downtown."

"An S.O.B. Well, la-dee-da."

"Yes, but you live on the Pleasant side of the Cooper River."

She laughed delightedly. "Very true! What brings you here?"

"My husband and his cousin have a shrimp boat that ties up at Shem Creek. They're putting in a toilet today."

"Is it a Toto?"

"*Toto*lly not. On a shrimp boat? We're not *that* la-dee-da. Anyway, I'd rather spend my time walking around the Old Village than handing them wrenches."

"You've obviously been here before."

"Off and on for the last forty-some years. I'm originally from Rock Hill, but my family used to vacation at the beach. How long have you lived here, Miss Dora?" As a native Southerner, I knew that many ladies of the older generation, whether married or single, preferred to be addressed by the honorific "Miss" when called by their first name.

"Three hundred years—give or take."

151

That was what I needed to hear to make my day. "So you're a native."

"Uh-oh, you're not going to hold that against me, are you?"

"I'll try not to. But I must confess that ever since I moved to Charleston I've suffered from a mild case of *aboriginal envyitis*."

"Abby, the church folk are about to let out. Would you like to come in and have a cup of tea? This is my house right here—and I would so enjoy your company. I am a widder woman, you know."

"A what?"

"A widder woman; my husband is deceased."

"That's what I thought you said. I didn't know the locals still used such a quaint expression."

"They don't, but I do. I think it's colorful."

That did it. Here was an eccentric older woman, one unconnected with Buford the Timber Snake, one who might possibly know Lady Bowfrey—or at least know of her. Bad reputations, like pebbles tossed into ponds, have far reaching spheres of influence.

"I'd be happy to have tea with a widder woman," I said. Although my game plan had changed slightly, my mission was still the same.

You can always tell a family's history by the amount of silver that is displayed in the dining room. Dora's sideboard was groaning from the weight of a bath-size sterling punch bowl and cups the size of margarine tubs. A massive tea set took up most of the dining room table, and two glass cabinets were so full of silver odds and ends that it was impossible to keep the doors securely latched.

But instead of using her heirlooms to make and serve the tea, Dora boiled water in a red enamel kettle and poured it into a blue and green painted mug that had once belonged to Truman Capote.

"I bought it at Disney World," she explained. "There's a shop there that sells all kinds of things that were once owned by celebrities."

"Were you a fan of his?"

"Not so much—not really. I just thought it would make a nice story."

"And so it does." I sipped from the same spot where presumably Truman's lips had once pressed. "Ah, that's good tea."

"Here's to Lady Grey," she said, and held aloft an orange mug of humbler origins.

"I bet you must know everyone in Mount Pleasant."

"Of course, dear—well, anyone who is anyone. I mean, I certainly don't know all the carpetbaggers. And the Mexicans," she added in a low voice.

"By carpetbaggers, may I assume that you mean Northern retirees?"

"You may. I suppose that I've met a few good ones along the way. I must have, don't you think? But they so look down on us. Because *they* think we speak with an accent, therefore we must be uneducated."

"I believe that attitude is changing. My husband's cousin, by the way, is from an old Mount Pleasant family. They don't live in the Old Village, but farther north along Rifle Range."

That certainly got her attention. "What is his name?"

"Booger Smith. His daddy is Estus Claybill Smith and his mama is Rae Lee—shoot, I can't remember her maiden name."

"Pinochet. I know the family well. I used to babysit for Estus and his five brothers when they lived in closer to town. Why, I'll be, Abby, you're practically family."

"Just as long as I'm not kissing cousins to Booger Smith; he comes by that name honestly."

Dora laughed. "Like father, like son. Oh, the stories I could tell."

I took another long sip of Lady Grey and carefully set Truman's mug down. "Miss Dora, do you know a family named Bowfrey?"

My new friend scowled just as sternly as that unpleasant author who has thankfully taken her bad attitude with her to Charlotte. "A family, no, but a single woman, yes. She calls herself Lady— some sort of foreign aristocracy—and I tell you, Abby, she is bad news."

I tried to adopt the demeanor of an eager young gossip. Sadly, it wasn't hard to do.

"What do you mean?" I asked. "Do you think she's like the head of a smuggling ring or something?"

Dora's pale blue eyes widened and she had to struggle to return her mouthful of tea into the cup, rather than spray it hither, thither, and especially on me. "*What* did you say?"

"Well she is very sinister looking, isn't she?"

"I can't say that I've ever thought of that. Harriet—that's Lady Bowfrey's real name—is the sweetest woman this side of Heaven. When Rutledge died she couldn't have taken better care of me. She insisted that I come stay with her, had her cook make my favorite meals—not that I was ever hungry—"

"But you say she was bad news!"

"She is, my dear: at poker! Harriet is a fabulous bridge player. A group of us used to get together every Wednesday night and play. Then someone suggested poker, so a couple of us widows who had nothing to do on weekends started adding Saturday poker to our schedules. And oh what fun we've had. But let me tell you, dear, Harriet Bowfrey is the most formidable poker player you will ever hope to meet. She is absolutely inscrutable. I lost my shirt to her again last night."

"Aha! How much was that?"

"Eight dollars and thirty-six cents."

"Surely you're joking! I mean—isn't Lady Bowfrey rather well off?"

"Oh my dear, you must be nouveau riche, like the carpetbaggers and most especially the developers. We play for pennies because—well, what else is there to do with them?"

There is an old saying in my family: "If the ugly baby is yours, embrace it." Mama says she heard it from her mama, who heard it from her mama. I've given that saying some thought over my forty-eight years, and have come to the conclusion that either we've given birth to a plethora of ugly children in our family's history or else we have refused to hug them.

Mama claims that nary a one of her ancestors was anything less than photogenic, and that the saying simply means own up to your shortcomings. Instead, I decided to own up to one of Dora's shortcomings, and that was her obvious distaste for developers.

"Just so you know, I am not entirely nouveau riche, because my family did have money before the Late Unpleasantness."

"Well, that is an improvement."

"And I *despise* developers."

"Then we see eye-to-eye."

"But speaking of Lady Bowfrey—"

"She's the salt of the earth; the savory substance that adds that special exotic zing to the Old Village. Ah . . ." She sighed, and sipped deeply from the orange mug. "Of course there were a few old fossils—like me—who didn't cotton to her from the beginning, but I think most of us have eventually come around. Did you know that on the first Wednesday morning of every month she serves an enormous breakfast buffet that is open to the entire community?"

I was stunned. "No, I didn't. How?"

"She doesn't actually cook it herself. She has it catered. White tents and everything. It's become an Old Village tradition. Wednesday Mornings with Lady Bowfrey. Perhaps you saw it on the *Today* show?"

"I prefer *Good Morning America*."

"You know, dear, you should come as my guest."

"I'd be delighted."

She cradled the orange mug in her mottled hands. "I don't suppose that you—no, I couldn't possibly ask you to do that."

"To do what?"

Dora looked down and shook her head. "Please forget that I said anything. It was just an old foolish woman talking."

"I doubt that. And anyway, I love foolish talk, so talk away!"

"In that case, would you be willing to pose as my daughter? At the breakfast next Wednesday?"

That caught me off guard. "Uh—"

"Abby, my daughter, Clara, hasn't been home to see me in thirty-two years. We had a falling out, you see, and—"

"Stop, please. You don't need to explain."

157

"Just once, Abby, I don't want the neighborhood to look at me as the woman whose daughter won't even come home to see her old mama." She took a deep breath, which sounded a bit like a gut-wrenching sob. "I'm so sorry. I shouldn't even have brought this up."

"Can we say serendipity?"

"No, dear, her name is Cassandra."

"I'll do it!"

"I don't know what got into me. Marilyn Douglas, that's what—or I should say, who. She's always bringing family from out of town. She brings so many, and so often, why it's even occurred to me that she might be dragging in tourists from the streets."

I grabbed one of Dora's hands. It was as light as biscuits. And even though she'd been cradling a warm coffee mug, it was cool to the touch.

"Miss Dora, I said that I'd *come*."

"Oh Abby, really? I wouldn't want you to go to any trouble."

"It wouldn't be much trouble," I said, while lying through my teeth, "it will be fun. But since I own an antiques store downtown, there's a good chance that some of your neighbors have been in it, and might even know me. I'll have to wear a disguise. And anyway, I am a little shorter than most people."

"Abby, my daughter was a dwarf. Aren't you a dwarf?"

158

"I'm four feet nine inches."

"Which officially makes you a Little Person, right?"

She was right, of course. The definition of a dwarf includes anyone, male or female, who is less than four feet ten inches tall.

"Miss Dora, how old is your daughter?"

"About your age, I suppose. She was fifty-eight in October."

"Let's not suppose, sweetie. I'll just add some temporary gray to my hair."

Dora smiled happily. "When I went on my walk this morning I was feeling lonely, practically dreading the week ahead. Now look at me: I have a daughter to come with me to Wednesday Mornings with Lady Bowfrey."

"Just think," I said, "Marilyn Douglas will be absolutely crushed."

Dora giggled.

The truth be told, I missed Mama terribly. Yes, she could be a pain in the tushie at times, but at least that kept life interesting—in a mildly entertaining sort of way. When Greg and I returned from Mount Pleasant we found Sunday supper in the oven, and a note saying that Mama planned to be out for the evening and that we shouldn't wait up.

While that kind of news is far from boring, it didn't make for an evening of good entertainment. After we ate, Greg kept asking if I'd finally show him what jumpy-jumpy was, and again I was simply in no mood to be jumped. By the time Monday morning rolled around (I fell asleep before Mama came in) I was actually looking forward to going to work.

Don't get me wrong; I love what I do, and my dear friends with whom I work. It's just that there are days when I'd like to knock about the house in my pajamas all day, maybe even sprawl across the couch and watch *The View* while eating chocolate-covered bonbons. Or maybe read. Who has enough time to just read? *Eat, Pray, Love was* a good book, but I needed to get beyond memoirs and self-help books, and tragic Oprah picks, and above all, books that scream: *this book is literary, punctuation optional.* Maybe someday I'll get it together to read something that has a beginning, a middle, and an end. Maybe someday I'll read a good novel—like a mystery.

Perhaps it was the theory of reciprocity at work, but when I got to the shop—early, mind you—I found Wynnell Crawford already there. The poor woman was pacing up and down in front of the register like a caged tigress.

"Abby, can we talk?"

"Yes, of course."

"Can we go someplace private?"

"Wynnell, the shop doesn't open for another forty-five minutes. It's just you and I, and a bunch of old things."

"A collection of preowned treasures, Abby: that's what you taught us to say."

"Good for me." I steered her into the Den of Antiquity's holy of holies: my private office. This windowless room is literally smaller than the walk-in closet I had in my home up in Charlotte when I was married to Buford the Timber Snake. *Much* smaller. It's just big enough to contain a desk (topped by a computer, of course), three filing cabinets, and two chairs.

Both my employees have unlimited access to the break room (such as it is), but except for the days on which they are hired, or fired, entry to my office is restricted to this Big Cheese alone—or perhaps I should say this Mini Gouda Wheel. Thus it was that when I bade Wynnell sit, she took her sweet time staring at the wall art first.

"Gracious me, Abby, are those calendar pictures you have hanging on your walls?"

"Yes, but they're nicely framed, and the pictures themselves are quite striking, don't you think?"

"I suppose—if you like kittens. And I know you do, Abby, and that's all right with me. But personally, I prefer dogs. There's nothing cuter on God's green earth than a Pomeranian puppy. I personally believe that's the breed He gave Adam and Eve in the Garden of Eden."

Wynnell is a Southern Baptist of the literal persuasion, and while I have nothing against these good folk, I have long since learned that it is a waste of breath to try and convince them that there were no dogs present at the moment canines were created. If indeed creation happened in six twenty-four-hour days, there were wolves present, but no dogs. Dogs were bred from wolves, just as tomorrow's dog breeds will descend from today's dogs.

"Pomeranian puppies are adorable," I said agreeably. "Now tell me what's on your mind."

"Is the door locked?"

I got up and locked it.

16

A re we expecting terrorists, Wynnell?" I asked. "No—well, you can never be sure, can you? Anyway, *she* might barge in at any minute."

"She who? Is there an Apparition American living in my shop that I don't know about?"

Wynnell's hedgerow eyebrows met as she clucked impatiently. "No, Abby, I mean C.J.! *She's* what I want to talk to you about."

"What about her?"

"*What about her?* I can't believe you just said that. Abby, you and I used to be best friends—"

"We still are."

"But lately you've been taking C.J. with you everywhere and taking her into your confidence. It's like what you did with me in the old times, Abby, and I miss it. Am I jealous? Yes! Am I a lesbian? No! Besides, your boobs are way too small for my taste."

"What?" Surely I hadn't heard right.

"Just kidding!"

"Wynnell, you don't have a funny bone in your body. That's one of the things I've always liked about you. You're deadly seriously, and slightly boring—to the point of endearment, of course. I mean, funny people are a dime a dozen. But with you, well, I always get strong opinions—albeit a little to the right of George Walker Bush—but at least I know where you stand."

The eyebrows parted like the leading edges of the Red Sea. "Thanks, Abby—I think."

"You're welcome!" Enthusiasm can go a long way to confusing an issue, which was exactly my intention.

"But, Abby, you still think that C.J. has better decorating skills than I do, don't you?"

"Decorating is for cake makers, dear. We stage vignettes; we stage rooms; we stage entire houses; why, I bet you could upstage anyone if you set your mind to it."

"You really think so?"

"Absolutely. Upstage, engage, enrage, Wynnell Crawford is incomparable."

My shaggy-browed buddy beamed. "Right back at you, Abby."

"Thank you. Wynnell, did C.J. fill you in on what we did Friday?"

"No. Except that the two of you had fun together, and then C.J. came back here and earned a huge commission."

"Well, I wouldn't call it fun, exactly. I'd asked C.J. to help do a little undercover work in my quest to catch the ivory smuggling ring, but she wasn't able to stick with the assignment. And do you know why?"

"Why?"

I lowered my voice and put my finger to my lips. "Because our big galoot, as bright as she is, lacks your maturity."

"Really?"

"She's only twenty-six. And you're how old?"

"Old enough not to answer that question, Abby."

"Anyway, while C.J. was earning her commission, you were earning time and a half for holding down the fort."

"I *was?*"

"Make that *double* time."

"Oh thank you, Abby!"

"You're very welcome, but you have to keep this between the two of us. *Capisce?*"

"Okay, now you've confused me; what does this have to do with fancy lettuce?"

"Huh?"

"It was bad enough when folks started putting spinach into salads, then along came this ridiculous radicchio stuff, and now there's *capisce?* Abby, I'm telling you, it's the Yankee influence.

We used to boil our greens with fatback—except for bib lettuce, which was so bitter you had to put something on it—Mama let us put sugar on it. Then along came the snow bunnies with their salad bars and now the sky's the limit for what constitutes a salad. Last night we ate supper down at Hush Puppies, that new restaurant on Route 17, and they have Snickers bar chunks in their fruit salad section. And folks wonder why they gain weight when they only eat salads."

I love it when Wynnell goes off on a tangent—if the timing is right—and this seemed to be just such an occasion. C.J., and the favoritism I'd appeared to be showing her (believe me, it was unintentional on my part), seemed to have been put behind us. I would do what I could to pave over that sore spot with more quick-drying concrete.

"And speaking of Yankees," I said, "I read somewhere that there is a grassroots organization that believes building a wall along the Mexican border, while basically a good idea, should take second place to building a wall along the Mason-Dixon Line. The trouble is what to do with the border territories, not to mention all the people who already live in the South. Should they receive compensation for their property? What do you think, Wynnell?"

"I think you're trying to play me for a fool, Abby, that's what I think. Now tell me, when do I get to play sleuth with you?"

"Uh—well—"

"I'm not letting you off the hook, *best* friend."

"How good are you at applying makeup? I mean, like stage makeup?" As far as everyday makeup went, Wynnell's skills rated a minus two on a plus scale of one to ten—and I say that charitably. Her "old man" bushy eyebrows were actually a blessing in that they kept one's eyes focused above the scene of most of her artistic damage, which was just about anywhere on her face.

"Abby, before I met you I used to do makeup for various Charlotte community theaters, and before that I did makeup for church and school plays."

"Why Wynnell, you're just a barrel of surprises!" Now what was I going to do? I really didn't want to use her, yet I was in need of someone.

"Oh, and I forgot, I worked behind the makeup counter at Belk's Department store—but I got fired. They said I made the customers look like clowns."

"Did you?"

"That was back in the 'natural look' days, Abby. It was so boring; I was just trying to spice things up a little."

"Hmm. Wynnell, Wednesday morning I need to look like I'm at least ten years older. Do you think you can pull that off?"

Wynnell squinted and cocked her head, first one way and then the other. "The good news is that you already look a good deal older than you are. The bad news is that Wednesday is my day off, remember? Ed and I were going to drive up to Georgetown and kayak on the Black River. Our goal is to kayak on every stretch of black water in the state before the mosquitoes come out again."

I shuddered, having almost lost my life to alligators in the Black River, but that was another story. It was good to hear that the Crawfords were doing things like this together. Several years ago when their marriage hit a dry patch, Wynnell ran off to Tokyo to become Japanese, a venture that didn't quite work out. Still, some valuable cultural lessons were learned: she became an aficionado of sumo wrestling *and* installed a squat toilet in her house.

"Wynnell, dear—*best* friend—I'll buy you both dinner at Frank's up in Pawley's Island if you stop by on your way up to Georgetown and turn me into a believable fifty-eight-year-old woman."

"Frank's? You've got a deal."

"But keep it subtle."

A cheerful Wynnell is a worrisome thing. It's like driving on a limited access highway, without a spare tire, when suddenly a large bulge appears on one of your four radials. What do you do? Pull over and wave down some help? Stop the car and run before it blows? Kick yourself for the millionth time because you let your AAA membership lapse, and besides, your cell phone isn't charged? I found myself giving her wide berth, lest I be in too close proximity when she exploded.

In fact, smiling is so foreign to Wynnell that by lunchtime she had the beginnings of a migraine, so I let her go home. Being that it was the slow season anyway, C.J. and I could handle what little street traffic there was, and finish marking down our red dot items. A lot of antiques stores—especially high end shops—don't have clearance sections—but I have found that most customers—even the very wealthy—like to think they've gotten a bargain. What they don't know is that I've already taken the discount into mind when I assigned the original price. As the Rob-Bobs would say, "Our little Abby knows more ways to make a buck than a herd of does in heat."

I was putting a sale tag on an Edwardian era armoire when I became acutely aware that I was being scrutinized by someone, or *something*. My first thought was that I had somehow disturbed an Apparition American—perhaps one associated with the armoire. This is not such an uncommon event amongst Charleston shop owners. Bed and breakfasts are particularity vulnerable to visits by former tenants who have been unable—or in some cases, unwilling—to depart the premises. This entity was behind me, but standing so close that I could hear him breathe, although I had heard no footsteps.

There are two kinds of people in this world:

those who pull the covers up over their heads and scream, and those who grab the broom in the corner and give the boogeyman under the bed a good thrashing. Through no credit of my own, I'm the kind who screams *while* they thrash with the broom. I've also been known to exaggerate, so it wasn't that bad this time. Still, it was awfully rude of Phillip Canary to sneak up behind me on cat's feet.

"Hey, hey, easy now," he said.

"You couldn't cough or something? I think I just used three of my lives."

The handsome young man chuckled. "That's all?"

"That's all I have left. Now if a silverfish runs across the floor tonight on my way to the bathroom, I'll drop over dead—all because of you!"

"They're the nastiest critters, aren't they: silverfish? Did you know that they can go a year without eating?"

"That bit of arcane knowledge is just the thing your girlfriend can put in one of her books. Isn't that the kind of experience that readers want? To learn something while they're being entertained?"

"Yeah, but I think they want to learn about something that has to do with the subject of the mystery. Let's say it's set in an antiques store—kind of like yours—why the heck would they want to learn about bugs?"

"No offense, Mr. Canary, but you can be a very contrary man. I was only making small talk."

"You were being sarcastic, and you well know it."

"I suppose right now sparks are flying off the page—so to speak."

"Don't you be flattering yourself, Miss Timberlake."

"Aha! So at least you've got my name right this time. Sort of. I am, in fact, Mrs. Washburn. Miss Timberlake is merely my business name. You know, like a stage name. Or a nom de plume."

He scowled and put his hands on his hips. "If my wife used her divorced husband's name just to make a few extra dollars, I'd tell her to keep it. Permanent-like."

"Well, what I do isn't any of your darn business. Now, how can I help you?"

"I want to see that ivory you advertised," he said without missing a beat.

"First, you tell me how you managed to track me down."

"There wasn't any tracking needed. *I* didn't recognize you because I'm working in the market all of the time, and I don't ever shop on King Street, most especially not in fancy antiques stores. But after you stormed out of there—Wanda, she has the stall next to mine—told me all about you. Said that not only were you a big-time, up and up, antiques dealer, but that she'd seen your picture in the paper lots of times—on the society page. So I figured that you have too much to lose to be scamming anyone. As for finding you, heck, once Wanda told me the name of this shop, it was easier than finding my own big toe."

"You have such a charming, colloquial way of speaking, although a copyeditor would defecate a brick."

"What the heck is that supposed to mean?"

"I don't know—it just slipped out. I visited a lot of European castles last summer; maybe I contracted turret's syndrome."

"Miss Timberlake, I may not be as educated as you, but I can tell when I'm being played for a fool. You don't have any ivory to sell, do you?"

I took a deep breath. The newspaper ad had been such a stupid ruse. It had been like throwing a chunk of bacon into the harbor and hoping to catch a tuna. Instead I was pulling up crabs. Not there's anything wrong with crabs—but meanwhile the tuna was swimming free and would probably get away.

"You're right, Mr. Canary, I don't have any ivory to sell. I apologize for wasting your time."

He looked stunned. "That's it? That's all you have to say?"

"What else can I say? I didn't ask you to come to my shop."

There, I felt immensely relieved. Now, if only he would go away. But Phillip Canary didn't seem to want to let me off the hook that easily. His dark brown eyes narrowed and his nostrils flared.

"Something doesn't exactly smell right."

"Look, I said I was sorry; what more do you want?"

"How about the truth?"

That did it; that hiked my hackles. I'd barely taken any of this man's time at the market; I surely didn't owe him an explanation for my behavior, and I certainly didn't owe him the *truth*.

"How about you get out of my shop?"

"Why? Aren't I free to look around, and maybe buy something, just like anyone else?"

I pasted on my best saleslady smile and drew on a remnant of holiday cheer. "How may I help you, Mr. Canary? Are you looking for anything in particular?"

"Yes, ma'am. I'm looking to buy some ivory."

"Why I declare, Mr. Canary, you're beginning to sound like a broken record. But with a name like yours, coming up with a new tune shouldn't be all that difficult. Do you sing, Mr. Canary?"

Much to my astonishment, he grinned. Then he threw back his head and sang, in a lovely baritone, a rousing rendition of "Bess, You Is My Woman Now" from the opera *Porgy and Bess*. As I watched open-mouthed, a small crowd gathered: first Wynnell; then customers who were browsing in my shop; then folks from off the street.

17

B ravo!" Wynnell cried, clapping vigorously.
There were, in fact, many "Bravos," and even some "Encores." By then it was with pure pleasure that I watched Phillip Canary sing "Old Man River" from the musical *Showboat*, and a couple of gospel numbers that got a bunch of folks clapping and tapping their feet. At this point news of his performances must have traveled via the famous "Charleston phone line," because my store was packed.

"Who is this guy?" Wynnell whispered loudly in my ear.

"He does the velvet paintings in the market," I said.

"Oh, I thought he looked familiar. He's the one who donated fifty thousand dollars of his own money for new playground equipment for his neighborhood elementary school."

"That's *him?* Then why is he selling velvet paintings of Madonna and Elvis in the same one-person kayak?"

"Abby, that's what made his story so newsworthy—he made the money for the playground by selling those paintings. Mr. Canary is a very generous man—and cute too." She'd stopped whispering now.

"I hadn't noticed."

"Liar."

"Wynnell, I'm a happily married woman."

"So am I. I'm also postmenopausal, yet my heart's going pitty-pat-pat. I could just eat that young man up with a spoon."

Unhappily for Wynnell, the young man in question finished his song a second or two before her brain could react, and thus recall her licentious words. This was also during that narrow window of time before the crowd had a chance to cheer and whoop their approval of Phillip Canary's stellar performance.

Instead, there was a smattering of applause, and then a roar of laughter that shook the dust mites from the highest tiers of nineteenth century chandeliers. Poor Wynnell's face turned Shiraz red and she fled into the storage room. I felt my face turn at least a champagne pink as I followed suit.

Neither of us had expected Phillip Canary to follow us. Nor did I ever in all my born days imagine that I would witness a celebrity fight back fans at the door of my stockroom, but that's exactly what happened. Although I do use the word fighting in the most general sort of way, for after signing a few autographs on road maps and paper towels from the restroom, Mr. Canary was able to convince the assemblage to stay in the showroom and do some shopping for his sake. Of course that meant that one of us had to be there—

and since C.J. was still nowhere to be found, that meant it had to be Wynnell.

You can bet that she protested mightily, but a bear hug from Mr. Canary got her as far as the door, and another hug and a few pitty-pats (sans spoon) eventually got her out on the floor. As soon as she was gone, he turned to me.

"Well, you did sort of challenge me," he said with a laugh.

"Indeed I did. Well sung, Mr. Canary. Are you a professional?"

"In fact, I am. I did *Porgy* in a touring company— but not the lead—*Showboat* at dinner theaters, and I sing in the church choir. I don't get paid for that. My dream is to get a starring role on Broadway."

"With that voice, I'm sure you could."

"Yeah, maybe. I studied at Juilliard, you know. Six years. Full scholarship. Then just when I was starting to get me some parts, my daddy keeled over dead from a heart attack. Then just six months later Mama passed. I'd come home to be with her, which meant dropping out of Juilliard. Anyway, I've made Charleston my home base ever since."

"How come?"

"My parents were my encouragement—the wind beneath my wings. With them gone, I didn't much feel like beating my head against the walls in New York City. That's why I do these gigs closer to home; they're easier to get. And, of course, I paint my pictures."

"You're a very talented young man, Mr. Canary. I read somewhere that people who are talented in one of the arts are often talented in another. Supposedly that's why you find so many actors who paint, or authors who play in bands, etcetera. Is it true that your author friend, Ramat Sreym, paints, draws, *and* plays the piano beautifully?"

He laughed while shaking his head. "Look, I'm not here to talk about her."

"That's right; the ivory. What do you want to do with all this ivory, Mr. Canary?"

He recoiled slightly, the smile replaced by a frown. "I can't believe that you're asking me this. What if I was buying a cupboard or a chair? Would you be giving me the third degree then?"

I reached out and lightly touched his forearm. It felt surprisingly hot.

"No. And I'm sorry; I was just being nosy. Some of these ivory pieces are exquisite, and I wanted to imagine them in their new home—unless, of course, you planned to resell them. But that's your business; it certainly isn't mine."

"Miss Timberlake, I find it very strange that you're wanting to imagine the ivory pieces in their new setting when I'm trying to figure out if these dang things even exist."

The little voice that sometimes speaks to me in the back of my head had been screaming at me for some time now. *This crazy idea of C.J.'s is going to blow up in your face,* she said (my little voice is female, of course). *Drop this nonsense before you use up your remaining life; I can't keep on protecting you forever.*

"Please shut up," I said. I said it sweetly, because a Southern lady must treat everyone kindly, including herself.

"What the hell did you say?" Phillip Canary's eyes were flashing and the veins at his temples bulged.

"Uh-oh. I'm sorry, Mr. Canary. That just popped out; I really wasn't talking to you."

"Is that supposed to be your so-called turret's syndrome again?"

"Something like that, yes. But I don't blame you for being mad enough to chew nails and spit out rivets."

His frown was again transformed into a smile. "Sometimes Mama used to say she was mad enough to spit tacks. Between the two of us, we could have opened a hardware store."

I laughed. I laughed far too long, and far too loud. Meanwhile my poor brain was trying desperately to figure out a way to get my big fat mouth out of trouble.

"Just because I shared something my mama—"

"Ooh, Abby!" C.J. said, bursting into my office. "You won't believe what happened to me."

"Deus ex machina," I said quietly.

C.J.'s stories are always fantastic, in every sense of the word. I used to think that she pulled them straight from the pages of supermarket tabloids, but—and this is almost too creepy to contemplate—I've come to discover that most of them have more than a kernel of truth to them. Some might even have a large ear of truth.

Without being asked to share, and before any introductions could be made, C.J. launched into a strange tale of alien abduction. (These were aliens from outer space, by the way, *not* amigos from south of the border.) At some point during the night she'd awakened to find four small beings gathered around her, as she lay on a platform of some kind, and these strange beings were probing her with index fingers that were over a foot long. C.J. got the distinct impression that they were on a spaceship. When I asked her to describe the aliens further, she said that they had large smooth heads, huge almond-shaped eyes, and they were all about my size.

"Just think, Abby," she said, "if you ever get abducted, you'll have no problem finding clothes that fit you."

According to the big galoot, the aliens performed all manner of medical tests on her, and were particularly interested in her problematic DNA. Apparently it had shown up on some of their monitors.

"When I told them that I might be part goat, they got real excited," she said, breathless from her recitation. "They made a beeline back to earth and to a pasture I told them about near Shelby where this couple raises a huge flock of Nubians. The next thing I know, I'm back in bed in Charleston, and it's the middle of the afternoon. After I got dressed I came straight over here. Sorry again for being late."

I glanced at Phillip Canary. He was not only staring wide-eyed at the poor gal, I could tell by his posture that every muscle in his body was on standby for the fight or flight command. Frankly, I was tempted to shout *Boo!*

Instead I said, "C.J., this is Mr. Canary. Mr. Canary, this is Mrs. Washburn, my sister-in-law."

"Soon to be ex-sister-in-law," C.J. said, and giggled.

"Nice seeing you ladies. 'Bye." With that the talented artist (as well as supertalented singer) fled my office like palmetto bugs when lights get turned on.

A good friend is someone who will listen to your troubles. A true friend is someone who loves you enough to set you straight, even if it means straining the friendship. As C.J. and Wynnell were already up to their armpits in the trap I'd set for the importer of illegal ivory, I decided to come clean to Bob Steuben.

Bob is like a gay priest who came out of the closet but never sought the holy orders, and never abused anyone. That is to say, he walks as straight

179

and narrow a path—so to speak—as any man I know. Bob doesn't gossip, Bob doesn't lie, Bob doesn't cheat (not even on his taxes), Bob doesn't wish anyone ill will (not even his partner's mother), Bob is slow to anger, Bob doesn't judge—well, the list goes on and on. And although the Rob half of the Rob-Bobs is really my best friend, I know that when it comes to unvarnished truth, Bob Steuben is my man.

Just as I was fixing to mash the doorbell on The Finer Things, the man with the oversized head and steady moral compass came stumbling out into bright Charleston sunlight. He slapped himself around his pigeon chest until he located the sunglasses in his pocket and put them on.

"Abby!" He said it as if suddenly surprised to see me. "What are you doing here?"

"I was about to come in and see you."

"What about?"

"I need to talk."

"Does it involve What's-his-name?"

"Who?"

"You know, that tall, dark, and handsome half of the duo—the one who is immensely more popular than I?"

"Bob! You shouldn't say that."

"But it's true, isn't it?"

"That is beneath comment."

"I know what everyone calls us: the Rob-Bobs. Am I right?"

My face burned. "It's just an affectionate nick-name."

"Ah, but whose name comes first?"

"Yes, but Bob-Robs wouldn't sound right, would it?"

"At this point it would be impossible to tell, your ears are so used to hearing it the other way around."

We were standing on the sidewalk, where God, tourists, and whoever else might be passing down King Street could see us, and possibly overhear us. This was not the cozy sort of confession I had in mind.

"Can we go someplace more private? How about the bar at the Charleston Place Hotel? I'll buy you a drink."

"You're serious? You really want to see just me?"

I nodded. "I need to run something buy a non-related person with a mature perspective. I pick you."

Even the most homely person takes on a mod-icum of attractiveness when they smile. "Abby, I'd love to stay and have a drink with you, but I have to drive out to Folly Beach to measure a client's dining room. So far she's given me three sets of dimensions over the phone. I'd send one of our interns out to do the job, but this is potentially a huge sale, involving not only a table and twelve chairs, but two credenzas and a corner cupboard—all part of a suite."

"Wow. I didn't know there were any houses that big on the island."

"Say, if you've got the time, why don't you ride along? I can always use someone to hold the other end of the tape measure; someone other than this mathematically challenged woman."

"Okay," I said, needing no further prompting. It was, after all, a beautiful afternoon for a drive.

When God made Charleston, He blessed it with water and declared it "good." It seems as if you can't go a hundred yards in any direction without getting a glimpse of a river, a marsh, or even the open ocean. We left the peninsula via the James Island Expressway, and although it was indeed a sunny day, a stiff breeze was blowing, bringing the sailboats out in force.

"Isn't it to die for beautiful?" Bob said.

"I couldn't imagine living anywhere else, could you?"

"No," Bob said. "Not really."

"Wait a minute; I heard hesitation in your voice."

"Well, I do miss Toledo."

"Toledo?"

"Abby, it's not a swear word."

"But it's cold and industrial, and you yourself said that at this time of the year it's as brown as a pair of old shoes."

"Yes, but it's where I spent my formative years—like in those old Wonder Bread commercials. I'll always feel connected. Don't you feel that way about Rock Hill, South Carolina? Or should I pronounce it 'Raw Kill,' the way the locals do?"

I laughed. "Watch it, buster."

We crossed over Wappoo Creek, which is part of the Intracoastal Waterway. From the elevated roadway we had a fabulous view of the marsh and the Country Club of Charleston.

"Okay, Abby," Rob said, "maybe now would be a good time to get down to brass tacks."

18

Was it my imagination, or did a cloud suddenly obscure the sun? I swallowed hard but barely made a dent in my pride.

"Bob, I may have done a stupid thing: I put a bogus ad in the paper—"

"We saw that."

"You *did?*"

"Darling, we're gay men. We're antiques dealers. Of course we scan the ads for antiques and collectibles. And since you're Rob's best friend—after *moi*—you can bet we recognized your cell phone number. Did you stop to think that every other dealer in town recognized it as well?"

"Uh—"

"But don't let me stop you, darling. This is your story, not mine."

"Well, as dumb an idea as it seems, I thought that if I advertised a large stash of ivory, I could draw the attention of whoever is smuggling ivory into Charleston."

"How so?"

"Like maybe I was competition—either that or a new source for them."

Bob is a very careful driver and didn't comment until we had safely turned left onto Folly Road. "Did this strategy work?" he asked.

"Not entirely." I filled him in on the particulars of each of my encounters, and he was suitably horrified, or disgusted, by my stories.

"You're lucky you didn't get hurt by some crazed stranger or sex maniac. And you're lucky the real smugglers are too lazy or stupid to read the *Post and Courier*. Abby, somebody who is in the business of smuggling large quantities of ivory into this country via the ports is not going to fall for a newspaper ad. Frankly, we all think it wasn't the best idea you've ever had."

"Wait a minute! Who is 'we all'? Are you saying that everyone's been talking about me?"

"Abby, we all love you. I haven't heard a single negative word—not about you personally."

"Just that my ideas suck. Which means—" I sucked in a mouthful of pluff-mud-scented air. "—that I don't have a cotton-pickin' brain in this little ol' head of mine."

Bob's hearty guffaws sounded like a base drum

at a high school band practice. "Abby, whatever am I going to do with you? *I'm* supposed to be the one with the self-esteem issues, remember? Besides, I can't think of anyone in the antiques community who is more respected and beloved than you."

"Oh yeah? What about What's-his-name?"

"So it's a tie in the respect department, but you win hands down in the beloved department. Didn't Mozella teach you not to be greedy?"

"Can one really teach a lesson that she hasn't learned herself?" Believe me, I instantly felt guilty for saying that.

"Touché," Bob said. "Now tell me, Abby, if you could redo the last couple of days, what's the first thing you would do differently? Not place that silly ad?"

I stiffened. "Heck no! I would place that darn ad all over again in a heartbeat. I don't care what everyone thinks. I seem to have sunk my hoe into a nest of baby rattlesnakes, and I aim to find the mama. The only reason I came to you, Bob, is because I thought you might offer a shoulder to cry on." At that, I actually started to cry, and I mean *really* cry.

I boo-hooed, I blubbered, I wailed, I sobbed, I gnashed a few teeth, and plain old just had me a good old-fashioned, snot-producing crying marathon. Trust me, there isn't a man alive, gay or straight, that can stand up to a Wiggins woman's meltdown.

Poor Bob had to pull to the side of the road so he could gesticulate nervously with both hands.

"Abby, stop, *please!* I'm begging you. Besides, you didn't give me a chance to tell you that I totally agree with you."

Momentum is a hard thing to overcome. I couldn't help but snuffle a few times before I could achieve something that even approached speech. And of course I had to blow my nose a million times, and the only thing either of us had that came close to being a tissue substitute was an old AAA car map that Bob found under his seat. And then when I did finally speak, every other word or so was punctuated by a hiccup.

But Bob was patient and kind. He was also very firm.

"I meant it when I said that I'm behind you on this. Do you know why I am? Because you have good instincts. Trust your gut, Abby. I do."

"B-B-Bob," I blubbered.

He put his gangly arms gingerly around me. "Oh Abby, it breaks my heart to see you like this."

"B-Bob, c-can I ask you a-another q-question?"

"Anything."

"H-How b-badly is my m-mascara smeared?"

"You look like a drunken raccoon, darling."

I must say that I was pleasantly surprised by Wynnell's skills as a makeup artist. She met me at my office with what looked like a large fishing tackle box full of pencils, tubes, brushes, and small jars. In a plastic shopping bag she carried an assortment of wigs and hair extensions, and in a canvas tote bag that she'd toted (what else?), bottles of spray-on color and fixative.

We had a few tense moments, but only until I turned myself totally over to her control, which is exactly the way it should have been. This was a lesson I learned from watching *Project Runway* on TV, and should have remembered from the onset, instead of wasting valuable time. The gist of it is this: compromise is not always a good thing, so give the artist her head. Her vision is bound to be better than whatever hybrid the two of you can finally cobble together.

When Wynnell pronounced me "finished," I wouldn't have recognized myself. No kidding, I would have walked right past myself on the street and not given me a second thought. How creepy is that? Besides looking like a totally different woman, I looked convincingly older—no make that *disturbingly* older. If I asked for a senior discount made up like this, no one would have batted an eye—which might tempt me to punch him or her in the eye. But gently, of course, like a proper Southern sexagenarian.

"Well, what do think?" Wynnell said.

"You did a fantastic job, you really did, which makes it kind of creepy."

"It's my Aunt Marietta."

187

"She's a beautiful woman, Wynnell—far prettier than I . . . You made her prettier and older at the same time. How did you do that?"

Wynnell shrugged, but she didn't deny that her creation was prettier than her model. Oh well, she was still a good friend. Once, on a camping trip, I had to rely on her to remove a tick from my buttocks. Friends don't come any better than that.

"Abby," she said, "I know you think I see a conspiracy behind every tree. But why do you think the public saw almost nothing of Vice President Cheney during the last six months he was in office?"

"Why don't you just save us both time, darling, and tell me."

"Because his popularity ratings were so low. The Secret Service told him that since he was a lame duck, there was no point in him hanging around Washington anymore, given the security risks."

"No offense, Wynnell, but that's one theory of yours that just doesn't fly. Cheney may not have been as much in the news those last six months, but he was still visible."

"And all because of makeup!"

"Say what?"

She nodded vigorously. "My cousin Charlene owns a beauty shop in Washington, D.C., and—"

"Wynnell, darling," I interrupted gently, "we have a live performance to put on. We need to hustle if we're going to hit our marks on time."

"Whatever you say, Abby." But she was all grins.

I knew for sure that Wynnell had been a success when Bob stopped us as we were getting into my car. "Good morning, ladies," he said in that basso profundo voice of his that weakens the knees of many an unsuspecting lady of a certain age—the Liberace crowd, he calls them.

"Good morning, Robert," Wynnell said.

Bob looked expectantly at me, then at her, waiting for an introduction. When none was forthcoming, he proffered a hand. "I'm Bob Steuben. I see that you know my friend, Wynnell."

I shrugged and shook my head. "No Eengleesh."

"This is Fatima, Abby's second cousin from Lisbon," Wynnell said, having only missed a couple of beats.

"Would that be Lisbon, North Carolina?" Bob said. I could tell by his tone that he was deadly serious.

"Portugal," I snapped and started the engine.

"Welcome to this country, miss."

"Tank you."

"Wynnell," Bob persisted, "where's Abby?"

"The little minx stayed home to do the jumpy-jump again. She asked me to show Fatima around."

"Does she have a license?"

"Why don't you ask her yourself?"

Bob turned to me. *"Voce tem uma licenca?"*

189

"Holy crap, Bob," I moaned. "You're not supposed to be able to speak Portuguese."

The poor man had turned the color of cigarette ash and was swaying like a pine in gale force winds. I jumped out of the car and helped him sit on the curb.

"It's only me—Abby." I put a warning finger to my lips. "Don't say anything about this to anyone. *Please.*"

"Darn if you don't look like—well, someone other than yourself."

"Why thank you," Wynnell said. She'd joined us at the curb and was all grins again.

Thanks to her deft hand there was no way my scheme in Mount Pleasant was going to backfire.

Dora was equally fooled by my appearance, and doubly delighted. She clapped her hands with glee and made touching chortling sounds. After an embarrassingly long time she turned to Wynnell.

"Who are you, dear?"

"This is my friend, Wynnell. She'll be coming along to keep an eye on my makeup. Is that all right, *Mother?*"

"The more the merrier!"

And quite a merry gathering it was. Of course one might imagine that a free catered breakfast in the middle of the week would be a festive occasion for your average retiree, but Lady Bowfrey's generosity knew no bounds. An enormous white tent occupied her entire backyard, and uniformed caterers scurried back and forth between two long white trucks.

Inside the tent, chatting and stuffing their faces, was the happiest cross section of Mount Pleasant faces I had ever seen. And why not? At one end of the three long rows of dining tables was the buffet table, which looked close to collapse due to the weight of food that it bore. At the other end of the tent a string quartet was softly playing light classical pieces.

Directly in front of the musicians, seated at her own table, was the formidable aristocrat herself. Although her hooded eyes gave the impression that she might be asleep, Lady Bowfrey proved to have the vision of an osprey. With some effort she raised a massive arm and pointed a pudgy, but bejeweled finger, our way. The music stopped on cue.

"I see some new faces," our benefactress said. "Dora, be a dear and introduce our guests."

The moment had finally come for Dora to put to bed a few rumors. The fact that it would create a lot more (what if childhood friends of her daughter were present?) had either not occurred to her or else she didn't give a darn. In any case, the dear woman gave me a squeeze and cleared her throat.

"Lady Bowfrey—everyone—I want y'all to meet my daughter, Clara van Aswegen. Clara, this is Lady Bowfrey, our hostess, and these are my neighbors."

There was a smattering of applause, and a sur-prisingly large number of people said "Welcome" —considering that most of them had food in their mouths. To be honest, it was terribly embarrassing for me until I glanced at Dora's face; she looked like my mama at the moment she'd held her first grandchild. From that second on I threw myself into the role of being Dora's daughter.

Lady Bowfrey tried to get everyone's attention by clapping, but getting gossipers to shut up is like corralling greased pigs. Finally she resorted to saying something to the bass viol player behind her, who in turn raked his bow across his instru-ment. The vile noise stunned the crowd into silence.

"Who is your other guest?" Lady Bowfrey inquired.

"My name is Wynnell Crawford," my pal said.

"Do I know you from somewhere? You look familiar."

"I own the Den of Antiquity, an antiques store downtown."

"Ah, that must be it. Welcome."

She clapped again and the merrymaking con-tinued. Wynnell, however, was not going to be quite as ebullient as the others—not when I got through with her. After helping Dora fill her plate and answering a few relatively benign questions, I steered my friend and employee outside by a pinch-grip to her triceps. It's a move every mother knows whose school-age child has had a complete meltdown in aisle five of Harris Teeter and on whom reasoning, psychology, and threats of an overnight stay at Guantanamo hasn't worked. Okay, so there are mothers who would never pinch their children, and they are right not to do so, and I salute them. Nonetheless, not only did I pinch Wynnell, I pinched her *hard*.

"Wynnell, that was a boldface lie!"

"And pretending to be an old lady's missing daughter *isn't* a lie?"

"I was doing it for *her* sake. Did you see how happy that made her?"

"Her sake, my eye! You were doing it—"

"Shhh! Okay, I'll go along with this nonsense for now, but what if one of these folks comes into the shop and asks to speak to the owner? What will you say then?"

"Abby, I'm not a fool. I wouldn't dare—"

I felt myself being gently nudged aside by a tall thin man in a green plaid sport coat. He was, by the way, addressing Wynnell, not me.

"Excuse me, ma'am," he said. "I was in your shop the other day and noticed a long case clock in the corner—the far left rear corner, I believe."

Wynnell's infamous unibrow appeared as she recreated *my* shop in her mind. "It's actually on the right-hand side."

"Ah yes. Is it for sale?"

"Everything is—for the right price."

Dang it! Wynnell had the nerve to steal one of my best lines. Even the tall thin man liked it, because he laughed annoyingly loud.

"Tell me," he said, "is it German?"

Wynnell massaged her chin while she forced her unibrow into a brush-filled vee. "Hmm. Carla, I showed the long case clock to you, didn't I?"

"No."

"Are you sure?"

"Positive."

The man in green plaid reached into his inner breast pocket and withdrew a business card. "My name is Pembroke Manning," he said. "I teach a class on appraising antiques through the Continuing Education Department of the College of Charleston. Perhaps you would like to register for the spring semester."

"But I—I'm not—"

"She's not able to sit through a class," I said. "She's got that 'going urge.' You've seen the commercials, right? But in her case the medication doesn't work."

I slipped my petite paw into the crook of his arm and tugged him gently away from a gasping Crawford. "So tell me, Mr. Manning, how long have you been attending these fabulous productions of Lady Bowfrey?"

Pembroke Manning's sexual preference was none of my business, but I got the sense that he was a latent heterosexual. That is to say, he may have been retired from the force awhile, but he seemed eager to reenlist.

"I've been coming every week now for the past year and a half. I only teach my class at night, you see. And that's only on Wednesday nights, at the Sheppard's Center. I'd have asked you, but you're obviously not in that age group."

"Obviously—oh, but I am. I mean, I *am* very interested in antiques. Are you a professional collector, Mr. Manning?"

"*Was*. I had a store up in Camden, and another in Columbia, but I got out of the business a couple of years ago when my daughter and her husband decided to settle down and take over the store in Columbia. So I sold the store in Camden and moved down here. I've always loved the coast. There's nothing like it, if you ask me."

"No siree, bob. Well, Mr. Manning, it's very nice talking to you, but I think I better go help my friend find a lavatory. Or does Lady Bowfrey supply those as well?"

"No, ma'am, but I live just catercorner from here—where you see those tall palms on either side of the front door. Your friend is welcome to use my bathroom."

"How very nice of you," I said wickedly. "And how very lucky of you to have such a generous woman as Lady Bowfrey as a neighbor."

I felt the tendons in his thin arm tighten. "One

might say that. Then again, if we, her immediate neighbors, did not partake of this weekly bounty, then we would feel used, wouldn't we?"

"Clara!" Wynnell called. "You mother wants us inside."

I forced a smile. "Just a minute, dear." I turned back to Pembroke Manning. "Would you care to explain, dear?"

19

Well, you see those humongous trucks that are all but blocking the street? Of course you do; you can probably see them from the space station. At any rate, those things come like clockwork every Tuesday around midnight so the crew can set up. With the lights and the noise, it's like setting up a carnival. Believe me, if I had my druthers, I'd rather stay home and eat a bowl of cereal after first getting a good night's sleep. I'm not a complaining man, Miss Clara, but I have to teach tonight."

Miss Clara? Who did he think I was? An octogenarian? I was only a faux sexagenarian, for crying out loud! Still, I knew I had better bite my tongue for the sake of my investigation.

"How do the other neighbors feel about this?" I asked sweetly.

"They're pissed as heck too—well, some of them. Others can't wait to kiss her behind. They think that because she's rich, somehow kissing up to her will benefit them as well. But I'm telling you, she's laughing down at all of us from her ivory pagoda."

"Say what?"

"That monstrosity of a house. Doesn't it look like a pagoda to you?"

"I would have described it as a three-story beach house with recessed floors. But yes, it is sort of ivory-colored. About those trucks and that terrible racket, have you tried talking to her?"

"Abby!" Wynnell shouted.

I pretended not to hear. "We have, but she insists that they're necessary. We even presented her with a straw poll saying that we preferred no breakfast over a sleepless Tuesday night, but she just scoffed. So our last step was to take it to the city council, but suddenly we lost three-quarters of our backers. Turncoats, that's what they are. You can hear them all in there now."

"Do you suspect her of bribing your neighbors somehow?"

Mr. Manning spit on the grass next to the sidewalk. That's when I disengaged from his arm.

"*Suspect?* She owns an apartment building in Orlando. She sent an invitation to everyone on the block inviting them to sign up for free time shares there with complimentary passes to Disneyworld. How could we refuse?"

"*You* signed up as well?"

"Yes, but I still have a right to grumble. This is America."

I didn't bother to excuse myself.

I must say that the food was excellent. It was prepared inside the grand dame's house and rushed outside under sterling silver domes. Nothing was ever too cold, or too warm, or lacking. It was the first buffet that I'd attended where I didn't feel like I had to hunt around to find a "good piece," or else feel guilty that I'd taken the last recognizable serving of that particular selection.

Not that I got much of a chance to actually eat. My new mother trotted me around the tables, proudly introducing me to a bazillion folks, none of whom seemed to care a stuffed fig's worth about meeting me. I got the impression that Dora, bless her heart, had outlived anyone who remembered that she had a daughter. Either that or the real Clara van Aswegen's contemporaries had moved away to larger towns, seeking opportunities that a sleepy fishing village in that day couldn't provide.

The only person who showed any interest at all was the indomitable Lady Bowfrey. When Dora brought me over, the self-proclaimed empress with the chopsticks in her hair snapped her pudgy fingers. The music stopped abruptly.

"Clara," she said, letting the word roll off her tongue almost like a European would. "Welcome home."

198

I had the urge to curtsy, but wisely refrained. "Thank you."

"How long will you be staying?"

"Well—I—"

"She's on her way to see the Dalai Lama," Dora said. "It's all very hush-hush, but when this particular assignment is over, you'll be retiring, won't you dear?" She put her arm around my shoulder and squeezed.

Lady Bowfrey closed one eye and regarded me with the other, which was now as round as a marble. "The Dalai Lama? I hope you're not involved with this free Tibet nonsense. You know, of course, that Tibet never was anything other than a province of China. All you have to do is look at a map to see that."

"I beg to differ. The Tibetan culture is distinct: first of all, the language is Tibetan, not Mandarin—"

The round eye narrowed. "Really, Clara, perhaps you should limit your conversations to subjects upon which you are qualified to comment."

That did it; that hiked my hackles—petite as they might be. "*Miss* Bowfrey, is it possible that your defense of Communist China is predicated on the fact that you do extensive business with them?"

Until that second I was unaware that virtually everyone in the tent, waitpersons included, was paying avid attention to our conversation. Now I could feel their eyes boring into my back. I tried to take a deep slow breath, but all the available oxygen had already been sucked from the air.

"You will not call me 'Miss,'" the grand dame hissed, as loud as an overheated boiler, one that might explode imminently. "In fact, you will never call me anything again, because you will leave this tent!"

Although she was unable to rise to her feet in her majestic and righteous wrath, Lady Bowfrey flung a great arm in the direction of the nearest tent flap. The movement of all that flesh created a small breeze, and a lifelong desire to refuse that third piece of Domino's pizza.

Dora's arm slipped from my shoulder. "My daughter isn't herself today," she said. She spoke so softly that the folks nearest the buffet tables rose in their seats in order to better hear our conversation. "She flew in from Quito, Ecuador, last night; she's suffering from jet lag."

"Foolish woman," Lady Bowfrey said scornfully to Dora. "How stupid do you think I am? Quito is in the same time zone as Charleston. Therefore you shall leave as well. I don't know what sort of scam the two of you are pulling, but I sure as heck can tell bad stage makeup when I see it. Whoever did this shouldn't even be allowed near a high school play."

Wynnell had been lurking within easy earshot, and I glanced over to see her reaction. As I suspected, the poor dear was crushed. Absolutely humiliated. I looked away quickly, so as not to draw attention to her, but alas, some folks were already making the connection.

"You're despicable, *Miss* Bowfrey," I said, and grabbing Dora by an arm, dragged her out of the tent and away from the sideshow that one exceedingly wealthy newcomer had managed to create in an otherwise still very pleasant town.

Wynnell joined us on a run, her head down.

My heart broke for Wynnell. I honestly thought she'd done a masterful job. What's more, she'd passed the "Bob test" with flying colors. To be so cruelly exposed in front of a hundred or more people was just more than she could bear. Before we even got back to Dora's house she was crying so hard I had to help her walk. When we got there, we made her lie on the sofa, with her head elevated, while I called Ed and Dora made us all cups of herbal tea.

Ed, bless his heart, was Johnny-on-the-spot. He was also a very convincing liar, or else he too didn't know who I was. At any rate, after he and Wynnell left, I stayed long enough to have a second cup of herbal tea while I tried to comfort poor Dora. The Wednesday morning breakfasts had been the highpoints of her weeks. They were the only thing she looked forward to anymore—except for Heaven.

Dora told me that she was a Presbyterian born

and bred. She told me that her church was only two blocks away. However, lately the Presbyterian Church seemed to have gotten a mite too liberal in its views, so she was thinking of joining the Mount Pleasant Episcopalians. What did I think about homosexuals?

"I think that some are tall, some are short, some are fat, some are thin, some are kind, some are mean—" My phone rang. "Excuse me, Dora." I turned away for a modicum of privacy. "Greg, this isn't a good time."

"Hon, turn on *Charleston Chats* right now."

"Huh?"

"The talk show; you're on it." He hung up.

I must admit that my brain misfired a few times, but within a crucial thirty seconds I managed to convince Dora to turn on the nearest television. The timing was perfect.

"Welcome back to *Charleston Chats*," a young beautiful black woman said. "I am your hostess, Keesha Pinckney, and today I'm talking to Pagan Willifrocke, private eye extraordinaire. Pagan has been on a secret assignment to ferret out a possible gang of ivory smugglers. Pagan, tells us specifically, how you set about doing this."

And there indeed was Pagan Willifrocke with her flowing blond tresses and her movie star good looks. She had the temerity to toss those locks and smile coyly before beginning her breathy explanation.

"Well, Keesha, I knew that contraband ivory—

lots of it—was entering the Port of Charleston. I just didn't know who the mastermind was. Then I read an ad in the *Post and Courier* that seemed as if it might have been written by the mastermind herself. So I agreed to meet this person for dessert at Poogan's Porch."

I gasped.

"Were you wired?" Keesha asked.

"You betcha."

I staggered to the closest chair. It was already taken by Dora, so I sat on the armrest.

"Would you mind playing that tape for us?"

"I'd be delighted."

PAGAN: "What shall I call you?"

ME: "The name is Sweathog."

PAGAN: "Good afternoon, Miss Sweathog. I understand that there will be certain consequences if I cross you. Can you please elaborate? By the way, I don't handle pain well. What's the best I could hope for?"

ME: "Hope to die."

PAGAN: "Oh my, I see that we're getting down to the nitty-gritty right away. In that case, do you head up the ivory smuggling ring?"

ME: "Yes."

PAGAN: "Please tell how you operate."

ME: "Once I sell this shipment, then I'll turn to my supplier, and he'll turn to his source, which is the poacher."

I couldn't push the Off button fast enough. "Uh—that wasn't who you think it is," I said to Dora. "Miss Sweathog—what kind of childish stunt is that?"

"Why Abby, that was you!"

"No way, José! I mean, how can you be sure?"

She eyed me warily for the first time. I could almost hear her heart race as she leaned away from me in the chair.

When I called Greg back he told me the boat was still docked in Shem Creek and I should meet him there. Since I was only five minutes away, I expected him to be waiting for me—or at least for the cabin door to be unlocked. Understandably, then, I rapped rather sharply on the glass pane with my car keys.

Booger opened the door. "Yes, ma'am?"

"Hey, Booger," I said as I tried to slip past him.

Booger blocked the door with his sturdy frame. "Whoa there, little lady. We ain't buying none of what you're selling today."

"I'm not selling anything, Booger; let me in."

"Sorry, ma'am." He started to close the door.

It's a little known fact that Booger and George W. were twins separated at birth, and therefore only God and a stick of dynamite can get them to change their minds once they're made up. When I saw that door starting to close, I knew I had no choice but to act. Despite the fact that I was wearing a skirt, I threw myself at the space left open by his knock-knees. My head made it through, as did my shoulders, but alas, my hips acted as bumper stoppers. To any slightly inebriated tourist who happened to be strolling along the dock that morning, it might have looked as if a bowlegged deckhand was riding a squat pony—backward.

Of course at that very moment Greg came charging up the stairs that led from the hold. "What the heck?"

Booger struggled to turn around, and in the effort stepped on my foot. "This woman just barged in here. You think she's a terrorist?"

Greg stared me in the eyes. "Yes," he drawled. "I believe she is."

By then I was all the way inside and on my feet. "I am not a terrorist!"

"Booger," Greg said. "Close the door and prepare to cast off. We'll take this one out to the Gulf Stream, give her a life vest, and if the sharks don't get her, she gets a free ride all the way up to the coast of Scotland. Did you know, ma'am, that they can grow palm trees on the coast of Scotland thanks to the Gulf Stream?"

"Greg," I screamed. "It's me, Abby!"

My beloved laughed merrily, but poor Booger was blown away. "What the heck is going on?" he said. His expression reminded me of C.J.'s cousin Orville, who got his head stuck in a window fan for a mite longer than he'd planned.

"It really is my Abby," Greg said, enfolding me in his arms. He smelled like a combination of diesel fuel, ship's paint, and fish, but with a slight overtone of Liquid Plummer.

"Well I'll be dippity-doodled and hornswaggled," Booger said. "And here I thought you was just some pushy old lady trying barge her way in."

"And now," Greg said, "you know that she's *my* old lady, right?"

"Right."

"Booger," I said, "if I weren't a lady, I'd punch you in the nose." I caught my breath. "So guys, what gives? Why are you still in port?"

20

Greg and Booger, bless their hearts, had not gone to sea that day because they'd had too much to eat at the Seewee Restaurant on Route 17N the night before. The Seewee, named after a now tragically extinct Indian tribe, serves up the best home cooking south of Norfolk and north of Jacksonville. A fried grouper, a fried flounder, a chicken fried steak, and two basketfuls of hush puppies were no match for the boat's new plumbing. Once the men got everything shipshape again they collapsed in front of the TV, and that's when Gregory heard my voice on local chat TV.

"Booger," Greg said when we were caught up, "seeing as how the morning's shot, and the tide is running against us, and the wind's picking up, why don't we just call it a day?"

"Nah, this ain't nothing. Besides, we caught ourselves a huge mess of shrimp that time we took Jimmy Estes out with us, and the weather was a lot worse than this."

"Okay, let me put it another way: I don't want to go out."

"But we'll lose money!"

Greg shook his head and sighed. "Abby, hon, I'm sorry."

"That's all right, dear."

"No, it's not," my husband said, and turned back to his cousin. "Look, Booger, give us ten minutes. And stay inside. If I see the whites of your eyes, I'll punch you in the nose myself. Is that understood?"

Booger nodded, whereupon Greg took my hand and led me back on deck. Although there was enough of a breeze to raise whitecaps on the distant harbor, the sun felt good on my cheeks. The screams of the swooping sea gulls was music to my ears. In many respects, it was a typical day at Shem Creek—but it was not.

Greg held me tightly for a long time. Then, releasing me slowly, he looked into my eyes once more.

"Abby, what are you up to this time?"

"The truth?"

"The whole truth, and nothing but."

I gave him an edited, nutshell version, before they cut and pasted snippets so the interview would sound the way Pagan Willifrocke wanted it to sound. My beloved knew me well enough to fill in the blanks and construct the unedited version on his own.

He hugged me again when I was through. "Don't panic," he said tenderly. "First of all, she never used your name, which is a good thing for her. Because since she took your words out of context, she's made herself open to a lawsuit. But the really good news is, Abby, that your voice isn't that recognizable over TV."

"It isn't?"

"You sound disappointed."

"Maybe a little bit—well, you said to be honest."

"That's exactly right. You see, I recognized it right away, and I think that your mother would have—but Booger didn't. I called my aunt after I called you. She'd seen the show as well. She hadn't a clue what that little stunt was all about. She said it bored her to tears."

"Greg, why would Pagan Willifrocke record me like that? Do you think she's somehow connected to Mr. Curly? To the real smugglers? Or does she just walk around with a microphone in her blouse?"

Greg laughed. "You know, as strange as it might seem, I'd bet dollars to Krispy Kremes on the last one. She was scheduled to appear on the show, and didn't have anything juicy to talk about, so she was taping everything she could. That woman is a publicity hound pure and simple. Trust me—she'll go far one of these days."

"You think she's pretty?"

"Heck no; she's gosh darn beautiful." Actually, Greg's language was a bit more emphatic than that. Since I prefer instant karma over the slow variety, I delivered a sharp kick to his shins.

"Ow! What was that for?"

"Watch your language when you're talking to a lady, even if she is your wife. Besides, I've seen Pagan close up. Her legendary bosom contains more petroleum by-products than the Exxon Valdez spill, and yes, her hair color is natural—to some species of dried prairie grass."

"Why Abby, I think you're jealous of my relationship with someone I haven't even met."

"See that you keep it that way, tiger."

His response was a kiss that nearly removed my tonsils.

The problem is that Greg trusts me too much. Okay, I suppose I could cop to being too hard-headed, but I won't. Greg's advice (he knew better than to order me to do anything) was to drive straight home, scrub off all traces of Carla van Aswegen, and eat a nice lunch while I watched *All My Children*. It was, in fact, good advice, and for once I fully intended to follow it, but life got in the way.

The name of this little roadblock was Mama. She'd been gone so much lately that when I walked through my own front door, I nearly had a heart attack to see another woman standing in my living room, dusting the shades on my floor lamps.

"Ack!"

"Why Sadie Sue," Mama said, "it is about time you showed up."

I patted my chest. "You about gave me the big one, seeing you standing here."

"Why on earth should that scare you, Sadie Sue? I live here, remember?"

I eased my tired bottom into the nearest chair, a genuine Louis XIV. "Mama, are you feeling all right?"

"Of course I am. It's you I'm worried about. You look a trifle peaked. Isn't all that supposed to be behind you?"

"Mama," I whined. Here I was, forty-eight, and still uncomfortable about certain things with my mother.

"Well, you don't look very happy for a woman who's spent the last sixty-five years in heaven."

"What?"

"Frankly, dear, you're a bit of a disappointment."

"Mama, what in heaven's sake are you babbling about?"

"Why that's just it, dear. On your deathbed, Sadie Sue, you promised to take one peek at Heaven and then come back and tell me if it was worth playing for. So what's the deal, did they keep you there until it was time—Oh, no you don't, Sadie Sue! I'm not going anywhere with you!"

Mama turned as white as her famous meringue, and I got the distinct feeling she was going to faint. In a flash it all made sense to me: my minimadre was thinking that I was her long since deceased great-aunt to whom, I've been told, I bear a family resemblance.

"Mama!" I shouted. "I'm not your great-aunt Sadie Sue—I'm Abby! I'm your daughter."

But it was too late. The chain of events that precipitate a proper faint had already been set in motion. I could no more reverse them than I could stop a baby from being born. All I could do was try to minimize the damage to her noggin—and my floor.

I rushed over to Mama and threw my arms around her just as she was going down. She might be an itty bitty woman, but I'm even ittier, so the two of us ended up half on the floor and half sprawled across a sofa cushion I managed to pull off as we made our final descent. She was, of course, on top of me. By the time I pushed free of her, she came moaning back to her senses.

"Abby, is that really you?"

"As big as life, Mama, and twice as ugly."

"Abby, I've always hated that expression, but since nobody but your daddy—may he rest in peace—ever used it, I must therefore conclude that it is indeed you." She struggled to a sitting position and scrutinized me at arm's length. "Abby, what year is it? How long have I been asleep?"

I couldn't help but laugh. "Come on, Mama. Let me help you up. You haven't been asleep; this is makeup. Wynnell made me up to look like I was ten years older. I'm also not supposed to be looking like myself, but apparently I do. Greg recognized me, and you saw a family resemblance."

"Wynnell? What's going on, dear? You're not having another one of your adventures without me, are you?"

Bless her heart. Mama sounded positively hurt. She loves my friends and they love her, and there really are times when we all pal around together. But what was I to tell her now? That she could be a part of the investigation if she quit sneaking around with my slimy ex-husband, Buford?

"Mama, you could be part of this investigation, if you weren't sneaking around with my slimy ex-husband."

"Aha, so you *are* having an adventure!"

"It's hardly an adventure, Mama."

"I guess this explains that handsome young man who came to see you this morning."

I sat on the couch, and Mama followed suit. "*Who* came to see me? When?"

"He was African American. I don't like that term, Abby. Not unless you use European

American every time you describe a white person. If you don't, white people become the norm—"

"Mama, I know your feelings on the subject. What did he want? Besides wanting to see me."

Mama smiled. She wears dresses that have fitted bodices, tightly belted waists, and full circle skirts. They are dresses that Donna Reed and Margaret Anderson would have worn—and of course the Beave's mom. These are not the kind of clothes that can be bought off the rack; my mother pays Mrs. Castelli good money for each one. Now where was I? Oh yes, Mama reached down into the fitted bodice of her navy and white polka dot dress and withdrew from the damp prison of her bosom a tightly folded piece of paper.

"He left a message, sweetie. But if you want it, you have to take me with you."

"Take you where?"

"Wherever it is that you're going from here. You know that after reading this note you'll shoot out of here like a bat out of *Hello Dolly.*"

"Mama, that's blackmail!"

"Indeed it is. I gave birth to you, Abigail; I have the right to take special liberties."

I sighed. "Okay, I give up. You win."

Mama giggled as she handed me the note. "Oh Abby, I always have so much fun when we play together."

"You mean when we almost get killed together?"

"Don't be such a sourpuss."

I unfolded the note.

I found my own source for ivory. But hey, it was nice meeting you.

"What the heck?" I said.

"Let me see," Mama said, and snatched the scrap from my hand. "Abby, what are you doing? You just got arrested for importing illegal ivory—"

"Mama, it's not what you think. Look, I'm sorry I scared you earlier, but I really have to go now."

Mama grabbed a hank of my hair, something she'd never done before, not even when I was a child. "Oh, no you don't. You're not going anywhere without me. You promised."

"But that's when I thought the note was more promising."

"Abby, either I'm coming with you or I'm telling Greg what really happened to his car on Christmas Eve."

"*What?* How'd you know?"

"And before you give your unequivocal no, answer me this: wasn't I instrumental in apprehending that rug lord up in Rock Hill last year?"

I sighed. "You were invaluable, Mama."

"Good, then it's all settled. Just give me a minute to rob my piggy bank. There's always something worthwhile buying at the market and putting away for Christmas."

Phillip Canary must have said more than "Hello" and "Boo" to Mama, because she knew exactly which shed to hit, and where in that shed his stall was located. Furthermore, she knew the location of a praline vendor, which was good, because I was starving.

Again the area around his stall was crowded, but we amused ourselves at a nearby pocketbook vendor until Phillip took what looked like a much needed break. At that point two very attractive, much older women showed up.

"Mr. Canary?" one of them asked.

"Yes, ma'am."

"I'm Sadie Sue Wiggins," I said. "I'm Abby Timberlake's, uh—great-great-aunt."

"No," Mama said. "That would make her too old, unless she'd be kept on ice—or really *was* back from beyond."

"I meant to say that I was her aunt. And this"—I poked Mama in the ribs—"is my twin sister Mozella. She has the same affliction that her daughter has, so I've come along to act as interpreter."

"You mean she has that mysterious European castle disease?"

"It's a syndrome, not a disease. Mr. Canary, my sister wants to know what you plan to do with Abby's vast ivory collection."

"So it does exist, does it?"

215

"Would my daughter lie?" Mama said.

"Well," Phillip Canary said, "frankly, I'm not interested in buying a vast collection of ivory. I'm more interested in viewing and photographing different pieces, and trying to match them to country of origin. It's for a research paper I'm writing." Perhaps I had a funny look on my face, because his gaze zeroed intently in on me. "I guess I forgot to tell Abby that I'm getting a master's degree in Environmental Studies. My thesis is titled 'The Depletion of Species for the Vanity of Mankind.'"

"No, you didn't tell me—I mean, Abby," I said.

He smiled. "You're one of a kind, Miss Timberlake—whoever you are. And folks think that Savannah has its share of eccentric characters!"

Mama bumped me aside with her crinoline padded hips. "She isn't the only eccentric Charlestonian, dear, or haven't you noticed?"

"Oh, I've noticed all right. You're definitely one of a kind as well, Mrs. Wiggins. It's clear to me that in this case the apple didn't fall far from its tree. But I'm sure that you're both aware of the fact that, if apples are left lying on the ground too long, they start to decay."

"Did he just call us rotten apples?" Mama said.

"So how did you know it was me?" I demanded.

"Your eyes; the window to your soul. You're a woman who approaches life full throttle, Abby. By the time you reach your mother's age—or thereabouts—your eyes are gonna show a whole lot more than they do now."

I felt uncomfortable; it was time to leave. "You have certainly been a bushel of surprises yourself, Mr. Canary."

"That's it? You're not gonna tell me what your gig is?"

I glanced around. We were starting to attract a knot of curious onlookers, no doubt attracted to the emotion in our voices. Mama noticed them as well.

"Shoo," she said, and waved her arms at them like she was chasing chickens off her porch.

Some of the tourists laughed and moved on casually. Others practically ran, and I can't say that I blamed them. When only the pocketbook vendor was left staring at us, I beckoned Phillip Canary to stand closer.

"I received an illegal shipment of ivory that was clearly intended for someone else. It came from Hong Kong. It seems that someone in the area is using Charleston as their base for their clandestine ivory importing business. I was hoping to out them with that ad."

He laughed, then noting the expression on my face, quickly sobered. "Sorry about that. But just out of curiosity, did you find that needle?"

"What?"

"In the haystack," Mama said. "Abby, sometimes I wonder if I forgot to eat on the days that your brain was forming—bless your heart."

Phillip Canary laughed again. "Abby, I really like your mama."

"Good, then you can have her," I said. "She is, after all, almost potty-trained."

"You know something else?" he said. "If I was gonna set my mind to a case like yours, I'd start back at the ship. Like could any of the crew be in on it? After all, ivory just doesn't get up and walk out of the harbor on its own. Somebody's got to be down there to collect it. So what are they driving? What kind of a system do they have going?"

"System?"

"Poor Abby," Mama said. "She doesn't have time to watch old movies. He means like smuggling the ivory in and out in a laundry cart, don't you, Mr. Canary?"

"*Or—*" I began.

"Abby, be polite and wait for Mr. Canary to answer."

"Mama, you asked a rhetorical question. Besides, we have to run!"

"Run?"

"Mama, if my hunch is right, then Mr. Curly can cross me off his list of suspects with ink!"

21

My dilemma was whether or not to fill Mama in on all of the details of our destination while on the way there (and scare the bone marrow out of her), or do the kind thing and let her draw her own conclusions. I decided on the latter. After all, Mama had expressed a desire to share more adventures with me, had she not? Besides, experience has taught me that she really does perform better when not overrehearsed.

"Abby," she said as the houses whizzed by, "in this part of Mount Pleasant they're very strict with the speed limit. My friend Cheryl got clocked here last year going six miles over the dang thing and got a ticket."

"That's nice, Mama."

"That's *nice?* That's all you've got to say? There's supposed to be a grace period of nine miles per hour. I thought you might want to know that, seeing as how your tootsie is mashed down about as far as it can go."

"I'm in a hurry, Mama. Time, tide, and criminals wait for no woman."

Mama chortled with glee. "This sounds like it's going to be fun. Do I get to pack heat?"

"I don't know. Did you bring one of those gizmos from the drugstore that becomes warm when you peel off the tape?"

"It means a *gun,* dear. Honestly, Abby, some-times I wonder which century you're living in."

We turned a corner and my heart leaped both with joy and terror. Sure enough, there they were: the two large white trucks. The large staff was still quite busy tearing down and loading outdoor fur-niture. Much to my relief, however, the queen bee was nowhere in sight.

"Abby," Mama said, "this is Lady Bowfrey's house, isn't it?"

"Yes. How do you know?"

"She goes to Grace Church. I've been here for a foyer dinner."

"Imagine that: a criminal attending church. Do you think it's ever been done before?"

"Abby, this isn't because she outed you this morning, is it?"

"*Au contraire,* Mama. This goes much deeper than that. Lady Bowfrey—and I doubt that's her real name—is the head of the ivory smuggling ring."

"Your Aunt Marilyn said there would be prob-lems if I started you on solid foods too early, but since she never had any children of her own—not that she kept, at any rate—I just chalked her advice up to the ravings of a jealous aunt."

I pulled over to the corner behind an SUV, where—if we conducted ourselves properly—we could remain somewhat inconspicuous. "Look Mama, after all we've been through together, it's about time you trusted me. The pieces of this puzzled have already clicked together in my head."

"That's nice, dear, but did it occur to you to consult your sweet old mama before you glued those puzzle pieces in place and sent it out to be mounted?"

"Frankly, no. I'm not a real detective, and neither are you. I've been doing this on my own time, and you've been busy making a fool of yourself with my ex-husband."

It was a cruel thing to say. Of course I regretted it. But people who love each other can hurt each other the most, precisely because they know where the soft spots are. Apparently my tiny dagger was successful in hitting its mark.

Mama's lips disappeared and her eyes narrowed behind her lenses.

"I'm sorry, Mama," I said quickly. "And I'm consulting you now. Okay?"

The dear woman never could hold a grudge. "Abby, the thing is that I know Lady Bowfrey; she isn't the smuggling type."

"What?"

"You do say 'what' a lot, dear. Have you noticed that?"

"Can we get back to the Lady, please?"

"She's hardly that, dear; she's a very much respected member of my church—or I should say, was. What I mean is that she was when I still belonged to Grace Episcopal, but as you know, I'm now in flux. Oh Abby, flux is a terrible place to be. What if I should die whilst I was in flux? Why you'd be flummoxed as to where to hold my funeral, wouldn't you?"

"Mama, *please,* can we stick to Lady Bowfrey for just a second? After that we can digress all you want."

"Ah, her. Well, she is the nicest woman you'd ever hope to meet, except maybe for Princess Diana or Mother Teresa, which at this point I'd just as soon not meet. But my point is that everyone loves her."

I was stunned breathless. Neither could I hear very well. Mama, however, had no trouble continuing to babble. After I was able to breathe again, I was forced to interrupt her.

"Excuse me, Mama, but kind in which way?"

"I swear, dear, don't you listen to a word I say?"

"Upon occasion I do try, Mama. I *really* do."

She sighed dramatically. "All right, dear. But don't make me repeat it again. I find talking about others so boring."

"Yes, Mama."

"Now what was I supposed elaborate on? Oh yes—she was kind. You'd think she couldn't get around very well, but she has this powerful electric wheelchair that she's actually named. 'Zippy,' she calls it. She says it's a boy. On account of that, she can do just about anything—so she does. She helps out with Altar Guild, serves as a lay reader, works in the church kitchen, she welcomes visitors, she fills in for sick Sunday school teachers, and she always, always, has a warm smile for everyone and something thoughtful and comforting to say to those who are down in the dumps."

"Wow."

"Oh, and she sends cards with personal notes to everyone who is on the sick list, or in special need of prayer, *plus* she sends cards to each and every member who has a birthday or anniversary."

"Sounds like a superwoman to me. So how well do you know her personally?"

"I'd say fairly well—a six on a scale of one to ten. We were in the same adult Sunday school class."

"You mean that touchy-feely one called 'Issues with Tissues,' where y'all are crying all the time?"

"Abby, it's healthy to vent with your peers. You'd be surprised to learn just what kind of problems a rich woman like Lady Bowfrey has. Money can buy you a lot of things, but it can't buy you a decent twelve cup rice cooker."

"Excuse me?"

"Are you going deaf, dear?"

"No, but I thought you said rice cooker."

"I did. The one I have makes four cups of steamed rice, but the largest one I've been able to find makes only eight. Abby, how am I to make enough rice to feed thirty people when I have the group over for the spring luncheon?"

"Mama," I said patiently, "let's return to the subject of Mrs. Bowfrey; what kind of problems might she have?"

"Shame on you, Abby. I would never break a confidence."

"How can it be a confidence, Mama, if she shared it with your 'Yankees with Hankies' group?"

"That's my 'Issues with Tissues' group," she said. She sighed. "Okay, but if karma comes back around to nip me through my crinolines, it's your fault, Abby."

"Blame accepted, Mama."

"She's all alone in this world, Abby, except for this spaced-out nephew who runs a shop on King Street but doesn't do half the business you do, because the poor kid doesn't have an ounce of salesmanship in his vein."

"What's with this 'Lady' stuff?"

"Oh, she really has a title—well, that's what she says, at any rate. She's originally British, I think, but grew up in one of those African colonies that later became independent. Some of the Brits hung on, and hung on to their titles too. Unofficially, of course. But hers is from her husband, Lord Something Something Bowfrey. You'd think that would make her all stuck up, but she's really just as sweet as brown sugar pie."

"And to think that brown sugar pie used to be a favorite of mine," I mumbled.

"What was that, dear?"

"Nothing. Mama, where's her husband now?"

"He died in that African colony's fight for independence. That's when she decided to come to America and make a new life for herself. She said that she found the American entrepreneur spirit so refreshing. And I can see why, because she's as smart as the dickens too."

"I bet. Mama, have you been to the Wednesday buffet breakfasts?"

"At the Charleston Place Hotel? Abby, you know that I don't have that kind of money—"

"No, here, Mama. That's what these trucks are here for, and these white tents. Every Wednesday morning Her Ladyship serves breakfast to the hoi polloi of the Old Village of Mount Pleasant. You wouldn't believe the quality of the food. Really top drawer! Oh, and she even has a string quartet play."

"I don't believe it. I'd be invited if this was the case."

"It's true, Mama, but it's just for neighbors."

"I still don't believe it."

"Okay, but it's true."

"It's not! I'll prove that it isn't." With that Mama scrambled from the car and, despite the fact that she was wearing three inch heels (as is her custom), strode straight to Lady Bowfrey's house.

I know this because I slipped out of my side of the car, and still using the SUV as cover, maneuvered to where I had a better view. Mama cut diagonally across the street—to the left of the white tent and the nearest white truck—and clickclacked her way up the torturous steps of the beach-style house without pausing to catch her breath. (One advantage to having played Donna Reed for the last fifty years is that it has built up her calf muscles.)

I couldn't tell exactly what transpired at the door, just that a few seconds after she arrived, it was opened, and then she slipped in. A faithful daughter—that is to say a good Abby—would have chased after her, maybe even called 911. I didn't as much as call Greg.

Instead, I saw this as the perfect opportunity for me to do what I do best: I snooped. There was chitter-chatter coming from the tent, and it occurred to me that it might be the wait staff finishing up what was left of the buffet food. I peeked in the tent, and sure enough, there was food being downed. Not only that, but the air was thick with the pheromones of good-looking young men and women in high-flirtation mode.

Having survived that stage of life, I knew the help was temporarily oblivious to what was going on outside, so I turned my attention to the truck. It was one of those ultra long, eighteen-wheeler jobs, the kind that come within a prayer's width of running you off the road between Charleston and Rock Hill. The back doors were closed, and besides, I would have needed a pole-vaulting pole, or a step ladder, to reach them anyway.

Keeping the truck between me and the tent, I walked casually down the street. Now that the residents had been served their customary Wednesday breakfasts, they were off to the golf courses, tennis courts, or (I hoped) shopping. The shady streets of the Old Village—indeed of virtually all of Mount Pleasant—are generally deserted while school is in session during the winter.

Imagine my excitement when I discovered that the windows were down on the driver's side of the cab. If only I could hoist myself up to the running board . . . well, it never hurt to try, and try I did. On my first attempt I landed hard on my petite, but rapidly expanding, patootie. The second time, I managed to get the door open, but it rudely knocked me back on my aforementioned patootie (there is something to be said, however, for being bottom heavy). But as they say, the third time is indeed the charm; at last I had gained access to the high-riding command center of the eighteen-wheeler.

Despite the fact that the cab's exterior was shiny and white, the interior of this one smelled of old leather, cigarette smoke, sweat, and the essence of flatulence. It was exactly how I remembered Greg's apartment smelling when we first started to date. I took a quick look around, hoping to find nothing unusual, because if I did, I wouldn't be able to breathe. But silly me, every truck with an extended cab has a compartment behind the seats where the driver and/or his companion can sleep and/or engage in activities that might help keep them refreshed on a long haul.

This cab was no different. There was a fiberglass wall behind the seats that contained a fiberglass door. Wait—the door wasn't locked. And behind it was—uh—darkness. But not for long. Between the seats and the wall there was a huge mound of filthy magazines (literally and figuratively), a toolbox the size of a small coffin, and a pair of well-worn soft-sided suitcases.

What jumped out at me was a flashlight lying on top of the toolbox. The battery case was as long as my forearm, and the reflecting head almost as large as my own noggin. It was a torch for those who took their flashlights seriously, and it was therefore something that I could respect.

I picked it up and turned it on. Good! It was in perfect condition. I aimed its intense beam at the portal that led into the compartment behind the seats.

"How very interesting," I said aloud.

"What is?" a voice said just above my ear.

22

Mama! You just took ten years off my life!"
"Since I gave you life to begin with, dear,
I dare say that's my prerogative."

"Not according to your church. The Lord giveth,
and the Lord taketh away."

"That's all very nice, dear, but the Lord didn't
become a widder woman in the prime of His life
and have to raise children on His own."

"That's blasphemous!"

"Oh Abby, you really need to take that adult
Sunday school class. You'd learn all about situa-
tional ethics. Like, what if this was only a book,
and we were just characters in it? Would it be blasphemous then?"

"Mama, quit wasting my time! How did you get
up here? What happened with Lady Behemoth—I
mean, Bowfrey?"

"Of course I climbed up here, Abby. How else do
you suppose I got here? Flew? As for my friend, I'd
really appreciate it if you'd stop with the fat jokes.
They aren't funny! They hurt people's feelings."

"I'm sorry."

"Just don't do it again, dear. Now about my
friend—the truth is—well, she isn't. Not anymore!
I thought we knew each other so well from 'Issues
with Tissues,' but she doesn't recognize me from
Adam. Tell me, Abby: has our culture become so

multifaceted that someone like me goes totally unnoticed these days?"

Someone like me. My how those words hurt my heart. Was my poor little mother really that aware of just how eccentric she was? Was this a "costume" she put on every morning to mourn my daddy's passing, or perhaps to make a statement, or was she merely vying for attention? Nonetheless, I opted for the coward's way out that day.

"Mama, how could anyone *not* notice you? After all, you're the cat's pajamas."

"*Really?* That's what I thought! Anyway, she told me to vamoose. To amscray, or she would sic the cops on me."

"How awful." And how relieved I felt.

"So, I trotted over here to have a good cry. And here you were. So dear, now it's my turn to ask: what are *you* doing here?"

I didn't have time to answer Mama. I heard the voices when they seemed to be only feet from the cab. Therefore I had no choice but to do what I did: I grabbed my mother by the lapels of her shirt dress and pulled her over the armrest of the passenger seat and into the hollow that I occupied. Then while she was still too startled to react, I pushed her head first into the black hole that was the hidden compartment at the rear of the cab. I immediately dove in after her, and apparently just in time. Someone slammed the compartment door shut and the truck roared to life.

. . .

Picture, if you will, two not-so-wily Wiggins women floundering about in a dark smelly hole. I reckoned that I felt pretty much the way poor Jonah must have felt when he was swallowed by the whale. Granted he probably had moisture issues to deal with, but at least he didn't have Mama's flailing limbs smacking him across the face willy-nilly.

I pressed as flat as I could against a wall of the compartment in an effort to avoid serious injury, and that's when I felt the switch just inside the door. I flipped it on, flooding the small space with an eerie orange light.

"Abby!" Mama cried. "It's only you."

"Shhh, Mama," I said, mouthing my words more than speaking them, *"they might still hear us over the engine."*

Mama nodded and looked around, as did I. We were in the driver's sleeping quarters, nothing more. No deposits of illegal ivory. Just dirty twisted sheets and a pillow so stained it looked like it had been salvaged from the harbor. The walls of the tiny metal cubicle were papered with pages ripped from girlie magazines depicting air-brushed women with bosoms so large it was painful just to look at them. The floor was a single thin mattress that had been custom-made to fit such a small and oddly shaped area.

At least I could stand erect; Mama, on the other

hand, had to stoop. This fact, more than any other, seemed to get her goat.

"Memorize the maker of this truck, Abby. I'm going to write the CEO—I'm going straight to the top. If a little old lady who has been abducted can't stand up, then how is she supposed to fight for her life on an even footing with someone who can? It isn't fair, I'm telling you. It's discrimination. Heightism. And I'm not going to stand for it!"

The truck lurched and Mama prophetically fell down. Being a Wiggins (even by marriage counts fully), Mama struggled to get back on her feet. After all, no one keeps a Wiggins down involuntarily, even another Wiggins. Anyone in doubt should ask my brother Toy, who tried in vain to drool on me when we were in elementary school but never could succeed, even though I was just half his size.

"You're better off staying down there, so you won't get hurt."

"But Abby," Mama objected, "this mattress is disgusting!" She clawed at a corner of it, in an attempt to flip it partway over. Who knew what lay under it, but even if it was just rusty truck parts, it had to be better than this.

We spotted the clipboard simultaneously, but Mama reacted first. "They're conducting political polls," she said.

I gave up trying to stand. The truck must have been turning a corner, because I felt like I was riding a mechanical bull, but one without stirrups. Once down, I grabbed the clipboard from Mama.

"You don't have to be so rude," she said.

"Sorry," I said, as I fell back on the filthy bed. The rocking and swaying of the cab made any other position just too rigorous to maintain. Mama joined me.

First I scanned the pages; then I studied the top one carefully. Slowly the columns and figures began to make sense. The more I comprehended, the faster my heartbeat.

"We're headed for Georgia," I said. We were already about twenty minutes into our trip.

"Isn't that terrible what the Russians did? And right during the Olympics too."

"Not *that* Georgia, our Georgia. Mama, why aren't you taking me seriously? "

"I knew what you meant, dear, but of course I can't take you seriously because you're the one who told me that Lady Bowfrey holds these teas every Wednesday morning. And even though I don't live in Mount Pleasant, I don't think I'll ever forgive her for not inviting me to one. As if she's the cat's pajamas. Ha! Why I'll have you know she wore the same outfit to church two Sundays running, and it wasn't even summer, but high season. And those chopsticks she wears in her hair! Give me a break, Abby, that look is so retrohemian. That *is* a word, isn't it?"

"Perhaps it is now. Mama, this paper is a manifest

of the ivory shipment that arrived in the Port of Charleston on Tuesday, and was delivered via this truck to Lady Bowfrey's residence—where we were, right up until a few minutes ago—on Tuesday evening. Also on Tuesday evening a crew—presumably arriving via separate transport—set up the humongous tent and cooked the breakfast buffet."

"And you know this how?"

"This is a record of arrival and departure times. Our next stop is the Port of Savannah, by the way."

"You mean after this stop?"

"Excuse me?"

"The truck just stopped."

"Stoplights don't count," I said, slightly irritated.

"Yes, but even if your guess is right, Abby, why would she have two trucks in motion all the time? Why not just one?"

"Maybe it's a bit like a shell game. Who knows? Maybe the other truck is loaded with the ivory this time. Maybe this one is empty."

"Yes, but what's with the neighborhood breakfast in the first place? Why have the ivory brought into a peaceful upscale neighborhood to begin with? Isn't that risky?"

"*Au contraire, ma mère.* What better place to have a warehouse full of contraband than right there, in an historic village? That despicable woman has bought her place in the neighborhood with weekly portions of eggs Benedict and Virginia smoked ham."

"She's too d-despicable to be Episcopal," Mama said, sounding for all the world like Sylvester the cat. "So Abby, what do we do now?"

"We think."

"Think? You tried that before, and just look at the mess you dragged me into!"

"Mama, I didn't drag you into my mess; you jumped into it willingly, like a frog into a lily pond."

"That's been drained," Mama said. "Abby, I have a bridge game tonight, so I'm getting my hair blued at two. Did you hear that, dear? I just made a rhyme. Anyway, if I'm as much as ten minutes late—"

"Mama! This is no time to worry about your bluing. We need to think about getting out of this truck undetected and to a phone. Maybe we can trick them—"

"Silly Abby, tricks are for kids."

A second later the door to our hideaway was rudely flung open. One has a right to apprehend interlopers lollygagging about on your bed, but shouldn't one do it with a modicum of manners?

"Do you mind knocking first?" I said.

"Whoa! The little lady's a spitfire; I like that." The rude man was probably in his early twenties; quite handsome, with lots of sandy-brown hair and green eyes, and good dental hygiene. I think a lot can be said about a man by the way he cares for his teeth.

"Which little lady?" another man, who I couldn't see, asked. "All I see is two old bags."

"Why I never!" Mama said.

"Yeah, I bet you didn't."

The two men laughed uproariously at the coarse joke. So much for my good teeth theory. I tried pushing the door shut with my shoulder, preferring self-imprisonment for the meanwhile over whatever freedom these two goons had to offer.

"Oh no you don't, grandma."

A pair of callused hands grabbed me under the armpits and I popped right out of the sleeping compartment like a queen olive from a tall narrow jar. Again, Mama was right on my heels. Simultaneously we were plopped on the ground some distance from the truck, on a sandy patch beneath a scrubby oak.

Much to my amazement, we were no longer even in the city. My how time flies when you're shut up in someone's smelly sleeping hole. My guess was that we were in the Francis Marion National Forest. I decided I had nothing to lose by asking for confirmation.

"Yeah, so what?" said Thug Number Two. He had gray eyes and a salt and pepper goatee. He also had a tattoo of Barbara Bush on the back of his bald head. THE MOTHER GODDESS was inscribed in a ribbon beneath the portrait.

"We were only curious," I said. "I'd never seen

an eighteen-wheeler up close. I'm sorry if I offended you."

"I'm sorry too," Mama said. "I tried to raise her better. But kids these days—go figure."

The thugs must have thought Mama was a stand-up comedienne; they roared with laughter. "Right, like you two old ladies is mother and daughter? Tell us another," Thug Number Two said.

"Well," Mama said, "there was the time Abby asked me to help her write her own thank-you notes. Can you imagine that? What would Emily Post have had to say about that? Oh, how I miss Emily Post. These modern-day columnists can't hold a feather duster to her. But speaking of Emily, I think she would have a lot to say about you."

"Me?" Thug Number One said. "I ain't the one who called you an old bag."

"Nevertheless," Mama told him, "you could use a little work. Abby," she said, "don't you think this man could be a model?"

I cocked my head this way and that, taking my sweet time to answer. "Yes—*if* he stood straight, put on a decent wardrobe, and turned away from a life of crime. There isn't much call for modeling orange jumpsuits, is there, Mama?"

"Mama?" Thug Number Two said. "What's with that again?"

"She really is my mama," I said. "I'm wearing stage makeup. See?" I licked a finger and rubbed vigorously at the fake wrinkles at the corner of my right eye.

"Why, slap me up the side of the head and call me whopper-jawed!" Thug Number One said. "So what are you, actresses of some kind?"

"You might say that," Mama said.

"We're scouts for a game show," I said (unfortunately, I have the ability to lie quickly on my feet).

"It's called 'Singing for Your Sandlapper Sweetheart,'" Mama said.

"Huh?" Thug Number Two grunted. "What the heck is a sandlapper?"

"It's a South Carolinian," I said.

"Yeah? What's that?"

"Never mind. My mama was just funning with you anyway. The game show is called 'Bobbing for Bimbos.' You take a bunch of hoochie-mamas in bikinis, put them in a tank of saltwater, and then a couple of guys have to go in there blindfolded with their hands tied behind their backs and choose the one with the biggest—well, you know what I mean. You want to audition?"

"Heck yeah!"

"Me too!" Thug Number One was equally as enthusiastic.

"Great. I'm going to need your names, addresses, and phone numbers. You got anything to write on?"

"Yeah, here." Thug Number Two took a greasy

receipt out of his back pants pocket and commenced writing.

Meanwhile I scanned our surroundings. We were in a clearing off of a logging trail deep within the Francis Marion National Forest. The "forest" is named after the Revolutionary War hero (also known as the Swamp Fox), and covers over a quarter of a million acres. It is comprised of second growth pine forest, oaks, gum trees, magnolias, bay trees, swamps, hiking trails, and three small towns connected by a couple of sparsely traveled highways.

The wildlife is varied but includes poisonous snakes, wild boars, bobcats, coyotes, and quite possibly black bears. *Plus,* I've even heard rumors of a remnant panther population. None of the aforementioned critters were on my "must see" list, especially if I were to encounter them at night, while Mama and I were making our great escape. But again I was jumping the gun, à la Magdalena Yoder; we weren't officially anyone's captives. So far there wasn't a gun to be seen.

"It is turning out to be a beautiful day," I finally said. "Although frankly, I'm rather hungry. When do we start the picnic?"

The Thugs had a good laugh. "Here's our names and addresses," Thug Number One said, handing me the slip.

"But now that we're done with that," Thug Number Two said, "we gotta tell ya ta shut up."

"How rude!" Mama said.

"Hey, old lady, it ain't my fault; it's hers."

"Speak of the devil," I said. Thundering toward us in a cloud of red dust was a Humvee twice the size of Rhode Island.

23

Sure enough, when the dust settled some, I could see its occupant, Lady Bowfrey, who was only one and a half times the size of the Ocean State. Perhaps it was lingering dust, or perhaps it was her mood, but her eyes were mere slits, and her jowls appeared to shimmy with rage. One could easily imagine her head as a huge mound of flan, topped with a wig and a pair of chopsticks, set on a vibrating plate. Even the Thugs seemed suitably cowed.

"You little brats!" she roared. "How dare you infiltrate my private affairs!"

I nudged Mama. "Say something," I mumbled. "She's *your* friend."

Mama gulped, and then excused herself for such an unladylike action. "W-Why Lady Bowfrey. What a pleasant surprise to see you out here. Abby—that's my daughter, and she really does look younger most days—and I were searching for truffles. Would you care to join us?"

"Good one," I whispered. In the heat of the moment I actually thought it was.

"Truffles? You need pigs for that! Which one of you is the pig?"

Let's face it, it really was all my fault that Mama was in trouble. Just in case Lady Bowfrey decided to slip a harness on one of us and make the victim root around in the dirt, I needed to take the blame. My nostrils probably had a few more years left on them than Mama's did.

"I'm the pig," I said.

"Ha. Just so you know, Miss Timberlake, honesty won't get you anywhere with me. I despise you."

"*Excuse* me?"

"Oh, are you surprised that I recognize you? If I could, I'd squash you like an ant—"

"I bet you could," Mama said.

"Mama!"

"Oops, I forgot to say 'bless your heart.'"

Although Lady Bowfrey didn't budge from behind the steering wheel of her Humvee, nonetheless she was obviously enraged. She shook a fist at Mama, and her massive face progressed through several color changes—from strawberry red to whipped cream white.

"Perhaps you can amuse your daughter tonight with your jokes as you stumble about in the forest, getting more lost with each step."

I stepped in front of my minimadre, although I was even more mini than she. I also slipped into a dialect the Thugs would be able to understand.

"Just what *is* your beef with us, Lady Bovine—I

mean Lady Bowfrey? Yes, we were caught hitching a ride in the sleep compartment of yonder truck, but can you blame us? Just take a gander at them two studs you employ as drivers, and then compare them with our husbands. For starters, my husband is as ugly as a stump full of spiders, and if brains were dynamite, he wouldn't have enough to blow his nose."

Mama pushed me aside. "That's true," she said loyally. "And as for *my* husband, he was so ugly that when he was born, his mama had to borrow a baby to take to church."

Just like I thought, the Thugs thought that was hilarious. Unfortunately, their state of amusement made Lady Bowfrey even angrier.

"Get those ladies up closer," she said, and waved a delicate little hand that seemed oddly out of place, as if it had been grafted onto her following some freak accident. It was then I noticed for the first time that her hands didn't match in size; they didn't even come close.

"Sorry," one of the Thugs said, and although I was pushed, the treatment I received wasn't as rough as it might have been.

In the meantime Lady Bowfrey had managed to slip on a pair of sunglasses. It is amazing just how much a person can hide of herself just by donning shades. It's no wonder drug dealers and street toughs wear the darn things. It certainly doesn't make for a level playing field.

Not that we had had a level playing to begin with; that was pretty clear when I saw the gun finally make its appearance. "Well, Miss Smarty Pants, I was hoping it really wouldn't come to this, but you leave me no choice."

"We always have a choice," Mama said. "Weren't we just talking about that in Sunday school? In fact, wasn't it you who said that there was never a point at which we couldn't decide to face up to our mistakes, pay the consequences, and get on with our lives?"

Lady Bowfrey smiled, and it was a lovely one at that. It was evidence that she, for one, had listened to her mama's nagging and worn her retainer when she was growing up—unlike someone I know.

"You're quite right, Mrs. Wiggins. We can indeed face up to our mistakes and fix what needs to be changed. In this case I should have gotten rid of you the day you first came snooping around my house. 'That little twerp is harmless,' I said to myself. 'She can't even run a decent antiques store—' "

"I beg your pardon," Mama said, stamping her foot. "I'll have you know that my Abby owns the best antiques store south of the Mason-Dixon Line."

"Ha," Lady Bowfrey snorted, "as if that's saying much."

One or both of the Thugs grunted in apparent disapproval. They were, I knew, good ol' Southern boys, and she had just insulted their heritage. *This* was useful information. But since it didn't feel like the right time to use this information, it behooved me to quickly change the subject.

"In any case," I said, "I deserve to get thrown to the wolves—quite possibly even literally. Nearby Cape Romaine has a red wolf reintroduction breeding program, and although it is contained to Bulls Island, there have been escapees."

Those asinine, highly reflective sunglasses were pointed in my direction for an eternity before Miss High and Mighty deigned to speak again. "Shut up, Timberlake. You talk too much."

"Yes, ma'am, but I can't help it. I have infectious verbalitis. It's a horrible disease that I would wish on no one, not even you."

"I've never heard of it."

"She caught it at a Toastmasters International meeting last year," Mama said. "I can vouch for that."

"You would: you're her mother."

"Very well," I said, "I'll come close, so I can breathe on you. You won't like the initial symptoms. First you'll start to feel all warm inside. Then a strange compulsion to seek out other people . . ." As I spoke I advanced on the Humvee and the smug smuggler from across the pond.

"Back off and shut up."

"Yes, sir—I mean, ma'am. You don't have to get your panties in a bunch."

The Thugs shook with laughter, prompting the owner of the sunglasses to turn briefly to them. "And you too, you worthless twits."

Actually, Lady Bowfrey used language that was far coarser than that. Ever since arriving, she'd used words that Greg, even when he stubbed his toe, would probably not have used. I'd heard these words before—probably in college—but so infrequently that now they were a shock to my ears. As for Mama, bless her heart, the sewage that came from Lady Bowfrey's potty mouth appeared to sail right over her head.

There is nothing dishonorable about talking out of both sides of one's mouth, especially if it means not having to move one's lips. "Listen up, you twits," I hissed softly. "We're in a woods, for Pete's sake, and she's in that ridiculous gas guzzler. And we know she can't chase us on foot. So let's all make a run for it—on the count of three. We'll split up in four different directions, and we'll run through the most closely spaced trees we come across. She can't follow all of us. In fact, she won't be able to follow any of us for more than a hundred feet. How does that sound?"

"It ain't gonna work," Thug Number Two growled.

"Hey!" Lady Bowfrey bellowed. "What's going on down there? What are you dunderheads doing? You better not be planning a revolt."

"No ma'am, we ain't," Thug Number One said, and bowed in the most groveling way.

"Chickens," I clucked disapprovingly. "Mama," I whispered, "let's at least you and I make a run for it."

"I heard that!" Lady Bowfrey extended her reach as far as she could. It took a lot of effort, and the exertion showed on her face, but she managed to pick something up off the seat beside her.

I swallowed hard as my eyes adjusted to my fate. "It's Operation Shock and Awe," I moaned. "She has an Uzi."

"I love ouzo," Mama said. "A nice helping of moussaka, a dolmades or two. I have such fond memories of your daddy and me in Greece. Oh dear, just think, what if your daddy had passed on while we were on our tour, I'd have to dress like a Greek widder woman for the rest of my life: all in black. While it is a slimming color, it's just too hot for the South. Of course it's hot in Greece too, so it must be our humidity that makes the difference."

The dust stirred up by the Humvee must have gotten on Mama's glasses, because clearly she wasn't seeing straight. "An Uzi is a gun, Mama, not an anise-flavored drink. We make one false step and she mows us down with a squeeze of the trigger."

"Why you wicked, wicked woman," Mama said as she waggled a finger at Lady Bowfrey. "You, of all people, should know that 'Thou shalt not murder' is one of the Big Ten. In our 'Issues with

Tissues' class we specifically covered that one, seeing as how Taiga Fünstergarten—that's with an umlaut—killed her own parents, and then threw herself on the mercy of the court because she was an orphan."

I gasped. "You know Taiga Fünstergarten?"

"With the umlaut?"

"Yah, yah! Do you?"

"Of course, dear; she's in our Sunday school class as well."

"Oy vey, I need to start attending. If she killed her parents, then why is she not in jail?"

"Well, the court didn't take mercy on her because she was an orphan, but they did look the other way because she has more money than Oprah Winfrey. Money will get you anything you want in America. That's what makes this country of ours so great, Abby. Leave your first wife when she's been maimed and marry a rich one. Isn't that what it's all about?"

"Taiga was married to a woman?"

A blast from the Humvee's horn made me jump into Mama's arms—well, not quite. But it certainly scared me. I observed that Thug Number One and Thug Number Two got a lot closer to each other than they might have consciously intended.

"Knock off the jabbering down there," Lady Bowfrey bellowed. "Boys, you have your orders; now get to them. Or do you want *mommy* to do your job for you?"

"She's not really our mama," Thug Number One muttered.

Apparently Mama wasn't quite through waggling her finger at the behemoth behind the wheel. Pulling herself up to her full five feet, she fluffed up her crinolines before advancing on the vehicle, one hand on her hips, the other practically a blur as the index finger got a power workout.

"For shame, Lady Bowfrey," she said, sounding a wee bit like a high-pitched Gomer Pyle. "For shame, for shame, for shame. You're from some British colony, aren't you? Didn't your mama teach you any manners over there? Assuming she didn't, here's a crash course. For starters, I am older than you. That means that you should come down here when you threaten me.

"And for another thing, I haven't heard a single 'ma'am' out of you. In Sunday school class you said you loved living in the Charleston area and didn't want to be one of those immigrants who stick out like a sore thumb because they are incapable of assimilating into the local culture. So don't be like one of them: mind your manners as you prepare to send us off into the arms of Jesus. After all, you don't want us to give a bad report to Him, do you? Somehow I think not. Therefore from now on address me as 'ma'am.'"

"Mrs. Wiggins—ma'am! I've had enough of your shenanigans!" With great effort Lady Bowfrey turned, and whilst ignoring even more of

Mama's lecture, managed to extract a pair of shovels from behind her seat and pitched them out the open window.

One of the shovels barely missed Mama's hoary head. "And another thing," Mama said. "A lady doesn't throw things; a lady *hands* things."

"Make them dig their own graves," Lady Bowfrey barked, and off she roared in a second cloud of dust.

24

W hy don't that beat all," Mama said, in a temporary lapse of grammar. She did, I believe, have a valid excuse.

"I'm certainly not going to dig my own grave," I said.

"You is," Thug Number Two said. Frankly, he was even more unlikable than his companion.

"And where were *you* raised?" Mama said. "A Southern woman is supposed to sweat in only two venues: a garden and her marital bed."

"In fact we don't even sweat," I said, "we merely 'dew.'"

"Do what?" Thug Number Two said.

"Wear gloves," Mama said. "You can't ask any old lady like me to dig a hole without wearing gloves. I'll blister."

Thug Number One saw where Mama was headed and stepped in. "That ain't his problem, ma'am."

Mama turned to him. "Thomas, would you want your grandma to develop blisters on those spotted wrinkled old hands that rocked you as a baby?"

The thug squirmed. "My name ain't Thomas, ma'am—it's Delbert. And my grandma ain't that old. I reckon she's only 'bout as old as that one." He'd picked up a shovel and was now pointing it at me.

"I'm ninety-eight," I croaked.

"Bet me," said Thug Number Two. He turned on his companion. "What for did you have to tell 'em your name?"

"It's already on that paper we gave the younger one, you idiot."

"Hey, dirtbag, don't you be calling me no names."

"I'll call you what I want to call you, scumbucket."

At that, Dirtbag took a swing at Scumbucket and missed, which sent him sprawling virtually at my feet. Needless to say, Scumbucket was not amused. The next time he went airborne, it was to tackle Dirtbag, which he managed to do. Like angry fifth-grade boys on a school playground, the two grown men all but disappeared in a blur of arms and legs as each attempted to pummel some frontier justice into the other man's hard head.

Mama and I couldn't help but watch, spellbound, for a few precious seconds. Then I grabbed her by the arm and pulled her into the woods. I'd like to say that we slipped away as quietly as two city women could, but because the woods was second growth, it contained a lot of underbrush. For Mama, making progress in her full skirt with its myriad petticoats was like trying to drag a parachute upriver with your teeth while doing the breaststroke.

"Mama," I whispered after we'd barely gone ten feet into the bushes, "you need to strip."

"I most certainly will not!"

"We can't continue this way. They'll catch up to us in two seconds the moment they quit fighting. Besides, you're leaving scraps of cloth behind like bread crumbs."

"What do you propose that I do? Run through the woods in only my brassiere and panties? What if they catch us? I'd die of embarrassment."

"If you don't, they'll catch us for sure, and then they'll have all the time in the world to see you in your bra and panties."

"Abby, where did you learn to be so crude?"

"The morning newspaper. The eleven o'clock news. Take your pick. These things happen, and these are the guys who do it."

"Okay, I'll take off my crinoline," she said, fighting back the tears. "But that's it."

I kissed her hurriedly on the cheek. "Way to go, Mama."

"Abby?"

"Yes, Mama," I said. I'd grabbed her hand and was already pulling her deeper into the forest.

"Do you think we should go back and give them the Lizzie Borden treatment?"

"You mean pick up the shovels and give them forty whacks each?"

"Well, they aren't paying attention."

I had to stifle my laugh.

My first inclination was to circle around so we would be near the dirt logging road, just not so close that our clothing would give us away. Then keeping the road to our left, we would follow it back to Highway 17, or to a human habitation, whichever came first.

I'm not a brainiac, like my friend Magdalena, but I did graduate from college in the top half of my class, and I have seen enough movies and nature shows to know that it is easy to get disoriented in the woods. Sometimes ridiculously easy. I admit to watching these programs with incredulity, not comprehending how someone can be practically within spitting distance of their starting point and still be "lost."

Take us, for instance. No—take just me: Mama is not to blame. If she'd had her way, we'd have been back in the clearing digging the graves for Dirtbag and Scumbucket, or at least tying them up with her panty hose (after giving them the requisite forty whacks). But me! What a failure as a Girl Scout I was.

I'd spotted a pine tree that had somehow missed harvesting and towered over its neighbors. Since it was opposite the sun, it had to be in an easterly direction, which meant that beyond it was Route 17 and the Atlantic Ocean. Why then should we even bother risk being seen by following the logging road out of Francis Marion National Forest? Why not just make a beeline straight for our goal? Isn't that what they taught us in geometry class? The shortest distance between two points is a straight line. As long as I kept that pine tree in my line of sight, we were on track.

Nature, however, abhors a vacuum, including the one in my head. Not content to leave the space between my ears empty, nature filled it with fuzzy thinking. As a result I soon learned that an untended forest grows willy-nilly, and that a tree that is visible from a clearing at a great distance might actually disappear when a vantage point for viewing is no longer available. Unfortunately, Mama and I also learned that wild forests are rife with vines and prickles of all nature, and sharp sticks half buried in the dirt, and mysterious some-things that get startled by one's approach and go crashing off into the undergrowth emitting horrible Dantesque sounds.

After about an hour of trying to slip quietly into the gorse, we were merely thrashing about like a pair of great fish caught in a net. At that point all I wanted to do was find a clearing large enough so I could scrape aside the damp leaves and lie down. Thank God it was too early in the year for "no-see-ums" and mosquitoes.

"And most kinds of snakes too," Mama said.

I practically jumped out of my skin. "What do you mean by 'most' kinds of snakes?"

"Never say never," Mama said. "Even up in York County, if the weather's warm enough, some varieties will come out and sun themselves. Why once—"

"Mama, *please.* I'm a nervous wreck as it is." I still didn't have the heart to tell her that I hadn't the foggiest notion where we were.

"I suppose then you really don't want to hear about the Small Hairy Ones."

"Our cousins in Wilmington? No thanks, Mama. And I thought there wasn't anything scarier than snakes."

"Not our family, silly; South Carolina's answer to Big Foot. The local tribe used to call them the 'Srotideypoc,' which literally translates as a small hairy person. According to the story—this was told to my great-great-granddaddy when he first started coming down to the beach after the War of Northern Aggression—there were many Srotideypoc living in this forest at that time. You see, it was all virgin timber then. Anyway, the Indians described them as being about four feet tall, bipedal, and covered with reddish brown hair. It was said that their eyes displayed human intelligence. They apparently lived in small family groups and subsisted on raw deer meat and berries. The Native Americans mostly left them alone, except when the Small Hairy Ones caught one of their maidens and made off with her."

At that point my hair felt like it was standing on end and I was scanning the underbrush for reddish brown hair and bright eyes. "What did they do with the maidens, Mama? Did they eat them?"

"When times got tough, I suppose so. But mostly they wanted them as mates. Over the millennia the Small Hairy Ones became less hirsute and taller, and so it was easier for them to pass as humans, but they continued to live in isolation in this forest. There was a terrible forest fire here in the 1930s and they say that during the worst of it a band of about twenty or so short, dark, naked people staggered out of the forest, about half of them holding babies or small children. The forest rangers rushed over to give them first aid, but these people— everyone agrees they were Srotideypoc—were terrified by the rangers and rushed back into the forest and disappeared."

When we'd begun our foray into the woods, the sunlight streaming down between the second growth trees had created a dappled effect. Now the undergrowth was merging into one great shadow. It was also noticeably cooler.

"Mama, who told you this wild tale?"

"It's not a wild tale, dear. Your Grandpa Paw-Paw told me the story when I was knee high to a grasshopper. He said that his best friend Roy was one of the forest rangers who saw the Small Hairy

Ones that day. Besides, there have been reports since then. Why, just a couple of years ago some tourists saw one run across the road carrying a baby. That was just over in Berkeley County."

"No offense, Mama. But wasn't Grandpa Paw-Paw the one who got fired from his job at the newspaper on account of he made up half his stories?"

"That was only when he was drinking, dear, and the figure was more like a third."

"Mama! You've got me all worked up over nothing!"

"Aha, admit it, Abby. My story scared you, didn't it? Well, at least it got your mind off that horrible woman."

At that very moment the universe decided that Mama's not-so-funny joke could use a little embellishment. From somewhere to our left came a bloodcurdling scream. It was like nothing I'd ever heard before in real life. I'd heard peacocks, panthers, and jackasses all give forth on the big screen, and this was a bit like those three animals rolled into one and then amplified.

"Oh shoot," said Mama, but not in a ladylike way. "What in tarnation was that?"

"You tell me; you seem to be the expert on these woods."

The universe did not approve of the way I'd just spoken to Mama. From the other, opposite direction came the unmistakable cry of a human baby.

This was a loud caterwauling baby, one who refuses to be appeased by a bottle, by rocking, even by a citywide car ride. I'll swear the child— for that's exactly what it sounded like—cried for two solid minutes, then stopped abruptly. The second it did, the screeching to the northeast of us resumed.

"I'm getting out of here," Mama said.

"I'm with you there!"

But it was suddenly as dark as a well digger's buttocks, and unless we managed to dig our own well all the way to China, we weren't about to go anywhere. "Abby, will you hold me?" Mama said.

"Only if you hold me," I said.

"Deal."

So there we stood, two grown women, with our arms wrapped around each other, our hearts pounding against each other's chests. At some point we agreed to sit, but that made us feel vulnerable, so we stood again. After many hours the moon rose and remained unobstructed long enough for us to spot a hardwood tree that had fallen in some past storm. It appeared to have been stopped partway into its projected path by a dense grove of pines.

We clawed our way through the brambles and then, risking injury—should the hardwood complete its journey—scampered up its trunk like a pair of young coons fleeing a pack of bloodhounds. The moon's appearance was brief, and our climb was hazardous because huge patches of bark sloughed off everytime we shifted weight, but making it even just as high as a dozen feet above the forest floor was psychologically comforting. We assured each other that the screeching, crying beast—or was it really the Small Hairy Ones— couldn't climb trees. And of course it couldn't jump.

As we clung to each other in the dead branches of a felled tree, I decided to let it all hang out— metaphorically speaking, in a sixties sort of way. "Mama, I love you."

"I love you too, dear."

"More than anyone in the world?"

"At least as much."

"Who do you love as much?"

"I think that should be 'whom,' dear. The grammar police will get you."

"I'm serious, Mama. Is it Toy?"

"He's my son, Abby. I'm supposed to love him as much."

"But he's a ne'er-do-well—even if he is studying for the Episcopal priesthood. Besides, he never remembers your birthday, or Mother's Day. What did he get you for Christmas last year?"

"It's the thought that counts."

"Oh, poor Mama, I *knew* you were going to say that. Toy didn't get you anything. Not even a Christmas card. Did he even call?"

"Well, when I called him the next day, he said

that he was all set to call me, but he was playing this video game where you have to get to a certain level before you can stop, or you lose all your points—"

"In other words, his video game was more important than the woman who spent thirty-six excruciating hours in labor with him."

"Oh no, dear, that's what I spent with you; Toy just popped out like toothpaste when you squeeze the middle of the tube."

I was silent for a moment. Okay, if that's the way you want to play it, old woman, I thought; two can play this game.

"Mama, I'm kind of glad you're sticking to principle this time, because it makes it easier for me then." I waited for her inevitable question.

"What does that mean, dear?"

"First you have to understand that it's the Bible speaking, not me. It says that a man should leave his mother and cleave unto his wife and two should become one. That implies that the marital unit takes precedent over the bond between parents and their adult children."

It was Mama's turn to do silent strategizing. "Aha," she finally said, "it's the son who leaves his mother, not the daughter. So you still have to love me more than you love Greg, because I'm one of the Ten Commandments, and he's not."

"Yes," I said gently, "which means Toy left you, to cleave to C.J."

Mama pulled away from me, which was the opposite of what I'd intended. "How can you be so cruel, Abby?"

"*Me?* You're dating my ex-husband, Mama, the man who took everything from me, including my children! Yet, I continue to let you live in my house, and I've said nothing to the kids about the sordid, not to mention, icky conclusions one might draw from the hours you two keep."

Mama gasped indignantly. Had it not been so dark, I think she would have moved to another tree altogether.

"Why Abigail Louise Thunderbake! Somebody should wash your mouth out with soap. Buford and I have done nothing of the kind. I would never dishonor your father's memory. How dare you suggest that I would, and then set yourself up as a long-suffering saint who is able to move past such a horrible offense for the sake of your children?"

"Well, if you two weren't 'getting it on,' so to speak, what were you doing going out all the time, and even spending the entire night together?"

In the distance something howled. It was probably a coyote—they'd been moving into the area in greater numbers over the last decade—but if so, there was definitely something wrong with it. The mournful sound began on a canine register, then soared so high that birds roosting in neighboring trees began to twitter. I can't imagine that a banshee, should such a creature exist, could sound any more eerie.

Mama grabbed my arm. "What *is* that?"

"I'm not sure. Mama, I'm sorry I hurt you. I was just basing my conclusion on what I could observe."

"But you didn't see me in bed with that awful man, did you?"

"No, but you flirted with him, like he was Rhett Butler and you were Scarlett O'Hara."

"Exactly. But didn't Scarlett manipulate Rhett into giving her what she wanted?"

"Sort of; he walked away at the end."

"Which is what Buford did with me, and that's exactly what I wanted."

"So what did you manipulate him into doing?"

"Oh Abby, I can't tell you; it's a birthday surprise. Darn it all, see what you made me do." Mama burst into tears, something I've never known her to do since the day Daddy died. Even at his funeral she remained dry-eyed for the sake of the little ones.

I felt so awful upon hearing my mother cry aloud that I would have gladly jumped from the tree and into the mouth of a howling banshee. Not having one immediately available, I too burst into tears. Thereupon hearing me blubber, Mama returned to my arms, whereupon the two of us sobbed until we could no longer breathe and had to blow our noses on our sleeves like elementary school boys.

• • •

Of course sleep was out of the question. Several hours further into our ordeal we heard something stamping in the bushes directly beneath us.

"Wild boar," I whispered to Mama.

She squeezed my hand and nodded.

Then the stamping creature emitted a very humanlike moan. It's quite possible that my ears were playing tricks on me, so I wouldn't stake my life on what I heard next—or, come to think of it, *anything* that I heard that evening. At any rate, I'm ninety-nine point nine percent sure that I heard the creature below say, "Help us, please. We're the last of the Srotideypoc."

I sat, frozen with fear, unable to think or react for a long, valuable stretch of time. The stamping resumed, then I heard it move away from the tree, and then farther away until I could hear it no more. Later on, once just before dawn, I heard the devilish screams of the creature to the left again.

It was the sound of that creature that woke me with a start. Slumped against me, cradled in my arms, was my lightly snoring minimadre.

"Mama, did you hear that?"

"Huh? You mean that crow?"

"That wasn't a crow, Mama. That was the thing we heard last night."

Mama gestured skyward with her chin. She was a bit on the grumpy side. In all fairness, she is *not* a morning person, never has been. Plus, if she was anything like me, she had to pee like nobody's business.

"There's a crow right up there in that tree, Abby, just looking at us. Probably wondering which one of us he wants for breakfast."

"Okay, so maybe it was a crow that I just heard, but what about last night? Golly, I've never been so ding dang scared in my life. Have you ever heard such an unearthly sound?"

"As a barred owl?"

"That wasn't any kind of bird, Mama. I'd be willing to bet my business on that."

"Oh darling, you don't remember Paw-Paw's peacocks, do you? Those things could shriek like banshees."

"Shhh, Mama! Something's coming now."

25

Mama listened obligingly for a second, then glommed onto me like germs on a day-care doorknob. In keeping with the bird theme, now that the sun had risen we were sitting ducks up there on the fallen tree trunk. There really wasn't much higher for us to climb without getting snarled in the branches, and since we couldn't even tell which direction the new sound was coming from, jumping off the trunk could well be the wrong move. Instead, like the pitiful cowards that we ultimately were, we hunkered down together, our arms tightly around each other, our eyes tightly closed.

While the latter sounds like a childish response to danger, there may well be an evolutionary basis for it (I read somewhere that some animals also close their eyes when danger is unavoidable). After all, it certainly removes that "someone is watching me" factor from the predator's mind. On the other hand, I can certainly understand why someone might prefer to see a Srotideypoc before feeling its hairy hands as it grabs you for its much sought-after mate.

"Oh, Mrs. Washburn," this Small Hairy One called. "Is that really you up there?"

I opened one eye. I shut it, said the quick prayer of a lapsed Episcopalian, and then opened both eyes.

"Mr. Curly!" I shrieked.

"Lord have mercy!" Mama screamed. "Holy crap," she screamed again, as she slipped from my arms and subsequently from her perch.

Thank heavens it was indeed Mr. Curly beneath us, and not some diminutive prehistoric remnant with overactive follicles. I'd never paid a lick of attention to Mr. Curly's biceps, but Mama said he caught her as easily as if she was a feather pillow, and then set her down on the forest floor as gently as if she was a crystal chandelier.

"He smells like Chrome," she whispered after I'd been hoisted to the ground. "Isn't it wonderful?"

"I beg your pardon?"

"It's a men's cologne. By Azzaro. Honestly, Abby, sometimes it's *you* who's way behind the times. But anyway, isn't he just to die for? That is what you young folks still say, isn't it?"

"Ladies," Mr. Curly said, "is something wrong? Besides the obvious, I mean?" He not only sounded chipper, but looked fairly dapper, all decked out, as he was, in khakis and a matching safari vest.

"My mama thinks you smell nice," I said.

"Abby!"

"Well, it's true. And as neither of you are married, and since he just rescued you—well, I think we could dispense with a courtship altogether."

I said it with a smile in my voice. It was meant in a lighthearted way. Believe me, I would rather eat a bowl of cream of maggot soup on a TV reality show than have my mother marry a man who'd been responsible for me going to jail, even for just a few hours.

"Mrs. Washburn," Mr. Curly said, sounding not one bit amused, "I am already married, thank you very much. And as it happens, the woman I am married to is the light of my life."

"Oh darn," Mama whispered.

If the man heard my randy mama's comment, he didn't let on. "What in the name of all that's good are you two doing out here in the middle of the wilderness? Is this some kind of game I've wandered into?"

"Game?"

"One of those reality TV shows. Like the *Amazing Race*—now that's a TV show worth watching."

"Unless you've missed an episode of *All My Children*," Mama said, "and we need to catch up on Soapnet."

"That's why God invented TiVo," I said.

"No you don't," Mr. Curly said sternly. "I'll have no taking of the Lord's name in vain in my presence."

"It was only a harmless joke," I said.

"He's right," Mama said. "You are sacrilegious far too much, Abby. Sometimes I fear for your life."

"What?"

"If the far right gets into power," Mama said, "they'll round up infidels like you and burn them at the stake—or something like that. I saw them discussing that on the Triple Six Club."

"Mama has an active imagination," I said. "And just so you know, her delusions are nonpartisan: she's an equal opportunity offender."

"Are you going to answer my question, Mrs. Washburn? What are you doing out here?"

"To make a very long story short, Mr. Curly," I said, "I know who has been smuggling ivory into Charleston for the last five years. We were inadvertent stowaways on one of her trucks—don't ask—and her goons were given orders to kill us.

They, however, got distracted by fisticuffs, so we fled into the forest and spent the night being courted by the Small Hairy Ones—again don't ask."

"Why that's fabulous news!"

"It is?" I said.

"I mean that you've been able to determine the identify of the chief smuggler. Who is she?"

"Lady Bowfrey," I said. "She lives in Mount Pleasant."

"Ah, the breakfast lady! I should have known." He hit his forehead with the palm of his hand. "Every week those trucks are at the docks serving up complimentary breakfasts to the stevedores."

"On Tuesdays?" I said.

"How did you know?" he said.

"Because every Tuesday night they park in front of her house and carry boxes in and out, and then on Wednesday mornings they serve a huge breakfast to a grateful community. Keep the people happily fed, seems to be her motto, and folks won't care which ordinances you break."

Mr. Curly beamed with pleasure at the revelation. "Excellent work, Mrs. Washburn. Excellent. I will personally see to it that the Department of the Prevention of Illegal Imports awards you with a Medal of Good Conduct."

"Thank you, sir."

Mama raised her hand. "Excuse me, Mr. Curly, but—"

"Mr. Curly's a busy man, Mama."

"Yes, but—"

"Not now, Mama," I said.

Mr. Curly was still beaming and shaking his head in amazement. "Do you mean to say that you ladies spent the night on this log?"

"Indeed we did."

"No, we spent it at the Small Hairy Ones' Hilton," Mama said, sounding even more peeved than usual. "Now we're out on our morning constitutional."

"Never mind her," I said. "Her first morning on earth happened to her when she was very young, and she's never liked mornings since."

Mr. Curly stopped beaming. "Say, it really isn't that far to where I'm parked on a logging road. Would you ladies like me to show you the way?"

"Do most congressmen enjoy getting perks from lobbyists?" I said.

"Well, I wouldn't know about that."

"I think it's a safe bet," I said."

"Abby's always been my cynical one," Mama said. "If the sky really was falling, she'd probably say something negative about that too."

"Form a line behind me," Mr. Curly said, and gallantly led the way through the bracken and gorse.

Okay, so there really wasn't bracken and gorse to be found in the Francis Marion National Forest. The local shrubs and weeds undoubtedly possessed far less poetic names, but they were tough and scratchy things and that made progress very slow. I marveled at how far we had managed to come the night before—thanks to adrenaline. It was no wonder we were covered with welts.

For a while it looked as if Mr. Curly was lost as well. "Don't worry, ladies, I have a GPS—uh, well, I do own one. I *thought* I had it with me in my pack."

"We're going to die out here," Mama wailed.

I battled some bracken to be at her side and put my arm around her. "No, we're not."

"That's right, Abby, only *I* will die; your fate will be a life sentence at the side of a Small Hairy One."

"Mrs. Wiggins," Mr. Curly said sharply, "I resent that remark. I have successfully completed therapy and no longer expose myself."

"She's referring to South Carolina's answer to Bigfoot," I said. "Only they don't have big feet, because they're very small creatures. Apparently they live out here. When they can't catch deer, they dine on human flesh—if given the chance. We're a walking smorgasbord."

"And all because of that horrid Lady Bowfrey," Mama said. "Can we watch you arrest her?"

"No," Mr. Curly said curtly. "It's against regulations."

"But Abby was there when you arrested Abby. I don't even believe in the death penalty, Mr. Curly, but when I think about all those elephants—those magnificent intelligent creatures—being slaughtered so that greedy women like Lady Bowfrey can become even richer, why I'd be tempted to see her put up before a firing squad. Of course they'd only shoot rubber bullets, but I'd really like to see her sweat. Especially after what she's done to us! Do you know that she really wanted to kill us? No, I take that back—I think one of those bullets should be real."

"Mama," I said through gritted teeth. I also tried to make eye contact with her, but to no avail.

"Then again, maybe a firing squad is too good for her. I'm coming up on my sixtieth birthday—bless my heart—but my poor Abby here has barely had a chance to live. That hideous, self-centered woman with the chopsticks in her hair was going to murder my precious baby right here before her mama's eyes. I'm telling you, no punishment is too bad for her. Where is Dick Cheney when you need him now? Whatever happened to Donald Rumsfeld? I say get those men out of retirement and set up a new interrogation center. Lady Bowfrey can be the guinea pig upon which the new agents practice their interrogation skills."

My heart was in my throat. "You have to forgive her, Mr. Curly, because my mama suffers from a rare brain disorder brought about from inhaling too much dust mite feces. In layman's terms she's a nincompoop."

"Abby! You see, Mr. Curly, how she talks about her mama?"

"Yes, and I don't like it. And I don't like the way you refer to my wife."

"Your *wife?*" Mama said. "Donald Rumsfeld didn't turn into one of those intransigents, did he? You know, with the full sex change and everything?"

"Please forgive her, Mr. Curly. She's got a big heart, but she gets a little addled when she's stressed."

"I'm not addled, Abby; I'm merely confused."

"My wife is Lady Bowfrey," Mr. Curly said. He reached into his safari vest and withdrew a snubnosed .38 revolver.

There was no drum roll from me. The Department of the Prevention of Illegal Imports, my fanny. Mr. Curly had come to finish off a job that Thugs Numbers One and Two had botched. Just how he'd managed to arrest me at the dock was a story that could wait until Mama was safe. At the moment nothing else mattered.

"Miss Timberlake," he said, sounding disappointed, "you don't look surprised."

I sighed. "Don't you have a conscience, sir?"

He laughed. "Sir! I love it how you Southerners are always so polite! The proper form of address in my case, however, is Your Lordship—or Lord Bowfrey—take your pick. But the answer to your question is, 'No, I don't have a conscience.' And

I'll tell you something, Miss Timberlake, that's something I thank my creator for every week when I go to church."

Mama's eyes blazed. "That's a sacrilege!"

"Oh, don't be so self-righteous, you old bat. It's because of judgmental environmentalists like you that my wife and I have to attend separate churches in order to keep our connection secret. Not to mention the fact that I have temporarily suspended using my title, and that alone is causing me severe emotional distress."

Mama blinked. "A *bat?* Abby, he called me a bat; do something!"

"You just mentioned what you weren't going to mention," I said to Mr. Curly. "As for your title, we don't recognize titles in America."

"Sure you do. When Queen Elizabeth II comes over to visit, she's not addressed as Mrs. Mountbatten, is she?"

"Yes, but you had to give up your title when you became an American citizen."

"Ah, but I never became one," he said, and in the space of just that one sentence switched from a California accent to the one I've heard used by native English speakers from South Africa.

"Even better, Mr. Curly," I said, "it should be easier to deport you."

"Miss Timberlake, you might think differently about me if you had a chance to hear a bit about my background."

"I beg your pardon?"

"It will undoubtedly come as a surprise to you; I was born and raised in Africa. Although my father was the eldest son of an earl, he left all that behind to become a game warden in a small country that you've probably never even heard of. When I wasn't away at boarding school, I used to ride with my father on his rounds of the reserve."

"I'm sure you have a fascinating backstory, but you'll have plenty of time in Hell to tell it, so please save it for there."

"Good one, Abby," Mama said.

"Shut the hell up," Mr. Curly said.

"I won't have you swearing in my presence!" Mama snapped.

Mr. Curly brought the gun up level with Mama's head.

"Then again," Mama said, "a word is just sound, and since Abby just used it in a nonswearing context, who am I to judge?"

"As I was *saying*," Mr. Curly growled, "I got to know the animals on our reserve very well. My father had a first-rate team of black Africans working for him—sharpshooters all—and since Dad was committed to wipe out poaching, by golly, they were able to do it. But there were consequences."

"I need to sit down," Mama whined. "I'm getting a blister on my heel."

"There's a log up ahead," I interceded. "If you're

going to kill her anyway, can you at least let her get comfortable for a minute?"

"Okay," he said, "but only until I'm done with my story."

But poor Mama was suddenly limping so bad that I asked for, and obtained, permission to step out of line a few yards and fetch a walking stick for her. It was more of a walking club actually: a sun-bleached segment of a broken limb, one no doubt fashioned by Hurricane Hugo some twenty years ago. Much to my relief, Mama quit complaining and gamely struggled along until she got to the log. Now there, I thought, was the prime example of a true Southern lady.

Meanwhile, of course, our raconteur had resumed his spellbinding narrative. "The elephant population exploded," he said. "They can eat as much as two hundred pounds of grass and foliage a day and drink ten gallons of water. We had only one spring-fed watering hole on the entire reserve, and one year, during a particularly severe drought, it couldn't replenish itself fast enough."

"Oh my," Mama said, a look of genuine concern on her face.

"The elephants were hungry and thirsty, and despite my father's best efforts, they began to wander off the reserve into neighboring farms. One farm was particularly attractive, because it had lush banana groves. Banana plants, as you know, are about ninety percent water."

"I did not know that," Mama said.

"One night the elephants got into the banana grove and totally destroyed it—I mean nothing was left. Dad was aware it had happened; he and his men had tried to head them off, but were afraid of starting a stampede through a nearby village. The kicker is that the owner of the banana farm didn't complain; even though he was wiped out, he didn't say one word."

"Maybe he loved elephants and felt sorry for them."

"Hardly," Mr. Curly snarled. "He was a white man, fairly well off, with a swimming pool. *It* was something the elephants had overlooked on their first foray onto the farm. On their second visit to the farm, now that the banana plants were gone, the pool became their destination. Unfortunately the owner was ready and waiting: the water was laced with strychnine."

"How awful!" Mama cried.

"Indeed. The herd was decimated. Many of them died agonizing deaths right there on the farm. Legally, by the laws of the country, the banana farmer was able to claim the ivory of any elephant that died on his land."

"But he murdered them!"

"Yes, but we were never able to prove it. We did autopsies on the few that were able to make it back onto the reserve before collapsing, but by then the pool had been drained and cleaned. Besides—and more important—this fellow had friends in high places. Of course he had a problem disposing of the corpses, but the ivory more than made up for his banana crop. He even bragged about it in a letter to the editor of *Our African Republic*. His 'poison ivory,' he called it. Get it?"

"I'd like to 'get' him," Mama said. "With my cudgel."

"On second thought, you're quite a woman, Mrs. Wiggins. It's too bad I have to 'off' you."

"*Must* you?" said Mama. She removed her grimy spectacles and batted her unadorned eyelashes at her soon-to-be executioner.

"Yes, and I abhor whiners. Now, where was I? Oh yes, the banana farmer who made all the money on the poison ivory was to become my father-in-law. He became my idol, you know. Just look at how much smarter than my father he was."

"Since you're dumber than a post, bless your heart," Mama said, "we can hardly take your word for it."

26

Ha! Such moxie! If you were about fifty years younger, then perhaps *you* could be my Lady Bowfrey. After all, you do seem to possess a fine pair of breeding hips."

Mama spat on the leaves at her feet. "I'd rather be a serving wench," she said.

"A literal spitfire," Mr. Curly said.

"What happened to your poor father?" I said.

"He got fired from his post, of course. Took up a series of low-paying clerical jobs—of the kind suitable for a white man—but totally unsuitable for a man of his rank. He died ten years ago, a broken man. But the point I'm trying to make is that there is no future for elephants in the wild. In one hundred years mankind will marvel that their great-grandparents were able to see them roaming wild in the bush. No, make that fifty years."

"Because people like you kill them," Mama said. "If I had a hairbrush and was fifty years younger, you wouldn't be able to sit down for a week, young man."

"You're going too far, old woman. And it has nothing to do with greed; despite AIDS, famine, and constant turmoil over much of the area, the population of Africa keeps exploding. There simply isn't enough room for large animals like elephants and people both to exist. The same thing goes for Asia. The kind thing, the decent thing, is to euthanize the elephants now, rather than let them starve, or terrorize some native village.

"Back then—when I was a lad—it was an Englishman's banana plantation that was destroyed, and three hundred workers temporarily lost their jobs. But human lives could have been lost. Is that what you prefer to see happen?"

"Harrumph," Mama said. "Evil men can always

justify their ways. It's not like you care; you already said that you don't have a conscience."

"Get up, you old crone! You've had your five minutes of rest. I've got two properly dug graves waiting for the pair of you. I had to use a backhoe, since I couldn't count on you ladies to do the job. By the way, I hope you're not averse to sharing. Remember the fellows you met yesterday? You'll each get one in your grave—I hope you're not particular about who gets whom."

Mama stood slowly with the aid of her stick. She was trying to communicate something to me with her eyes, but unfortunately I didn't understand.

"I want the one in the plaid shirt," she said.

What an odd thing for her to say. Clearly she wanted me to respond, but how? Wasn't there some famous saw about not trying to overthink a problem? Perhaps I should begin by supplying her with the obvious solution, I thought, which was simply by being contrary.

"You can't have him," I said. "He's mine."

"No, mine."

"Over my dead body."

"Did you hear that, Mr. Curly?" Mama demanded. "Abby wants my dead body over hers."

"Ladies! You two are incorrigible. I don't usually enjoy offing women—call me sexist, if you like—but this is one occasion where I'll make an exception."

"Mr. Curly," I said, "I'll make you a deal. I'll go

278

along with whatever you want, easy breezy, if you let this old senile woman go. As a matter of fact, let's just leave the old bat right here in the woods— that should give the coyotes something to chew on for a day or two—and then you can do whatever you want with me. Turn me into shark chum if you like. I've been told that I'm very chummy."

"So that's what you really think of me, is it?" Mama abruptly stopped marching and stomped a pump into the leaf-strewn forest floor. The heel stuck into the accumulated detritus, and she came up shoe-free and even angrier than before. "Just an old bat, like he said, huh? Abigail Louise Wiggins Timberlake, shame on you!"

"Stop!" Mr. Curly barked. "I've heard enough of you two bickering. I'll shoot you right here, if I have to."

We stumbled after him in silence for a few minutes. Then, sure enough, it was Mama who braved his wrath again.

"Abby, do you remember those old Borden's milk commercials with Lizzie the talking cow?"

I sighed heavily. We were on a death march, and Mama wanted me to waltz down television memory lane with her. What was next? Liberace's candelabra?

"It was Elsie," I said irritably.

"No, it was Lizzie, dear. Lizzie Borden. Remember? Like before?"

"Before?" Before what? *Oh!* I got the picture.

"Mr. Curly," I said as I stepped away from him and to the right. "Is that a blimp above that tree?"

He put his free hand up to shield his eyes from the rising morning sun that sliced through the widely spaced second growth trees. His other hand still held the gun, but my imaginary aircraft held one hundred percent of his attention.

It took only three seconds for Mama to raise her trusty cudgel and give Mr. Curly a whack across the small of his back. It was enough to send him pitching forward onto the forest floor. Like two hungry Small Hairy Ones, my minimadre and I fell upon him and subdued him—well, with the aid of the snub-nosed .38, which had practically landed at my feet.

"It was just *horrible,*" Mama said. She shuddered dramatically, took a long swig of her Bloody Mary, before launching back into her skillfully embellished saga. She'd already been on *Good Morning America, The Tonight Show*, *Entertainment Tonight*, and a host of lesser shows. And although my name had only passed her lips once in all the various versions of the tale, that was truly fine with me. A gal deserves a little something extra when she turns seventy-five. Besides, I'd just as soon not have the real customs office breathing down my neck.

Since I'd not only heard all million-gazillion versions of her story, but lived it, I wandered into the

Rob-Bobs' spacious kitchen to see how her birthday dinner was progressing. Although Bob had issued instructions that no one (including the Messiah and the Buddha) should enter his kitchen while his masterpiece dinner was still being prepared, I didn't think the rules applied to me. After all, I was footing the bill, and I wasn't one of the thirty-six guests. I was the Guest of Honor's *issue:* I was her flesh and blood. Besides, I was Bob's best friend—after Rob, of course.

At my expense Bob had hired a team of chefs to serve under him for the evening, whereas he should have hired merely experienced cooks. The chefs were not responding well to Bob's somewhat dictatorial style of direction, which made him all the more stressed, and therefore all the more likely to bark out orders. Clearly, Rob's calming presence was needed, but the other half of the Rob-Bobs was too busy meeting and greeting and being the suave debonair host, a task at which he excelled. And anyway, at that point Bob would have resented the heck out of him for interfering.

I crouched behind a large plastic trash can to take it all in for a moment. Someone had just dumped a massive amount of onion skins into it; but tears can be a small price to pay for the joy of eavesdropping.

"I'm the meat chef at Maison de la Nez," said a tall thin man with a prominent proboscis and a questionable French accent. "And I am telling you, monsieur, that there *is* something wrong with these steaks."

At that very second C.J.—bless her large and unsuspecting heart—sailed through the swinging door. "Ooh," she squealed, "where did you get those lovely hippo steaks?"

"*You* know hippo meat?" Bob asked.

"Farm-raised pygmy hippo, right?"

"Right, but—"

"Hippopotamuses graze like cattle do, but they convert grass into protein at a much higher rate. The meat has a mild, porklike flavor. If people could learn to set aside their prejudices and try new things, hippo farms could be—*should* be—the wave of the future."

I popped out of hiding. My sudden appearance caused the faux Frenchman to produce a series of high-pitched squeaks and his face to turn as white as his three story hat.

"*Pardonnez-moi,*" I said. *"Je suis une imbecile grossier."* I turned to C.J. "Where did you learn about hippo meat?"

"Silly, Abby, don't you remember anything?"

"Uh . . . I forget the answer to that question."

"Cousin Loquacious Ledbetter was a Peace Corps volunteer in West Africa back in the seventies. When he returned to Shelby he brought a pair of pygmy hippopotamuses home with him. Passed them off as a new breed of pigs. Of course laws were less stringent then—"

Being the *imbecile grossier* that I was, I slipped back out of the kitchen and back into the Rob-Bobs' vast, and expensively appointed, salon. If you want to see Rob shudder, refer to the space as a living room or, God forbid, a "great room."

Every inch of the salon had been staged. Every fold in the heavy, floor-to-ceiling drapes was manipulated so the drape puddled just right when it hit the floor. The random stacking of books on the massive ebony coffee table was as random as planes landing at O'Hare. The various tableaux displayed on smaller surfaces around the room had been agonized over and reworked ad nauseam. In fact, I wouldn't have been surprised to learn that even the dust particles under the custom-covered sofas (should there be any) were arranged just so.

Therefore it was safe to assume that having thirty-six people over for a buffet dinner had to be stressful for an anal-retentive man like Rob. The sound of a thousand nails scratching across a chalkboard would probably be soothing by comparison. However, for Mama's seventy-fifth, he managed to keep it remarkably well together.

Just about every man looks handsome in a tux, but Rob looks especially dashing. He keeps himself trim at the gym, tanned on frequent mini-cruises, and I wouldn't doubt that it was Rob who turned John Edwards on to the four hundred dollar haircut. Although it was a "black tie optional" affair, most folks had opted to deck themselves out in their finest, so here and there I saw a bit of bling that put just the right amount of zing in the room. To top it all off, someone had thought to call the newspaper, which meant that come Sunday morning, Mama's momentous bash was going to be splashed across the society pages.

"That's M-o-z-e-l-l-a," I heard her tell the reporter from the *Post and Courier.* "My sixtieth birthday was really last Monday, but we had to postpone the celebration on account of I had to single-handedly apprehend a murderer."

Since the reporter didn't seem to recognize me, I felt free to horn in on the conversation. "Belated birthday wishes, Mozella," I said. "If you turned sixty last week, pray tell, how old are you this week?"

"Well, of course I'm still sixty—although maybe I'm sixty-one. I'm certainly not seventy-five like some people think I am."

"That's certainly too bad," I said.

"It is? I mean, I could be flexible."

"Mozella, let's say that you were really eighty—which is a preposterous idea in this case—folks would say that you were the youngest looking eighty-year-old they had ever seen. On the other hand, if a seventy-five-year-old woman—not you, of course—tried to pass herself off as sixty, or even sixty-one, there might be some who would think to themselves that she'd been ridden hard and put away wet—if you know what I mean."

"I get your point," the reporter said. "If you're going to lie about your age, then *add* years, don't subtract. Otherwise you might just be getting people to pity you."

"Exactly."

"Why Abby," Mama said with a laugh, "that's the silliest notion I've heard in all my born days, and believe me, there have been plenty of them. But I guess if your theory is true, then I should at least fess up to *real* age, don't you think?"

"Be proud, Mama," I said.

The reporter, bless her heart, leaned in, pencil pressed to her pad, ready to scribble away.

"I'm one hundred and three," Mama whispered in a breathy tone, more reminiscent of Marilyn Monroe than a centenarian. "Ask me what I was doing the day the *Titanic* went down. Go ahead, ask."

The clinking of a metal utensil against a wine-glass was like an angel sent from Heaven. "Ladies and gentlemen," Rob said, although he managed to get only half of us to shut up. Someone—I think it was a uniformed waitperson—slipped into the kitchen and retrieved Bob.

"May I have your attention!" Bob boomed. In the ensuing hush one might have heard a human hair hit the floor, had anyone been so thoughtless as to shed one at that moment. "Before we open up the buffet line, our guest of honor has asked to say a few words."

"That would be me," Mama said happily. To hearty applause, she pranced across the room to where the Rob-Bobs were standing. Then, as if it were choreographed, two muscle-bound men swung her up and set her gently on a dining room chair that was covered with Brunschwig & Fils cashmere (you can bet I wouldn't have been allowed to stand on it). There followed more applause.

"Doesn't it warm your heart to see her so happy?" Greg said.

I nearly jumped out of my dress sandals. "Where'd you come from?"

"Shhh, she's about to start her speech."

"Friends, family," Mama said as she looked slowly around the room. "Thank you so much for sharing my eightieth birthday with me."

Mama waved aside the inevitable gasps and murmurs. "Yes, I know, some of you thought I was younger than that—but, I've decided to take a page from my dear daughter, Abby, who's convinced me, via her own example, to be proud of my age. Abigail, tell them how old you are."

"Mama," I growled, "not now."

"Oh, come on, dear. It's only a number."

"Come on, *Abigail,*" some jerk said. "Humor your mother." Far too many people found this funny.

"I'm forty-eight," I said. "*There.* Are you happy?"

"Nonsense, dear," Mama said. "I was twenty-five when you were born. That makes you—uh—"

"Fifty-five!" the jerk hollered.

"My wife *is* forty-eight," Greg said. "I've seen her birth certificate."

Mama shrugged. "Nevertheless, what I'd like to say tonight is a big thank-you to my daughter for letting me be such an important part of her life. She didn't have to do it, you know. She could have left me up in Rock Hill to rot on the vine, like an overripe tomato—or would that be a cucumber in my case, since I always seem to be getting myself into a pickle?"

Surprisingly few people groaned, so I cut mine short.

"At any rate, I'm sure it puzzled my family when I started spending some time with my very wealthy ex-son-in-law not too long ago. I might even have stepped on a few feelings. However, I hope that a ten-day Caribbean cruise for everyone here in this room on his megayacht, the *Abby-Lone*, will help erase any hard feelings. Lord only knows, my daughter is the single most precious thing in my life. Oh, and did I mention that my grandchildren will be joining us on this cruise?"

"A *cruise?*" Rob shouted.

That was a cue for one of the uniformed waitpersons to begin beating a child's drum. At that, the doors to Rob's study opened and out marched my children: Susan, age twenty-five who lives in New York City; and Charlie, age twenty-three, who had obviously flown in all the way from Paris.

"Happy birthday to me," sang Mama happily. She was off-key as usual.

Everyone in the room joined Mama in singing the birthday song, even the waiters, and I doubt if there was a dry eye there. In fact, it sounded like even the chefs and their helpers were adding their varied voices; I thought I heard the meat chef from Maison de la Nez.

"Speech, speech!" someone cried predictably afterward, but Mama shook her head. She knew when to end a production.

It was then that I pushed Send on my cell phone and spoke to the man upstairs. I do mean that literally, by the way. Phillip Canary, who was being paid handsomely for his gig, was not at all put out about having to wait in the Rob-Bobs' media room with a cold beer and a large screen TV until he got my signal.

Eightieth birthday, or not, I'm telling you, it was a sight to see Mama's face as Phillip came down the stairs, serenading her with "You Are the Wind Beneath My Wings."

Epilogue

Mr. Curly (aka Lord Bowfrey) was charged with two counts of murder and impersonating a United States customs officer, as well as smuggling into the country just over three hundred tons of banned ivory. However, he turned state's witness in exchange for extradition to his home country of Zimbabwe.

Lady Bowfrey was convicted of two counts of kidnapping, as well as smuggling into this country just over three hundred tons of banned ivory. She was given a life sentence to a prison somewhere in the Carolinas. After a year on prison food she has lost 126 pounds and is no longer confined to her wheelchair. She has acquired a special friend named Tamika and reports being happier than she's ever been. She has also started a women's self-help group called Bitches with Stitches.

Afterword

I was born and raised in what was then the Belgian Congo (now the Democratic Republic of Congo), in the geographical center of Africa. It is a vast area of land that sprawls across the equator and contains a variety of wildlife habitats. In the northern region small herds of pygmy elephants follow ancient trails through dark, mysterious rain forest. But I was born in the south, where the sunlit savannahs butt up against the southern reaches of the rain forest and the elephants achieve normal size, like they do in East Africa.

My parents were missionaries to the Bashilele tribe, which at that time were renowned for their elusiveness (they were head-hunters who drank from human skulls) and for their prowess as hunters. They were *not* poachers; the men hunted game solely for their cooking pots. They hunted with six-foot, tightly strung bows, and were assisted by beautiful, but barkless, little hunting dogs known today as basenjis.

Larger animals could not be felled immediately by the arrows, but were chased on foot until they "bled out," much as Americans hunt deer with arrows today. Elephants and hippos, however, possess hide that is several inches thick, and arrows are generally only a mere nuisance to them. The traditional way to hunt them was to dig a large pit, into which sharpened stakes were positioned pointing upward. The pit was then covered with branches and leaves. With any luck the animals wandered into the pit, but barring that, they were driven to it by beaters. This method of hunting dates back to prehistoric times and was used by cave dwellers to hunt mammoths.

The Bashilele did not posses modern weapons of any kind. They owned no guns; in fact, it was against the law for them to do so. They were, however, very skilled at crafts. One observant man, a hunter named Kabemba, had been recruited as a soldier by the Belgian colonialists. When he returned to his village, he was able to perfectly reconstruct, by memory, a functioning musket, as well as musket balls. Where he got the necessary gun powder, I don't know.

One day a herd of elephant cows and their calves (the bulls are solitary) passed within two miles of our house. Upon hearing, via the talking drums, that the elephants were approaching, Kabemba climbed into the branches of an acacia tree. He had with him only three homemade musket balls. The unsuspecting herd walked single file beneath him, and as soon as the last cow passed, he fired the gun, hitting the elephant in the soft spot directly behind her ear. The musket ball entered the large elephant's brain and she sank quietly to her knees. She died instantly. It was truly one shot in a million.

The year was 1952. I was four years old. There

was great excitement in the village and on the mission; everyone ran through the bush to see the elephant and to congratulate the mighty hunter. Kabemba instantly became a hero, and a legend throughout the district. No man before him had ever been brave enough to attempt to shoot an elephant with a homemade gun. Killing an elephant was a community activity. No one had ever managed to do so alone; it literally took a village.

My daddy lifted me up and placed me on the dead elephant's back. He held me up so I could look in her ears. That night, and for days afterward, the entire village feasted on elephant meat, while the drums recounted the hunter's cleverness and bravery. If the bullet had only wounded the elephant, she could have easily knocked the small acacia tree over and trampled Kabemba. It is most unlikely that he would have had time to refire his homemade musket.

The next evening Mama served us elephant burgers for supper. She'd cooked them in a pressure cooker to make sure they were tender, before browning them in a cast iron skillet on our wood-burning stove. Mama didn't tell us that we were eating elephant meat until supper was over. And she waited another full day to confess that our portion of elephant meat came from the trunk. Mama had heard somewhere that the trunk was the tenderest part of an elephant, so that was what she had arranged to buy from Kabemba.

Mama's younger brother bought one of the elephant's feet from Kabemba. He intended to make an umbrella stand out of it. Unfortunately for all of us, Uncle Ernie knew nothing about taxidermy, or curing hides, and subsequently the foot stank horribly. Soon Mama, who was his big sister, ordered him to throw it out. Uncle Ernie threw the elephant's foot out, but not very far—just over the edge of the front lawn. That night a pack of jackals dragged the foot hither, thither, and yon, as they tried to scavenge the interior of it for meat. The next day Daddy commented that the poor elephant's foot had probably traveled more when it was off the elephant than when it was still attached to her.

The grassy hills among which we lived were well-watered, and many of the valleys contained small forest-rimmed lakes. There was a local legend of an "elephant graveyard," a special lake where old and injured elephants went to die. It was said that the elephants knew instinctively where this place was, and when death approached, they sought it out, but they did so only if they were not being pursued. A badly injured elephant might prolong its death for hours, maybe even days, until it knew for sure that it could enter the waters of this mysterious lake unseen.

My daddy was determined to find the "elephant graveyard." He reckoned that there must actually be several of them, and that after eons of time they must be chock full of valuable ivory. It was his dream to find one of these lakes, drain it, and become a multimillionaire. He would then use his fortune to buy a Bible for every soul in America (Daddy firmly believed that Americans needed saving just as much as did the Congolese).

Finding the "elephant graveyard," and claiming its ivory, became our annual New Year's Day quest. Armed with an elephant gun, as well as a double gauge shotgun, and accompanied by a "snake spotter" from the Bashilele tribe, my father would set out from the house every New Year's Day to seek his fortune. My two older sisters and I trotted along behind him. Mama, who was on the heavy side, never came along, but occasionally we were joined by other curious missionaries, those who were willing to thrash through the bush all day in search of a pipe dream.

One year a middle-aged American woman wearing high-heeled pumps decided that she would hike with us to investigate a little lake that had just been "discovered" in a valley about ten miles away by foot. There was no path, and Daddy and the "snake spotter" had to chop their way through head-high elephant grass. When we got to the special valley, there wasn't even a lake, much less a stash of ivory—but we had a fine picnic next to a termite mound. As for the lady in pumps, a heel broke off before she'd walked half a mile, so she turned around and limped home.

Daddy never found the "elephant graveyard." In the years since our New Year's Day excursions, this region of Africa has witnessed tribal war, civil war, and an almost unparalleled population explosion. Soldiers and political potentates have hunted some big game species almost to extinction with the aid of automatic weapons and helicopters.

Some areas that were once set aside as game preserves are now hemmed in on all sides by starving refugees, and as a consequence are heavily poached. To put it kindly: although there has been valiant effort given to conservation by many of the game wardens—some of whom have paid with their lives—the Democratic Republic of the Congo remains a land of conservation potential.

Center Point Publishing

600 Brooks Road ● PO Box 1
Thorndike ME 04986-0001 USA

(207) 568-3717

**US & Canada:
1 800 929-9108**
www.centerpointlargeprint.com